D0953349

THE MAGNOLIA SWORD

A BALLAD OF MULAN

SHERRY THOMAS

Tu Books

An Imprint of LEE & LOW BOOKS Inc.

New York

Text copyright © 2019 by Sherry Thomas
Jacket illustration copyright © 2019 by Christina Chung

TU BOOKS
an imprint of LEE & LOW BOOKS Inc.
95 Madison Avenue, New York, NY 10016
leeandlow.com

Edited by Cheryl Klein
Book design by Neil Swaab
Typesetting by ElfElm Publishing
Book production by The Kids at Our House
The text is set in Sabon, with display fonts in Majesty and Galano Classic
Vector illustration by TopGear / Shutterstock.com
Manufactured in the United States of America
by Lake Book Manufacturing, September 2019

10 9 8 7 6 5 4 3 2 1

First Edition

Library of Congress Cataloging-in-Publication Data
Names: Thomas, Sherry (Sherry M.), author.
Title: The magnolia sword : a ballad of Mulan / Sherry Thomas.
Other titles: Mulan shi. English.
Description: First edition. | New York : Tu Books, an imprint of Lee & Low Books
Inc., 2019. | Summary: When her ailing father is conscripted to fight invaders from
the north, Mulan dresses as a man to take his place in the army, but an old enemy
and an attraction for her troop's commander complicate her mission. |
Identifiers: LCCN 2019003668 (print) | LCCN 2019005748 (ebook) |
ISBN 9781620148181 (epub) | ISBN 9781620148198 (mobi) |
ISBN 9781620148044 (hardcover : alk. paper)
Subjects: | CYAC: Folklore--China.
Classification: LCC PZ8.1.T3776 (ebook) |
LCC PZ8.1.T3776 Mag 2019 (print) | DDC 398.20951--dc23
LC record available at https://lccn.loc.gov/2019003668

To X,
only the best for you
and this is definitely one of my best

1

"Hua *xiong-di*, it has been a while," my opponent murmurs. In the feeble light, his shadow is long, menacing.

It *has* been nearly two years since we last crossed swords.

But I am nobody's xiong-di. Nobody's younger brother.

"Time passes like water," I reply, drawing a shallow breath. "Have you been well, Nameless xiong?"

In those notes of his that somehow find their way into my hands, he has always referred to himself as the Humble Nameless. But I know who he is. I knew the moment I first laid eyes on his sword-lean, sword-sharp handwriting.

The one against whom I am fated to clash.

My hand tightens around the hilt of my blade—not the priceless family heirloom that lies at the root of the enmity between us, but only a bronze practice sword of identical length and weight.

"Hua xiong-di's swordsmanship must have improved greatly since our last meeting."

My opponent keeps his voice low, but his words reach me clearly, despite the cloth that covers the lower half of his face. A shrieking wind flaps its corner, just below his chin. We are three days past the Lantern Festival, which marks the end of New Year celebrations. In the South, the first stirrings of spring must already be felt, a warmth in the breeze, a softening underfoot. But here in the North, the air is as frozen as the ground on which I stand.

I exhale, my breath vaporous. "Nameless xiong will have, of course, improved even more."

It is the polite response—*and* my deepest fear. The two previous times we met, I held my own. But things have changed since my family's abrupt flight to the North. My training conditions have deteriorated; it will be a wonder if my swordsmanship hasn't.

"Hua xiong-di is too generous in his praise," says my opponent. "Time flees. Shall we?"

My insides twist. Icy wind scrapes my cheeks. A bead of perspiration trickles down my spine, leaving behind a damp, cold trail.

This is not the real battle, I remind myself. Our actual duel will take place next month, on a date set when I was still an infant. This is only an interim assessment, a test of my readiness—and his.

I incline my head. "Nameless xiong, please."

I am ceding him the opening strike. He is the one who arranges these predawn meetings, but I am, so to speak, the host, as our combats always take place near my home. I have, however, never been to this spot, a small hillside clearing next to a decrepit shrine, where two incongruously new lanterns hang before the battered gate. And he occupies the slight rise that I would have taken, had I arrived first.

All the same, etiquette must be observed.

My opponent salutes me with proper decorum and respect. I return the gesture. Those of us trained in the way of martial arts like to cloak our violence with as much ceremony as possible.

But in truth I don't mind observing the rules for men. They get to concern themselves with how things should be done, while women must comply with everything that isn't allowed.

We draw our swords, my blade leaving its casing with a soft metallic hiss. My stomach clenches again, but my hand is steady. I know this sword. I know what to do with it. I inhale, a measured intake of air, followed by an equally deliberate release.

He too breathes deeply, quietly. Above the cloth that conceals the rest of his features, his eyes are shadowed. Only the blade of his sword catches the scant light, a dangerous gleam in the darkest hour.

I have long wondered whether I would recognize him if I saw him elsewhere, without sword, without disguise. Sometimes strangers of similar height and build snag my attention and I find myself studying them. But I always know they aren't him—they lack his aura of deadliness.

His silence and stillness flood my awareness: I have been waiting for this day, for his abrupt return.

The moment he advances, I launch forward to slip past him to the higher ground beyond. But he sees through my feint and slashes toward my midsection. I point my blade at his left shoulder, forcing him to his right while pushing aside his attack with my scabbard. When his blade hits the scabbard, however, my heart recoils. That sound—it isn't an ordinary weapon glancing off wood and leather, but an extremely sharp edge cutting *into* my scabbard.

He is wielding Sky Blade, one of the pair of legendary swords our families have fought over for generations.

When our weapons meet at last, Sky Blade immediately notches my practice sword. The sensation jars my palm. I wheel around and attack his left shoulder again. "Yuan xiong is impatient to bring Sky Blade."

I use his real surname deliberately. There is little point in continuing to address him as Brother Nameless when he has shown me something that identifies him so plainly.

"With the duel so near, I'm surprised Hua xiong-di did *not* bring Heart Sea," he says.

What can I say? That I don't have access to Sky Blade's mate? That my father still hasn't entrusted it to me?

"Swordsmanship isn't about swords, but strength of will." I repeat what Father has told me many times.

When two opponents are equal in skill and weaponry, strength of will comes into play. But when his is a legendary sword and mine no more legendary than Auntie Xia's meat cleaver . . .

We exchange a flurry of strikes. Since my family arrived in the North, I haven't had a regular practice partner. Occasionally a friend of Father's passes through and works with me; still, I've grown rusty.

But as the match intensifies, my reflexes quicken. My footwork becomes more agile, my mind sharper and more focused. And with this engrossment comes a palpable pleasure: If I let everything else fall away, if I concentrate on only the physical aspect of our contest, then I can't help but delight in it. I love fighting well and he has challenged me to fight better than I ever have before. A lifetime of training flows through my sinews to produce a dexterity and lightness that would impress even Father.

But I can't let everything else fall away—I can never forget that what happened to Father could befall me too. And my opponent hasn't traveled goodness knows what distance to spar with me for fun. He is seeking my weaknesses.

I am tall; my height exceeds that of the average man, or at least that of the average man in the South. As a result of my training, I also possess considerable strength. But Yuan Kai has trained as much as I have—more, most likely, since he's older. *And* he's half a head taller, the width of his shoulders unmistakable even in the meager light.

Our contest must not become one of strength. Only in swordsmanship will I have any hope of besting him.

Since he's unwilling to give up his higher spot, I retreat slowly until we are on flat ground at the foot of the incline. Then I change tactics: Whenever I get a chance, I aim my blade at his knees, disrupting his footwork and destabilizing his balance.

Once, he almost stumbles, but rights himself and retaliates with a dangerously angled jab at my throat.

I leap backward. He advances, suddenly a lot more aggressive. He is steering me toward the half-dilapidated outer wall of the shrine. With my back to the wall, I will need to rely on strength rather than speed or cunning—exactly what I've been trying to avoid.

Somehow I am only one stride away from the wall. His blade is a blur of deadly edges, sealing me in place. With a shrill scrape our swords brace together, jolting my shoulders. I usually fight single-handed, but now I have both hands on the hilt, and even so he is slowly, inexorably pushing my blade inward, bearing down on me like a falling sky.

I scoot my right foot back half a step to gain better leverage. All the same, my arms tremble. My sword slants at an almost unsalvageable angle: If I allow my elbows to bend, I will not be able to straighten them again. But I also cannot hold out much longer, and I cannot move back any farther without being trapped against the waist-high wall.

We stare at each other. The wind howls. The flimsy light jerks with the violent swings of the lanterns. I can read nothing in his eyes, dark and becoming darker, but a blank intensity that makes my breath emerge with a sound halfway between a gasp and a sob. My entire body shakes with the effort of holding him back.

I yank my sword toward myself, dodging just in time as he staggers forward, unbalanced. He seems about to crash into the decaying wall. But with a hard slam of his free hand against the masonry, he vaults himself into a sideways somersault.

I leap to the top of the wall. As he lands on his feet, I dive from my perch and strike from above. He meets my blade with his own. I pivot as soon as I touch ground so he won't be able to trap me again.

He does not immediately attack. Three paces apart, we circle each other, our blades gleaming coldly.

Patience, Father has always counseled. *Patience and concentration.*

I don't find it difficult to concentrate when there is something to concentrate *on*—a weapon lashing my way always has my undivided attention. But in a lull my focus splinters. My ears listen to his footsteps to gauge whether he walks more quietly than I do. My gaze flickers over his clothes—what can their style and construction tell me? My fingers flex and tighten around the handle of my sword, and I'm again envious that he can carry his priceless blade into combat and I'm not allowed to use mine even at home.

"Hua xiong-di's footwork has improved," he declares softly.

My eyes narrow. He hasn't exactly paid me a compliment, as I had to rely on footwork to get out of an undesirable position.

"Yuan xiong's strength has also improved," I retort.

That is practically an insult, to comment on a swordsman's vigor rather than his skill.

He laughs. "It will be an epic battle, won't it, our duel?"

Father has taught me that I should feel only utmost vigilance toward the duel. But each time I've met Yuan Kai, beneath my trepidation, there has been a . . . *thrill*—as if some part of me wants a contest that lasts luxuriously, from dawn to dusk.

I spring and attack, my jabs quick and just a little agitated. I can't be sure, but I seem to have caught him off guard. He parries, but his blade meets mine a fraction of a second too late each time. If I were fighting like that, Father would have sharp words for me. In fact, I find myself tempted to tell Yuan Kai to do better.

Our swords brace. The previous time, he applied overwhelming force; now, just enough to ensure that I don't hack into him. We stand toe to toe, nothing but crossed blades between us.

He studies me—not my technique, but my face, as if he has forgotten the precise arrangement of my features. As if he would rather look at me than fight me.

I would rather look at him too—preferably with his face uncovered.

I think of him constantly. And when I do, it is often accompanied by a sharp pinch in my heart, a pang of loss. For what, I don't know, because we are only opponents and we can only *be* opponents. But sometimes my thoughts run away with me, and in my daydreams we roam the shores of Lake Tai in spring, as peach blossoms drift onto our path. Sometimes we even sit on the bow of a small boat and glide across the lake, under the golden and crimson sky of a summer sunset.

In my daydreams, the duel does not mark the last time I will ever see him.

Does the frail, flickering light seem to trace a line across his forehead? Is that a crease of concentration—or a scar? If it is a scar, how did he come by it in that perilous spot?

With a start, I realize I have lifted my other hand, as if I intend to touch that perhaps-scar. Our eyes meet again. He does not look away, and neither do I.

A gust roars past. The lanterns gutter, once, twice—and extinguish. The near-dawn plunges back into darkness.

We leap apart as if we've been caught in something illicit.

I inhale slowly. His indrawn breath too is carefully even. Silence spreads, broken only by the restless wind, bumping lanterns into gateposts and rattling the roof tiles that still remain on the shrine. In the distance, the Northern town that serves as my new home is almost uniformly dark, with only a few lit windows. And the city gate won't open for at least the time of a meal.

Abruptly he says, "I take my leave of Hua xiong-di."

I exhale. But my relief at not having lost to him is immediately superseded by the questions that always plague me at his visits. Does he have his family's permission to seek me out? How is it that he can find me, South or North? And why did he visit me twice in quick succession, making me believe that we would see each other regularly, and then disappear for almost two years—only to reemerge now, little more than a month before the duel?

"Yuan xiong must excuse me for not escorting him farther along his path," I reply, back to courtesy and politesse. "I trust we will meet again."

We sheathe our swords and salute each other. He walks to his horse, pins on a cloak, and mounts, his motion easy, fluid.

From atop his steed, he murmurs, "A shame, isn't it?"

I frown. "What's a shame?"

"That we were born into this rivalry." He gazes at me. "Had we met under different circumstances, we could have been . . . friends."

And then he is off, his cloak streaming behind him, a great wind-whipped shadow.

2

Half a month later

Only seven left.

I am to catch forty-nine pebbles Father fires at me, hit forty-nine targets he indicates around the courtyard, and intercept forty-nine projectiles in midair with projectiles of my own. All while blindfolded.

Father sets these exercises because the Hua family produces not only sword masters, but also experts in hidden weaponry, who can capture and deploy small flying objects under almost any circumstance. Today I have finished the first two sets without mistakes. Only seven are left in the third set, and I will have achieved a perfect record, which I haven't managed in a year and a half.

Of course Father makes me wait now.

Patience, I tell myself. *Concentration. Don't let your attention wander.*

Murong, my little brother, jumps in place to keep warm—whenever I practice hidden weaponry, it's his chore to pick up all the small objects that end up on the ground, and he is even more impatient than I am with Father's deliberate pause. In the kitchen, Auntie Xia's cleaver falls rhythmically on a wooden board. This morning Father started my practice late, or I'd be helping her. A cold wind skitters through, carrying with it the aroma of frying dough and the soft whimpering of a baby from several courtyards away.

Beneath it all, I hear the odd quietness in the marketplace, when it should be boisterous with bargaining shoppers and poultry in woven cages, clucking and quacking.

I wonder how Father will react if I manage to intercept the last seven remaining projectiles. The first time I accomplished a perfect record, I wept in euphoria and sheer relief. He said, *Let's see how long it will be before you do it again.* And when I succeeded again, after two years, he only said, *Took you long enough.*

Does Yuan Kai train with a similar rigor? How does he get away from home long enough to find me? Father doesn't like me to go anywhere by myself—even dressed as a man—for more than half a day.

Stop thinking. Practice isn't over yet. Listen!

I shuffle the small, soft projectiles I hold, four in my left hand, three in my right.

The air sings—Father has released his remaining projectiles at once. I launch all seven of mine, also in a single motion.

"You got them, *jiejie*!" cries Murong.

I already know—I heard seven soft collisions—and can't help a small smile. I don't always love my training, but I love what that training enables me to do. Today, it has facilitated perfection.

I undo my blindfold to the sight of our courtyard littered with tiny grain sacks, and Murong busy gathering them into a basket.

When we lived in the South, our house on Lake Tai was set apart, its spacious grounds enclosed by high walls topped with glazed tiles. Then it didn't matter what weapons I used or how much noise I made. But here in the North we've had to adjust our training methods. In theory, we still have our own home. But it's a small courtyard dwelling packed together with other similar courtyards, the alleys in between narrower than my wingspan.

In such surroundings, the black and white playing pieces of a go game, which I trained with in the South, would be much too loud. Auntie Xia, always resourceful, made hundreds of millet-filled sacks from fabric scraps, each no bigger than the pad of my thumb.

Murong brings me his basket, brimming with tiny sacks. "Can I keep a few to play with after I finish my calligraphy practice?"

I squeeze his shoulder. "Of course."

"Will you come and grind ink for me?"

Murong grinds better ink than I do—his always turns out

the perfect consistency, whereas mine can be either too sticky or too watery. What he really wants is some company as he writes his characters.

Before I can agree, Father says, "I need to speak to your sister, Murong. Go practice by yourself."

I have avoided looking in Father's direction, not wanting to know that my perfect record today has again made no impression. It's almost a relief to hear his unusually tense tone and see his drawn expression: He won't be addressing the matter at all.

Yet my heart lurches. He is going to speak of the duel. I know it. He has been quietly making arrangements for our travels, but he hasn't involved me, telling me only that I must devote all my time to practicing.

"I'll be there soon," I tell Murong.

He leaves with the basket. Dabao, Auntie Xia's stout son, lifts Father and heads for the reception room.

Father would have cut an imposing figure in his youth. Even now, with his sharp gaze and hawklike features, he appears every bit the great swordsman. It is only in times like this, when he must rely on Dabao to move even a few steps, that his weakness is revealed.

We spoke of his paralysis once and only once. I was ten, bored and fed up with the grueling training he put me through day after day. I wanted to jump on a skiff and punt through a forest of water lilies on the great shimmering Lake Tai. I wanted to read under the shade of banana fronds on the terrace. I wanted to go with Mother to the marketplace and examine the odd and fascinating wares that had come from far, far away.

I went through the motions, waiting for practice to be over and my day to truly begin. After issuing several admonitions, each terser and more severe than the last, Father finally said, with barely leashed anger, "Do you want to become like me? Do you believe I have always been a cripple? No. I walked into the duel and never walked again afterward.

"You will not allow this to happen to you. You must be so good that you will win overwhelmingly. Because if you don't, if you have any weakness at all, your opponent will exploit it ruthlessly. And you are already at a disadvantage because you are a girl. Do you understand?"

I stared at him, not because he'd raised his voice—he hadn't—but because of the sheen of tears in his eyes.

"Do you understand?" he repeated, his words quiet, almost inaudible.

I nodded, more in confused obedience than anything else. But I did practice much harder the next day. And the day after. And the day after that.

And I have never let up since.

I follow the men to the reception room. It's a narrow, cramped space—every room in this dwelling always feels narrow and cramped. At the head of the room is a raised platform. Dabao lowers Father onto the platform, behind a low table. Father manipulates himself into a cross-legged position.

"You can go back to your mother," he tells Dabao.

Dabao's face lights up with a wide smile—he is in his early

thirties but still has the mind of a child. He bows and hurries out.

Folding my hands in front of me, I lower my face. "Father has instructions?"

A long moment passes.

"I received a letter this morning. The duel is to be postponed."

My head snaps up. "Postponed? Surely nothing has happened to my opponent!"

Father hands me a letter. I immediately recognize the strong, sharp handwriting—at least Yuan Kai wrote himself. I glance at Father, hoping he hasn't noticed my disproportionate distress. He looks not at me but straight ahead. I swallow once before I begin to read.

To *the venerable and esteemed Master Hua,*

Pray accept the sincere greetings of this member of a later generation. The good fortune of calling upon Master Hua in person has yet to be granted this humble pupil, which makes it more regrettable that in this humble pupil's first missive to Master Hua, he must convey infelicitous news.

As Master Hua has perhaps heard, the situation near the border grows tenser by the day. Open conflict with the Rouran appears inevitable. When the fate of the realm is at stake, each man must step forth and embrace his duties. And national peril must, this humble pupil

hopes Master Hua will agree, outweigh personal obliga-
tions, however ancient and all-consuming.

This humble pupil deeply regrets that in fulfilling his
obligation to his country, he will not be able to par-
ticipate in the contest as originally scheduled. He begs
Master Hua's generous forgiveness and hopes to prove
himself at an auspicious later date.

This unworthy pupil extends his devout wishes for
Master Hua's peace and well-being and his highest
regards to Hua xiong-di.

Yuan Kai

I read the letter twice. It may be courteous, composed in the elaborate language required for formal correspondence, but it is no apology. It isn't even a negotiation. We have simply been informed that my opponent will not be there for the most important appointment of our lives.

Yes, there has been talk of trouble to the north—in the marketplace, rumors are rife. And yes, the whispers grow louder and louder that open war could erupt. But it hasn't happened yet. Not to mention, on a battlefield with thousands of horses, hundreds of chariots, and foot soldiers beyond count, where a general's strategy requires the movement of entire regiments, a single martial artist's skills at close-quarters combat are completely wasted.

It makes no sense at all that Yuan Kai has reneged on the

duel for the sake of some defensive effort to which he could make only a negligible contribution.

I hand the letter back to Father. "I wasn't aware that he had the power to decide when the duel is or isn't to be held."

My tone is scathing. At our meeting, he had given no indication that he was going to withdraw. I think back to his parting words—*we could have been . . . friends*—and feel personally betrayed.

"The situation with the Rouran may be more dire than we supposed," answers Father. He doesn't sound as angered as I would have expected for this insult. He only sounds . . . heavy. "I was highly displeased when I received the letter, and had to restrain myself from immediately composing a reprimand. But—"

Before he can continue, loud knocks erupt at the end of our lane.

"Every family must send one person to the marketplace!" shouts a man outside.

"Hurry. The imperial messenger will be here soon!" cries another.

My heart thumps, but I turn back to Father. "You were saying, sir?"

He shakes his head. "Go to the marketplace. We will speak later."

I bite the inside of my cheek. There is no use badgering him to tell me anything before he is ready. There has never been any use. "Yes, Father."

Back in my room, I change into men's clothes, put my hair up in a topknot, and cover the slightly too-large knot with a square of brown silk. In the bronze mirror that once belonged to my mother, my reflection is bright but somewhat distorted. Still, that's good enough: I only need to see that my topknot is neat and properly centered.

I would much rather go out as myself, a young woman, but Father has not allowed that in years.

Auntie Xia waits for me at the gate of the courtyard, the lines on her face etched deep with worry. "Hua *gu-niang*, you aren't wearing enough. Put this on."

Obediently, I let her wrap me in Father's thickest cloak before heading out the front door. Auntie Xia's admonishments follow me. "Turn your back to the wind. Don't catch a cold!"

The marketplace is full to the brim when I arrive. I stand unnoticed at the edge of the crowd as men speak to one another, their voices rising and rising until the guards shout for everyone to be silent. We wait for the time of an incense stick—blowing on our hands, stamping our feet, me wishing that my cloak had a hood—before I hear riders approaching from the west. Soon the guards order us to line up in neat columns.

The imperial messenger, flanked by four outriders, gallops into the marketplace. All the waiting men—and I—kneel. But I keep my face up, curious to see the messenger. He will probably be Xianbei, and I have never seen anyone Xianbei up close.

During the Qin Dynasty, a wall that stretches from the eastern sea to the western deserts was constructed, at the cost of a million lives, to keep out the nomadic tribes that roam the wastelands to the north. The Xiongnu, the Xianbei, the Rouran—in the South, these tribes are known as vast, warlike hordes with their hearts always set on the fertile plains inside the Great Wall. The illustrious Han Dynasty assiduously maintained and expanded the Wall. When that dynasty at last fell after more than four hundred years, the North splintered into many squabbling minor states.

So it is perhaps ironic that the power that eventually arose and unified all those Northern states under a single banner was nomadic in origin: the Tuoba clan of the Xianbei tribe. In the South they are referred to as "the barbarian court," even though as rulers they don't seem noticeably worse than anyone else.

I arrived in the North expecting to see barbarians everywhere. I haven't been out and about much—we've mostly kept to ourselves—but still, it has been plain to see that the Xianbei are few in number, compared to Han Chinese. Certainly I haven't met any in this town.

The imperial messenger, other than being a tall, broad specimen, doesn't seem particularly foreign. Nor is he dressed in furs or other exotic garments, but in a more striking version of the imperial livery, scarlet on black, with an impressive jeweled toque covering his topknot.

"The Rouran invade to the north," he announces. "By orders of the emperor, each household is to contribute an able-bodied male for the realm's defense. No exceptions! Conscripts are to report tomorrow at dawn."

Cries of dismay erupt all around me, but I'm too stunned to make any sounds. One man per household does not place an equal burden on all households. And of the three men of our small household, Father is disabled, Murong is still a child, and Dabao becomes anxious and difficult to manage when he is farther than twenty paces from his mother.

And then I do gasp. *Officially*, at least, Murong, Dabao, and Father are not the only men of this household listed on the sub-prefecture roster of residents.

There is another, by the name of Hua Muyang.

Muyang, my twin brother, died when we were still infants, not long after Father returned paralyzed from the duel. Perhaps the loss of his son and his mobility, coming one after the next, were too great for Father to bear. Muyang's name was never taken off the roster in the South. And after our flight to the North, Father again made sure that his name was duly recorded.

While mine was the one erased all those years ago in the South, and never registered here in the North.

That has long cast a shadow across my heart, but now it means . . . now it means that even if we could somehow convince the sub-prefect of the unsuitability of Father, Murong, and Dabao, we must still produce Hua Muyang.

Someone taps me on the shoulder. "Young xiong-di? Young xiong-di?"

I realize that I am panting, my hands over my face. A man of about Father's age peers at me, his eyes sympathetic. "Are you all right, young xiong-di?"

I manage a nod. "Thank you, Uncle. I'm fine."

The messenger and his outriders are already gone. The sub-prefect announces that at dawn the conscripts must report to the north gate, where their names will be checked against the rolls. Any family that does not submit a tribute can expect to have one seized, along with the family's home and possessions.

The reaction from the crowd is muted—or perhaps it is only the din in my head drowning out all other sounds. Did Father deduce from Yuan Kai's letter that a general conscription had been declared? Why didn't he say anything? We could have gathered up what we could carry and hurried out of town before the imperial messenger was even a cloud of dust on the horizon.

Wait—Father went out earlier in a hired sedan chair, the reason my practice session started late. And when he came back, he was silent and haggard. He must have gone to the town gates and found them already closed. Then he returned knowing that while I might be able to scale the town walls and leave in secret, everyone else in the family was stuck.

My nails dig into my palms. I am in danger of panting again, the panic in me rising and rising. I feel a wild urge to pivot and run, away from this wretched place, this wretched day.

And yet I cannot move a single step.

At least I'm not the only one rooted in place. All the men around me, even those who are talking fast and gnashing their teeth, are still trying to come to terms with the suddenness and severity of the conscription.

But when they recover a little from their shock . . .

I pivot and run. My feet pound on the cobbled streets, carrying me past the blacksmith's, which I visited not long ago—my practice sword, badly dinged by Sky Blade, needed its edge reworked—to the carter's next door.

I know how to ride and I've been taught a thing or two on judging horseflesh. A glance at the carter's pen tells me that there are no exceptional steeds to be had: They are dray horses, not bred for either speed or agility. I point at the sturdiest-looking of the lot. "I'll take that one. And you'll throw in the saddlery."

The price the owner names is three times the horse's worth. I pull out the large jasper pendant, almost the size of my palm, that I wear under my tunic. Mother used to stroke it when we sat together on our terrace overlooking Lake Tai. But there is no time to go home and get money—there will be no horses left when I return.

A horde of customers rushes in as I depart with my mount—and a void upon my chest, where the pendant used to nestle.

Some streets I pass are completely empty, quiet except for fits of sobbing from courtyards to either side. Others are clogged with townspeople frantically asking questions of one another.

Outside our front door, Auntie Xia is waiting for me. News must have already reached her: Her entire face is red and puffy. She takes one look at the horse and fresh tears leak from her already red-rimmed eyes. "But my Dabao—he can't ride."

I squeeze her arm. "I know that, but I can."

Auntie Xia stares at me. "What do you mean, Hua gu-niang?"

I give the reins of the horse to her and head to the reception room. Father is still in the same spot, Yuan Kai's letter in his lap.

"The conscripts are to report tomorrow at dawn," I say. "I bought a horse."

"I was afraid you'd say that." He does not look up. "Must you go?"

Must I go? My stomach hurts at the question. "The punishment is forfeiture of home and property if no one shows up. And there is no one else here who can."

Father's neck droops farther; his face is almost parallel to the letter. "Then you have much to do. Prepare accordingly."

◆ ◆ ◆

Murong clutches onto my arm. "Will you come back, jiejie?"

I wonder how many frightened children are asking this question right now, all over the North. And how many frightened conscripts are about to give the same meaningless answer. "Of course, silly."

"Really?"

I tap his still-chubby cheek. "What's this, Murong? Haven't you seen what your jiejie can do? Just this morning, I hit forty-nine targets in midair—while blindfolded!"

"I know that. But on the battlefield there will be thousands of arrows flying. How will you get them all?"

In my mind's eye I see huge swarms of arrows, so many that

they blot out sunlight. Of course there is no hope of deflecting them all.

I wrap an arm around my little brother. "Not everyone in an army fights on the front lines. I might become a messenger. Or a cook. I bet they'll need a lot of cooks for all those soldiers. And I don't even have to be good. Battlefield food is supposed to be awful, right?"

Murong blinks, his expression somewhere between wanting to laugh and trying not to cry.

I swallow a lump in my throat and rub his head. "It's all right. I'll keep myself safe."

"You promise?"

"I promise." And then, because I don't want to keep lying to him, I say, "Now help me prepare. Go find out from Father where he's kept our weapons from the South. Ask him which ones I can take, and bring them to me."

When Murong is gone, I close my eyes for a moment and exhale. Then I busy myself cutting and sewing a length of binding cloth, while wondering whether I should trim my hair. I'd lopped off a fair length when we first came to the north, when I needed to be out and about more ofen. Now, it's slightly long for a man but still short for a woman—and I decide against it.

I will allow myself this one nearly invisible act of defiance.

As I finish with the binding cloth, Auntie Xia comes in. "I gave your boots some extra stitching and put cotton batting inside so they'll be more comfortable," she says. "Try them on and see if they feel all right."

I peel off my ugly cotton-filled cloth booties—the things people wear in the North to stay warm—and pull on my newly improved boots. When I stand up, Auntie Xia falls to her knees, tears flowing down her wrinkled face.

"Auntie Xia!"

She might be a servant, but she has been a constant in my life. After Mother passed away, it was Auntie Xia I turned to for a lap to lay my head on, for deep, uncomplicated affection that came with no demands.

I try to pull her to her feet, but she remains on her knees. "We are in your debt, Hua gu-niang. My son and I . . . We already owe everything to your family, and now he owes his life to you!"

"No, you owe me nothing." I fall to my knees too. "You have looked after me—after all of us—all these years. Now it's my turn to look after you and Dabao."

"But you are a girl. You shouldn't need to go to war to look after us. And war . . ." She shudders.

I grip her hands. "My father was one of the best swordsmen south of the Yangtze River. I am his heir. Do you think any Rouran soldier can stand in my path?"

Are elderly women easier to fool than seven-year-olds? Which one wants more desperately to believe that a loved one will return against all odds?

Auntie Xia looks at me, half in astonishment, half in wonder—and I have my answer. Even more than Murong, she needs to believe I will come back safe and whole.

I lift her up. "I'm not afraid, so you don't need to be either."

She is still studying me, peering deep into my eyes. I face her as if she were Yuan Kai and the duel were about to start. *Often the outcome of a contest is decided before either party unsheathes a sword*, Father has told me time and again. *If your opponent believes you to be invincible, then it's almost as good as if you are.*

Auntie Xia wipes away her tears and squeezes my hands. "As you say, Hua gu-niang. Since you are not afraid, I won't be either."

❖ ❖ ❖

After Auntie Xia leaves, I sit down on the edge of my bed, breathing hard. This pretense of invincibility is draining. However nerve-racking the duel promises to be, I know I can take on one man, in broad daylight, under strictly controlled conditions. But in war, a single stray arrow can doom me—and I'm not ready to die on some frozen, desolate terrain, one corpse amoung thousands.

I shake off the worst of my dread when Murong returns. He holds several pouches of hidden weapons, but my skin prickles at the sight of the cloth carrying case on his back.

"What is *that*?"

"A sword. Father says to give it to you."

To Murong, it is merely another sword in a household full of weapons; he is far more interested in calligraphy brushes.

But this blade lies at the center of Father's existence—and mine.

According to legend, a master bladesmith once forged a pair of perfect and perfectly matched swords. They were treasured by his descendants, who looked after them with pride and reverence.

For eighteen generations, the swords were kept in the family. But their next guardian, a great swordsman, was childless and alienated from the rest of his clan. He chose to give one sword each to his two most beloved disciples, Hua and Peng, for them to pass down to their heirs.

But there was a condition: The keepers of the swords must meet in periodic matches. These contests would provide an opportunity for a "discourse on swordmanship," where both sides could demonstrate their skills, receive instruction, and improve their technique. And as inducement, the winner would be granted the honor of keeping both swords until the next match.

The matches were meant to be friendly. But in time, the friendly rivalry turned fiercely adversarial, even occasionally deadly. No longer contests, but duels.

The one that crippled Father ended in a tie, the reason the Hua family and the Peng family each hold one sword at the moment. Yuan Kai's mother is a daughter of the Peng family, and it is acceptable for a descendant carrying a different surname to represent the clan, if no one else can.

Carefully I remove our legendary sword from its black brocade cover. Sheathed, it doesn't appear all that extraordinary:

The pommel features a fish-scale pattern, the scabbard a carving of magnolia blossoms. The whole effect is elegant but age-worn, something an antique dealer might consider not quite worth his time.

But the moment the blade is exposed, the dealer would change his mind. I have never held a naked Heart Sea without feeling a chill slither across my skin, its menace unmistakable. Forged from bronze, it is strong yet flexible, unmarred by rust after long centuries. It is also beautiful, its surface adorned with a shimmering checkerboard pattern that the smiths of our lesser era no longer know how to produce.

I trace a fingertip over the inscription on the sword. The ancient, spindly script is difficult to read, but as somber and stately as an emperor's tomb.

A HEART AS LIMITLESS AS THE SEA

"Come here, Murong. Let me show you something."

"What is it, jiejie?"

"Hold the sword, edge up."

Murong does as I ask. I pluck a hair from my head. "Watch."

I drop the strand of hair. It falls gently across the blade and cleaves in two.

Murong sucks in a breath. "That is *sharp*!"

I take the sword from him. "Yes, it is." I smile. "Mother once said that the blade contains a bit of metal from a star that fell to earth."

He looks appropriately awed.

"Go to the kitchen and see if Auntie Xia needs help." I sheathe the sword and squeeze my brother's thin shoulder. "She'll be cooking a lot for tonight."

He leans against me for a moment before heading out. Carefully I cover Heart Sea, my fingers lingering for a moment on the carved magnolia on the scabbard. *Mulan*, I think to myself. Mulan means magnolia. I am named for the flower, which Mother loved for its noble beauty, rather than for Heart Sea. But still I feel a secret connection to the great blade, as if it were always meant to come to me.

I leave my room to speak to Father. But as soon as I'm in the courtyard, I hear his voice. ". . . my fault. I have ruined us. Whatever I do, I cannot escape the ill fortune that I have created."

The pain in his words is a hard pinch on my heart. I step back over the threshold of my room. I expect a reply from Auntie Xia. But her voice, greeting Murong, arrives from the direction of the kitchen.

Father is in his own room. He must be speaking to Mother's spirit plaque, hoping that her benevolent spirit from the beyond will help us in the here and now.

There is much that Father doesn't tell us. Sometimes I wonder why. It isn't as if I can't see that he still misses Mother desperately, or that he is deeply troubled he brought us to a lesser life in the North.

Then again, it isn't as if I tell *him* much, or anything at all.

Since Mother's passing, at Father's command, I have not gone out except dressed as a man. Or sparred with a partner except dressed as a man. Or represented him in any capacity except dressed as a man—and introducing myself as Hua Muyang.

Muyang is gone. No matter how I pretend, I can never be him. Why can't you see that? Why can't I be enough as Mulan, your daughter? What must I do so that you will stop treating me as the inferior imitation of your son?

But these words I repeat only to myself. To him I say, again and again, *Yes, Father.*

I take some time to collect myself before I cross the courtyard and enter his room. He is seated, grinding ink, a piece of paper weighed down on the low table before him.

He glances up. "I will reply to Yuan Kai and accept the postponement."

"Yes, Father."

When I do not say anything else immediately, he asks, "What is the matter?"

"Murong brought me Heart Sea, Father. Are you sure I should take it with me? What if—what if I don't bring it back?"

He frowns as if I've asked a stupid question. "Of course you will bring it back."

I bite the inside of my cheek. Do I really need to point out that I might die in this war?

But his expression is so forbidding I lower my head and say, "Yes, Father, of course."

"Use it well. Do not make me regret sending it with you."

The great swordsman has spoken. I have no choice but to bow.

"Thank you, Father. I will bring back Heart Sea safely."

◆ ◆ ◆

At dinner, wine flows freely. Auntie Xia becomes a little drunk. Father too, but he is better at hiding it. By and large, I refrain. At the end of the meal, Auntie Xia presents a steamed cake made from ground lotus root and osmanthus honey.

Murong, who has been quiet for most of the evening, gives me his portion. "Auntie Xia says you won't have anything good to eat in the army."

I'm much more worried about how to keep my true identity hidden, living among so many men. "They'll have to feed us something halfway decent. Hungry soldiers can't fight."

"Only dried flatbread and pickles, Auntie Xia said."

"Huh. Guess I'll be one of those soldiers who steal livestock, then. Or do you think they'll let us raise a few chickens in the barracks?"

Murong is intrigued by the possibility of a steady supply of eggs. Auntie Xia leaps in with thoughts on what scraps I can save to feed those chickens. Even Father contributes what he knows of animal husbandry. For a moment, this could almost pass for any other feast-day meal.

Then bleakness returns to Father's eyes.

When I first dressed as a man, Auntie Xia would study me and frown. *But you just look like a girl in boys' clothes.* I didn't want to look or act like a man, but I wanted even less to be given a task and not do well. I stood with my shoulders back. I pulled my hair into a tighter topknot and made my face more angular. I walked faster, moving my upper body aggressively, taking up a lot more room.

But nothing I did was enough.

Until the day I put on Father's expression. It is not the expression he wears most often, but it's the one that immediately comes to mind whenever I picture him in my head. A severe look, just short of outright disapproval. A hard, unyielding look. And beneath the refusal and the near belligerence, a bleakness that somehow seeps through.

A bleakness that makes me wish, despite my pride, and despite my resolute lack of any desire to be a man, that I were indeed his beloved son.

I eat the steamed cake in too-large bites and almost choke.

◆ ◆ ◆

The next morning, well before dawn, I dress and join the rest of the household by the altar. Father prays for the ancestors' blessings while I abase myself before their spirit plaques.

I barely slept during the night, lying in my bed, blinking up at the dark ceiling. And now a muddled fatigue has taken hold of me. Father's prayers seem to come from a great distance, and

I feel nothing beyond a woolly dread at what this day will bring.

It is still dark when I strap Heart Sea onto my back and take my leave. I squeeze Dabao's arm, hug Auntie Xia and Murong, and kneel before Father. "I'm going now. Everyone, please take care."

Auntie Xia sniffles. Murong sobs. But Father is as silent and still as the deepest night. I rise, brush the dust off my overrobe, and lead my horse out of the courtyard.

At the last moment, I look back, only to see that Father has covered his eyes with his hand. All at once, my false calm shatters. I walk away, my own tears falling.

3

At the north gate, I report to the officials in charge, give Father's name, and watch as they remove us from the list of households that have yet to contribute an able-bodied male.

"So you are Hua Muyang, nineteen years of age?"

I need only to nod. But I hear myself say, "No. There must have been a mistake. My name isn't Hua Muyang, but Hua Mulan—the same characters as the flower."

This does not please the official's scribe, who needs to correct his copy of the roll, and all the other copies back at the sub-prefecture. He sighs exaggeratedly, glances at my horse, and writes my name, the correct one, on a new list.

That list of conscripts who have brought their own horses is given to two weathered soldiers with broadswords and crossbows on their backs. One, named Gao, takes a hard look at us. "So, you are the ones who are too precious to walk, eh?"

The other riders glance at one another.

Gao grins, revealing a missing front tooth. "Don't worry. There'll be enough misery for everybody, and I'm not going to hold it against you for being luckier at the outset of a war. But I do have to warn you—I'll be handing over this list of names to the record keepers at the encampment. And if your names get there but you somehow don't, the news will go right to your sub-prefect, and he'll make poor men out of all the fathers and uncles who have generously supplied you with horses. And then he'll drag those fathers and uncles off to take your places.

"So if you're thinking of slipping away when I'm not looking, don't. Even if my colleague and I don't pierce you with arrows as you flee, you will have nowhere to return to and your families will curse you forever. Do you understand?"

Gao looks at us one more time and seems satisfied with the stricken expressions on the faces of the young men around me. "All right, then, let's waste no more time."

We set out in two columns. I glance back at this nondescript Northern town I'd never heard of before we arrived from the South. I feel no particular attachment to the place, but my loved ones are inside, behind the high brick walls.

I have been away from home, but never away from my family.

Will I ever see them again?

My earlier tears must have done some good: As I wrench my gaze away, my heart throbs dully, but I'm no longer overwhelmed by grief. I need to look ahead. I need to think about what I must do so that I can return home in one piece.

The day is bright and cold. We ride through a brown land-scape, some stretches still covered in snow. Every village and town on our way is quiet and empty, aching with the absence of so many fathers, brothers, and sons.

We pass groups of conscripts marching in the same direction. Peasants, merchants, even a few whose attire indicates that they are scholars. And so many boys my age or younger. Some appear scared, some excited, the rest simply bewildered, as if they still haven't grasped what is happening.

At noon Gao leads us to an abandoned temple by the side of the road. We stagger off our horses. Gao keeps watch on them; his comrade has his eye on us. Most of the conscripts relieve themselves by the front wall of the temple, but I walk toward the rear.

"Hey," one conscript calls to me, "where are you going? You want an arrow in your back?"

I give him a stare Father would be proud of. "I don't like other people around when I go. You have a problem with that?"

He blinks. His gaze flickers between my face and the sword at my back. Then he says to the other conscripts, as if to cover his own embarrassment, "I was just being nice. Guess that was wasted."

At the back of the temple, even though I hear no one approaching—and none of the men present can take a step without alerting me from thirty paces away—I hurry to empty my bladder, my heart pounding. I don't know what the punishment would be if I'm discovered to be a woman, but I'm not eager to find out.

When I'm done, I pant for a moment, relief coursing through my veins, and issue a silent apology to the god of wealth, to whom the temple is dedicated. Ironically, the god of wealth has fallen on hard times, the roof of his abode caved in, the gilt that covered his statue all gone. I am reminded of the dilapidated shrine before which I last fought Yuan Kai.

I haven't thought of him in almost a whole day, which hasn't happened since our first meeting more than two years ago. He must have been conscripted—that much is obvious. Is he also traveling in a group, under the watchful eyes of seasoned soldiers? Or is he already at an encampment, trying to figure out how to increase his odds of survival?

On the way back, I pass a well that still has a bucket on a rope and pull up some water to wash my hands. When I reach the others, they are eating their lunch. I turn my back to the wind so that I don't ingest a mouthful of dust along with the stuffed buns Auntie Xia packed for me. In the often treeless North, dust is everywhere, whirling along the ground, leaping high with every stir of the air.

By midafternoon, as we near the encampment, the road becomes congested. Long lines of conscripts, on foot and on horseback, are waiting to be let in.

The journey so far has been leisurely: Our soldier escorts, in consideration of our draft horses, haven't pressed us for speed. The sky has continued to be clear and cloudless and by now there is almost a hint of warmth under the sun. And we have just come through some low hills and descended into a wide valley—stony hills and a mostly barren valley, but still, more scenery than I've seen in a while—so the whole expedition has begun to feel like an unexpected spring outing.

But the sight of the encampment sobers me. Twenty thousand men can fit into the rows upon rows of tents, and more are being set up before our eyes. And this is only a regional muster. There must be encampments like this all over the North—hundreds of thousands, if not millions, of men herded toward the front.

Another conscript might feel a sense of relief at the scale of the muster, to be one among so many. But I have read plenty of histories. At Red Cliffs, two hundred and fifty years ago, Cao Cao had four times as many soldiers as his opponents did, yet they defeated him, killing a hundred thousand of his men in a single decisive battle.

What if I were one of the hundred thousand caught in that turning tide? To have no room to maneuver, all escape routes cut off, and only a sword against a forest of spears? I have promised everyone at home that I will return safe and sound. How do I do that? How do I take charge of my fate when all around me, men have submitted to theirs?

A good while passes before it is our turn at the entrance. The admitting officials examine the list of names, count us three times, and finally allow us through the gates.

"Better look lively," says one official to Gao as he stamps the list of names. "The princeling is here."

The term he uses—*xiao wangye*—refers specifically to a son of a royal duke.

"Who is this princeling?" one conscript wonders as we move into the encampment.

"Probably a useless braggart," mutters another.

My hands tighten around the reins. Young noblemen are the worst—or at least in the South they are, preying freely on those who are the most powerless.

We lead our horses to a pen. Then Gao marches us deeper into the encampment. "Where are we going, Master Gao?" asks one conscript.

"The sanitation trenches. You'll have to wait for your tent assignment. Better go now before I take you to the training ground."

Trenches? Is that how it is? I swear inwardly.

The trenches don't smell quite as offensive as I expect—there must be some unfortunate minions assigned to shovel dirt in on a regular basis. My fellow conscripts shuffle up to the edge and relieve themselves. I do not. Gao gives me a curious glance but makes no comment.

On the training ground, a wide, open space at the center of the encampment, around two thousand men wait. They sit in rows, some looking around, others quietly talking. The mood is relaxed. Everyone has had to leave home behind, but they've arrived safe and whole at their first destination and they'll soon be fed and given a place to sleep. Some appear to have even made a few friends.

I, on the other hand, feel grim. The war is becoming more real. There is no good way for me to navigate the sanitation trench. And I'm suddenly wondering whether, in taking Dabao's place, I've made a terrible mistake.

Half a dozen men on horseback ride onto the training ground as we approach. The one closest to me is in his late twenties, bold-featured, strapping in build, and magnificently clad in a shining breastplate and a crimson cape. In fact, five of the six riders are in such eye-catching uniforms.

Against this wall of splendor, the civilian who rides with them, front and center and all in black, should be practically invisible. But I stare at him the moment he turns to listen to an older soldier on his other side. It is a simple motion, but something about it is oddly familiar. And the way he handles his steed—or hardly handles it at all, since the horse is proceeding at a leisurely walk—

Why do I feel that I have seen him before?

"Is that the princeling?" asks someone behind me.

"That's him," Gao answers. "His father, the royal duke, is in charge of all the forces of the central commandery."

The older soldier who is talking to him must be highly placed, possibly the commander of the encampment. And yet he is deferential in his demeanor, leaning toward the princeling, bent a little forward at the waist. The princeling listens with a grave courtesy, not the sort of petulant impatience I associate with aristocratic scions.

I shake my head a little. What am I thinking—that a Xianbei royal duke's son met me three times in predawn hours to cross swords?

Yet I keep studying the princeling. He is young, close to my age. And he may be one of the handsomest men I have ever seen. But there is something else.

Just then the older soldier indicates the training ground. The princeling makes a slow survey of the sprawl of conscripts. And I see it, the barely leashed intensity behind his eyes, which contrasts sharply with his aura of calm self-possession.

Perhaps what I'm witnessing is no more than the confidence that comes of his extremely elevated station, of having been obeyed and catered to his whole life.

Still my eyes do not leave him. Still I cannot shake the unsettling sense of familiarity.

The seated conscripts are being told to get to their feet when a young man comes running down the wide lane at the center of the training ground. "Captain Helou!" he shouts. Judging by his drab uniform, he isn't a conscript, but a low-ranking soldier. "Captain Helou!"

The strapping soldier I first saw raises a brow. Helou is a Xianbei family name. The princeling is also, of course, Xianbei, as is the commander to his other side, most likely. I may be seeing more Xianbei this afternoon than I have in my entire life.

"Captain Helou, this lowly soldier learned only now that you are looking for exceptional martial artists for the royal duke," says the young man. "I am heartbroken to have missed the trials earlier. If it is not too late—and if the commander will permit me this impertinence—may I beg for a chance before Captain Helou departs?"

The commander frowns. But the princeling makes a small gesture with his hand. Seeing that, the commander bows his head. Captain Helou also inclines his head in the princeling's direction, then he turns to the young man.

"What makes you think you're good enough?" he asks. He speaks Chinese with a Northern accent, not a foreign one.

The young man puffs out his chest. "I've been undefeated my entire life."

Captain Helou smiles indulgently. "That could be because you haven't found good opponents. But very well, let's test that."

He dismounts in one agile motion; for a big man, his landing is incredibly soft. He carries a bow and a quiver of arrows on his back, but he does not bother to take them off.

"I use a broadsword," the young man declares.

"I left my broadsword at home," replies Captain Helou. "My fists will have to do."

"Then I will also fight bare-handed," says the young man.

I shake my head. He isn't good enough for that sort of pride.

They stand ten paces apart and salute each other. The young man attacks first. Nothing wrong with that, but he should have given himself a little more time to assess his opponent. As it is, he goes straight for Captain Helou's strong side. Captain Helou sidesteps the attack. The young man, hitting nothing, turns around and launches a kick.

I shake my head again. The young man has already exposed a multitude of his own weaknesses. When he didn't hit Captain Helou, he needed an extra step to regain his balance, which means that his stances aren't firm. The kick is too much for show: He is aiming for the neck of a taller man when he could more profitably go for a vital organ just beneath the captain's breastplate. And of course, with that questionable balance, a high kick opens him up to attack just about everywhere.

Captain Helou doesn't take advantage. He toys with the young man, letting him become more impatient, more frustrated that none of his blows are landing. But I can predict that by their tenth exchange, the young man will go down.

In fact, he lands flat on his back on their ninth exchange. And judging by his bewildered expression as he struggles to his feet, he barely felt Captain Helou's boot hooking his ankle, exploiting a moment when he was already off balance.

I half anticipate that he will demand a rematch. But he does himself credit by bowing deeply as he salutes. "My gratitude to Captain Helou for his instruction. I see now that I have been far too ignorant."

Captain Helou smiles again and returns the salute. "You have a good foundation and the road is long yet. I hope to someday learn from you, after you become an exceptional martial artist."

The young man makes himself scarce. Captain Helou places his hands behind his back and looks around the gathering. "Anyone else here think he is an exceptional martial artist? Better come forward now. His Highness and I are leaving."

"Where are they going?" I ask Gao. "And why would the royal duke seek martial artists?"

"I don't know—I just got here myself," says Gao. "Maybe to guard the princeling. You want to try?"

Do I? I do want out of this encampment—if I never see those sanitation trenches again, it will still be too soon. But in a smaller group, members pay more attention to one another. How well can I pretend to be a man under close scrutiny?

And if the princeling and Captain Helou should realize that I am a woman . . .

The crowd has fallen silent, waiting for someone to step up. But now murmurs stir again. Captain Helou salutes the gathering.

"If no other hero will come forward, then everyone please take care. Let us meet again on an auspicious day."

He heads for his horse.

"Wait!" I cry.

Captain Helou turns around, surprised and half-amused.

I stride onto the training ground, past my astonished companions, past ranks upon ranks of conscripts, their faces lit with anticipation, before coming to a stop fifteen paces from Captain Helou. "This lowly conscript is an ignorant nobody. But with His Highness's and the commander's indulgence, I would also like some instruction."

Compared to the niceties I've been taught, this request barely qualifies as polite. But it has been a long day, and I'm less inclined toward elaborate courtesy when I'm dressed as a man.

Captain Helou grins. The commander frowns. And the princeling stares at me as if I have challenged *him*—a look that could fell trees.

I stare back. In that moment, I do not remember his parentage or that I am hoping to perhaps become one of his protectors for the sake of my own safety. In that moment, he is only a potential opponent who must know that I am not daunted.

Often the outcome of a contest is decided before either party unsheathes a sword.

I come to my senses only when Captain Helou speaks. "Very well. Young xiong-di, do you have a weapon of choice?"

He means the sword on my back, but I am loath to draw Heart Sea. After a lifetime of being inculcated on its immeasurable worth, I don't want to let anyone see it unless absolutely necessary. However, I'm also reluctant to get into a fistfight with Captain Helou.

My gaze lands on the weapons on *his* back. "Captain Helou has a bow and arrows."

"I do. Would xiong-di prefer a shooting contest?" He sounds amused.

I incline my head. "Captain Helou, please shoot. I will catch."

His brows almost meet his hairline. "Xiong-di will catch arrows bare-handed?"

"Three of them at fifty paces—while blindfolded."

Captain Helou's jaw drops. A collective gasp rises. And then excited murmurs spread as men within earshot pass on the word to those who are too far away to hear what I said.

I don't catch arrows as a normal part of my practice, but at fifty paces—and I plan to make those big paces—an arrow's flight would be almost spent. Captain Helou looks up at the princeling, who considers me and says, "We will have our eyes opened today."

He is more soft-spoken than I anticipated, the Northern accent in his speech crisp rather than harsh.

"But won't it be too dangerous, Your Highness? It wouldn't be auspicious for something to happen here."

"Young xiong-di there isn't worried. You needn't be either, Captain," replies His Highness.

Still Captain Helou hesitates.

"The day grows late," the princeling reminds him. "We should leave soon."

Captain Helou bows. "Of course, Your Highness." He turns back to me and gestures at the avenue down the center of the training ground. "Let us proceed, young xiong-di."

He indicates where he will stand. Hundreds of men count softly alongside me as I measure out fifty paces. At my spot, I pull out a large kerchief, fold it diagonally, and cover my eyes, making sure the blindfold is wide enough that no one can doubt its effectiveness. And then, as a precaution, I take my sheathed sword in my left hand. Should I be completely mistaken about how fast the arrows will arrive, at least I'll have something I can use to deflect them.

The crowd falls silent. My heart beats fast, but I don't feel any more nervous than during practice sessions with Father. I inhale slowly and exhale with just as much care and deliberation.

"Watch out now!" cries Captain Helou.

The arrow leaves the bow with a soft twang, its calm flight producing a very gentle sibilance. The depth of my training is such that I need only a fraction of a moment to discern an object's speed and trajectory. And what I hear is Captain Helou's great chivalry. Not only has he drawn the bow just enough for the arrow to reach me, but he has aimed at least two handspans to my right.

I reach out and snatch the arrow from midair, its shaft smooth beneath my fingers.

The crowd cheers raucously. I drop the arrow and wait for them to quiet down, feeling just a little smug.

"Well done!" shouts Captain Helou.

This time he shoots without warning, but the arrow's flight is still leisurely and again a bit wide—to my other side. Still holding Heart Sea, I pluck the arrow with my left hand.

The cheering is twice as raucous.

"Magnificent!" cry Captain Helou and the commander in unison.

I hold myself back from smiling. This contest isn't over yet.

I exhale and focus. The third arrow will come straight at me. Faster too, as Captain Helou knows now that I am not putting my life in jeopardy. This, then, will truly be a test of my skills and reflexes.

But the arrow doesn't come.

The conscripts begin to whisper. "Look, look! My Heavens! Nobody can catch that!"

What is going on?

Abruptly silence falls again. I bow my head and try to loosen my shoulders. My heart thuds, not knowing what I'm up against, only that it has dismayed the entire crowd.

Thoughts begin to whirl in my head. I force them out. I cannot let my concentration lapse. I cannot—

The arrow releases.

No, not one arrow: three. Headed directly at me, with a velocity that freezes my blood.

I yank out Heart Sea and slash at the oncoming arrows, even as I bend backward to avoid them. The legendary blade is so sharp that I barely feel it slicing through the shafts. Somehow I catch one of the broken pieces in my left hand as the rest plummet to the ground all around me.

With difficulty, I straighten. I am panting. I throw aside the broken arrow and drag off my blindfold.

Only to see, fifty paces away, the princeling standing on his horse, lowering the bow in his hand. And it is not Captain Helou's bow, but a much longer, more powerful one.

The bastard!

I grab Heart Sea's sheath and carrying case from the ground and march toward him. How dare he put a conscript at risk for his own amusement! Few under the sky would have come through unscathed. Were my training a shade less intense, I would be pierced through right now.

The princeling leaps off his horse, a motion so gentle and casual it is as if he descended a single step on a flight of stairs. He hands the bow to a waiting soldier and faces me, his gaze stark yet fierce.

Bastard.

I grow aware of the profound silence, as if thousands of conscripts are all holding their breaths. It is only when Captain Helou steps in front of the princeling—and the latter gently but firmly pushes him aside—that I realize I am storming toward them with my sword drawn, as if I am about to skewer the princeling clean through.

I force myself to slow. Ten paces out, I stop and sheathe Heart Sea. "This humble conscript thanks His Highness and Captain Helou for their instruction. I caught only two and a half out of the five arrows. Would one of the elevated personages present please inform me how that should be counted in this contest?"

I have never spoken so rudely in my entire life. Then again, I've never had my life endangered till this moment.

The princeling considers me, even as the commander appears ready to have me disciplined for discourtesy. "Xiong-di, what is your name?"

"Hua Mulan." After a moment, I add reluctantly, "I offer my humble respects to Your Highness."

He inclines his head. "It is said that the Central Plain is a place of crouching tigers and hidden dragons—extraordinarily talented heroes everywhere. Hua xiong-di successfully challenged Captain Helou, who is an extraordinary talent himself. Does Hua xiong-di wish to come with us?"

I did. But do I? I'm still breathing hard, my heart is still thumping from afterfright, and my fist still longs to plow into the ridge of the princeling's nose.

Patience, I hear Father's voice. *Concentration.*

I must focus on the larger goal of survival. I want to be in a safe place as I serve out my time in the army, don't I? I will not find a safer place than in the princeling's service. And if that will require a lot of patience, a lot of holding myself back from slugging him? Well, as Father says, patience is a good virtue to develop.

I bow as I salute. "It would be the fortune of three lifetimes, Your Highness."

The princeling turns to the commander, who has by now also dismounted. "Commander Dugu, my apologies for poaching this young hero from your encampment. But I have cause to believe that he will better serve the country by my side."

That's a deft turn of phrase. Or maybe he actually believes that I will better serve the country by keeping *him* safe.

The commander looks relieved—the princeling hasn't been attacked in his camp, *and* he will be rid of a troublesome conscript. "It is difficult to let go of such talent, but let go I must, for the greater good. My congratulations to Your Highness on gaining a worthy hero in your service."

I, of course, am obliged to sink to one knee to reiterate my eternal gratitude.

When I rise, the princeling glances at me, a strange gleam in his eyes. "Well, Hua xiong-di, shall we be on our way?"

4

Even with the commander's blessing, it isn't an instantaneous process to release me from the regular army. My name must be formally struck off the encampment rolls and assigned to the princeling's command. A better horse also has to be found for me: The princeling and Captain Helou have a hundred *li* to cover before the end of the day.

At last we are on our way. Captain Helou grins at me over his shoulder. "We ride fast, Hua xiong-di. Don't get left behind."

"What if I need to stop?" I hurriedly ask.

The princeling gives me a look. "Then you had better catch up fast. You have no pass on the imperial road, other than as my subordinate."

Swine. I hope patience will not be too difficult a virtue to acquire.

I half bow in his direction. "This humble conscript understands, Your Highness."

Despite Captain Helou's warning, we do not travel at breakneck speeds. Still, I find it challenging. Unlike walking a horse, for which I need only to keep my seat, riding at a crisp trot requires me to rise up and settle down in rhythm to the horse's movement to avoid either jostling myself or hurting my steed's back. But thanks to my training, I have the stamina and muscular strength to keep up with my new superiors.

Occasionally we slow to a walk to rest the horses, and Captain Helou tosses me something to eat. The first time I catch a turnover stuffed with garlic chives and a sprinkling of scrambled eggs; the second time, much to my surprise and delight, candied lotus seeds, which I haven't tasted since I left the South.

The princeling has been silent since that warning to me to keep up. Captain Helou, taking a cue from him, has also refrained from speech, except to alert me to the condition of the road.

Evening is falling. In the North, twilight lingers. We push forward in the long gloaming, the air a blue-gray haze into which the road ahead disappears. Captain Helou's bright scarlet cape streams behind him. The princeling's black cape, by contrast, is barely visible in the deepening dusk, but my eyes are drawn to it.

Again a sense of familiarity assails me. Three times I have watched Yuan Kai ride away in a similar darkness. Of course I never saw him very well under those conditions, but from here, it would be all too easy to mistake the princeling for my opponent: the same lean, tight build, the same easy, secure seat, the same shadowlike cloak, melding into the night.

Minus, of course, a sword carried on his person.

It occurs to me that if the princeling *were* my opponent, then what he did this afternoon, while still calibrated to within an inch of actual mortal danger, would not be considered excessive, since he would know of my skill at capturing projectiles. However, Yuan Kai's family, as far as I know, is strictly Han Chinese. In fact, three generations ago, the Pengs left the war-torn North and resettled in the South—Yuan Kai speaks with a slight Southern accent. The princeling is clearly a Northerner—and Xianbei. So it's ludicrous that I'm even pondering the possibility.

We stop for the night in a bustling town and seek lodging at a large inn. At first the doorman refuses us entry, saying it is already dark and he is forbidden to admit guests at so late an hour. The princeling calmly displays an elaborate-looking pass. After that, the door opens immediately. The proprietor himself comes bowing and scraping, and shows us to our rooms.

But there are only two rooms left, one large and well-appointed, one much smaller but still rather nice.

"I'll take this one," says Captain Helou of the smaller room. "You can be His Highness's servant tonight, Hua xiong-di."

I blink. What does that mean?

The princeling says to Captain Helou, "You are not obliged to dine with us tonight, Captain, if you have plans."

Captain Helou grins broadly. "Many thanks, Your Highness."

His Highness addresses the proprietor next. "Innkeeper, a cot for this young xiong-di in my room."

In *his* room? I've never slept anywhere near a man to whom I am not closely related.

"Yes, Your Highness. I'll have one brought in right away," answers the innkeeper.

In the meanwhile, he pours water for the princeling and me to wash our hands and then escorts us downstairs and across a courtyard to a warm, crowded dining room, where a private area has been fenced off for the princeling with a pair of silk screens. After the princeling sits down, I remain standing to the side, unsure how a servant should act in such a situation.

He glances up. "You're going to eat like that, Hua xiong-di?"

"Captain Helou said I'm to serve you tonight, Your Highness."

"Have *I* ordered you to do so?"

"Ah, no."

"Then sit down. I don't like people hovering around me."

I sit on one of the mats that have been arranged around the low table—they are so new, they've probably been brought out for the very first time in honor of the princeling's esteemed posterior. The waiter, who has also been hovering, makes his approach and places small plates of marinated bamboo shoots and sliced salted duck eggs on the table. "We have some very fine sorghum wines, Your Highness, and some rice wines from the South. Which one should I serve Your Highness first?"

"We are on official business. No wines."

"Ah, of course. Your Highness's dedication is admirable. We have a ten-dish set, but for you, the cook can also prepare a special twelve-dish set, with—"

"We are only two people. A four-dish set will be more than good enough. Unless"—the princeling turns to me—"Hua xiong-di needs more?"

How can I possibly ask for more items than a royal duke's son? "No, Your Highness."

The waiter is disappointed, but he puts on his best smile. "We'll have everything out in no time."

He is back in a blink of an eye, with a pot of infusion. "These herbs are grown and picked by the innkeeper's wife herself. The drink will aid your digestion, Your Highness, and promote your general well-being."

He pours for us and leaves. The princeling takes a sip from his cup, then picks up a morsel from each small dish. He is the person of the highest stature at the table. Now that he has eaten, I can start. I'm hungry and everything looks delicious— but I hesitate.

He sets down his chopsticks. "The food does not please Hua xiong-di?"

"The food is highly enticing. It is merely that this lowly conscript has never sat at a table with as grand a personage as Your Highness, and doesn't know what to do."

I might as well play the part of the bumpkin. To the princeling, I probably am.

"Is that so?" he murmurs. "I would have thought Hua xiong-di is still angry with me."

I glance sharply at him, unsure how to reply. He's right that I am still wary of him—I have not forgotten that awful pulse of fear when I heard his three arrows speeding toward me. But he is the Northern emperor's kin, and I am a refugee from the South. And he could very well be the kind of person who enjoys being blunt himself but becomes angry when others speak half as freely.

But he does not appear to be baiting me. In fact, even though his expression is carefully neutral, something in his gaze makes me think he might be a bit—worried?

"How can I possibly harbor any ire toward Your Highness, when you do me the honor of believing that I can withstand the simultaneous assault of three deadly arrows?" I hear myself say.

His eyes widen slightly. "Did Hua xiong-di not realize that the arrows I used were blunt-tipped?"

What? "There are blunt-tipped arrows?"

"Commander Dugu has a great many conscripts to train. When hundreds of beginners practice archery at once, blunt-tipped arrows are far safer than battlefield ones."

I think back. At no point did I ever look at the three arrows I sliced in half. I simply assumed them to be the normal, deadly kind.

"I see," I murmur, caught between relief and embarrassment. Not knowing what else to do, I eat a piece of marinated bamboo shoot, then a slice of salted duck egg.

"And how does Hua xiong-di find the North?" asks the princeling.

My Southern accent has become much less pronounced since my arrival, but there is still enough to give away my origins.

I consider my words. "Has Your Highness ever been to the South?"

"One of my uncles served as envoy to the court of the Southern emperor. I accompanied him and stayed for some months."

"What did Your Highness think of the South?"

His lips curve slightly, as if he is amused that I've turned the conversation around to him. I notice that he has a faint scar on his chin—and a longer and equally faded one on his forehead.

I immediately think of Yuan Kai. But even at the time I wasn't sure whether what I saw was a scar or a trick of the inadequate light. Do I have anything concrete to tie him to my opponent— or am I indulging in wishful thinking because he is handsome, and I wouldn't mind if Yuan Kai looked exactly like him?

"The South is as beautiful as I was led to believe, a lingering, poetic beauty," he replies. "The people of the South are not as haughty as I was led to believe—I found them thoughtful and friendly."

He pauses diplomatically.

Still distracted, a moment passes before I remember to prompt him. "But?"

"But there is such an undercurrent of fear at court. And even away from court, the people are afraid."

I expected a comment on Southern food or dialects, not this unsparing observation on the political atmosphere. Reflexively, I lean away from him, my eyes searching the dining room for anyone who might have heard us. But all I see are the silk panels that shield us from view, painted with court ladies frolicking under blossoming apricot branches. Beyond the screens, the dining room is noisy with travelers enjoying their evening meal, striking up conversations and exchanging information.

I take a deep breath. We are in the North now, where opinions on the South do not lead to unwelcome attention. And the son of a Northern royal duke can never be subject to the kind of consequences that forced my family's flight from our beloved home.

"You are still afraid," says the princeling.

An echo of my old fear.

After Mother died, when I was thirteen, Father took a much greater interest in politics. I didn't care for his new friends, who visited all day and discussed current events, court intrigues, and other matters of state. At first, it was because I overheard things I'd rather not have known about my beautiful South— the instability, the dynastic upheaval, the widespread rot that came of corruption and incompetence from the top down.

Then I realized that Father and his friends didn't want to only debate matters, but to act.

I begged him to stop associating with those loud-talking men. All it would take was for one of them to be less than discreet—or a spy for the Southern court . . . He listened, then told me I need not concern myself with his friends, in that soft yet resolute manner that let me know I was not to raise the subject again.

But someone did talk to the wrong person, and an edict came down to arrest all the coconspirators. We escaped with little more than what we could carry. And here we are in the North, exiles and refugees.

The waiter bustles in with our dinner. Despite the princeling's explicit request, I count six dishes and a soup, plus an assortment of nuts and dried fruits. He makes no comment. The waiter looks a little concerned as he leaves.

"The innkeeper would have been embarrassed to serve only four dishes to a royal duke's son," I say. Any subject that isn't the South.

The princeling picks up a piece of turnip from a bowl of mutton stew. "That's why I didn't say anything."

We eat for a minute in silence before I remember my manners and hasten to declare, "This lowly conscript overflows with gratitude at Your Highness's beneficence. Tonight's bountiful meal is a kindness never to be forgotten."

"Hua xiong-di is much too generous in his praise," answers the princeling. "I should not have darkened his palate with such coarse food and insipid tea. All the same, please forgive the inadequacy of this rough repast and deign to partake of it."

I blink. Given his frankness thus far, I did not expect him to spout this elaborate politesse. I did not even consider that he might be capable of it. But he is—and he makes all that formal drivel sound as ridiculous as I've always believed it to be.

I laugh a little, unable to help myself.

"Hua xiong-di still hasn't answered my question," he reminds me, after a few sips of his soup. "What do you think of the North?"

Am I not allowed to eat in peace? "Your Highness, I haven't been in the North very long."

"Does Hua xiong-di always wait years before forming an opinion?"

I could lie. But given how much I've tried to evade the question, any compliments at this point would ring false. "I have not yet become accustomed to the Northern climate—and it is a much harsher climate."

"So . . . the South is lost to you but you don't think you will ever feel at home in the North."

My chopsticks freeze halfway to a dish of braised carp.

He has articulated my feelings exactly. Except *I* have never been able to describe that chaotic mix of homesickness and alienation in my heart, not even to myself.

Somehow I detach a sliver of carp and put it in my mouth, tasting nothing. I approximate the sound of a lighthearted snort. "It's nothing so dire, Your Highness. I'm already pretty settled here in the North."

He does not reply.

I try to fill the silence with chatter. "In fact, I'm even getting used to the taste of Northern cooking. This carp is good—and I used to think I didn't like carp at all."

The princeling still doesn't say anything. Am I to broil in this awkwardness all by myself? "Captain Helou is going to kick himself for missing this meal. What plans does he have in this town?"

A hint of amusement animates the princeling's features. "Are you sure you don't know his plans for the evening?"

"I met him only today and he has said nothing of his plans to me."

The princeling smiles very, very briefly. And he is very, very spectacular when he smiles.

For a moment, I forget that I'm an exile who can never go home. I only want him to smile again.

He does when he says, "Captain Helou likes women."

So do most men. I fail to see how that is of any significance.

Then my face burns: Captain Helou isn't dining with us because he has gone to a pleasure house. "So . . . he knows where to find them?"

"We've been on the road together for months, and he never seems to have trouble."

"I see," I manage.

The princeling's eyes gleam. He looks at me in a way that makes something in me jolt. "I hope I have not kept Hua xiong-di here when he too would have preferred other plans."

"Ah . . . not while I'm on official business."

He laughs softly. "Good thinking."

I put a piece of savory walnut into my mouth, hoping that we're done with the subject. But it's also me who asks, barely a breath later, "Your Highness, you don't go with Captain Helou?"

"No." An unequivocal answer.

Why not? You don't *like women?* During the Han Dynasty, gentlemen's preference for one another was such that their wives' complaints made it into written records. I don't know if things have remained the same in the North—it isn't a question that has ever occurred to me before. "You . . . don't wish to anger your wife?"

"I am not married."

At his age, even if he isn't formally married yet, a match has probably already been arranged. "Then what could be the reason?"

"I don't like women smiling at me because they are paid to do so. Also, my master would have my hide if I frequented such places."

I laugh a little. "Now I can't tell whether Your Highness is noble or just afraid."

He does not clarify that for me, but asks, "What about you, Hua xiong-di? Why do you refrain?"

What can I say? "I am famously henpecked at home. My wife will beat me with her rolling pin if I so much as look at another woman."

The princeling raises a brow. "Really?"

"I should be so lucky." I sigh. "I would *like* a hot-tempered wife, but here in the North there is no one to matchmake for me."

"Contribute to the defeat of the Rouran, and I'll have my father vouch for you to the prettiest, fieriest girls in the North."

I am both entertained by the idea—and a little disturbed. On the surface the princeling has made no more than a wry remark, but I sense a stirring of glee beneath his seeming detachment. Not to mention, he and I are going to defeat the Rouran by sitting out this war. Right?

I take a sip of my soup. "I guess all that remains for me to do is to be the great hero of this age, and my whole life will fall into place."

◆ ◆ ◆

After some time, our talk turns to the war, and I learn that the Rouran attacks came as a surprise to the court.

The reunification of the North was achieved little more than a generation ago, after centuries of squabbling among warlords and self-styled sovereigns, and the peace since has been much cherished. Even the Rouran, in recent years, seemed content to keep to their territory outside the Wall.

The Northern court, foreseeing further peace, reduced its standing army to decrease pressure on the treasury. Then the Rouran launched large-scale assaults that seemed determined to break through the Wall. Faced with this sudden, grave threat, the court had no choice but to call for a general levy and conscription.

It occurs to me that from the encampment, we rode almost due north to reach our current location. Surely we are not headed to the border?

"Your Highness, where are we going?"

The princeling raises a brow, as if wondering how I haven't guessed yet. "The capital."

Relief washes over me. There will be no place as fiercely defended as the capital. "This has been a grand tour for me. I've never seen so much of the North."

I haven't seen much of the South either. But in the South I did not feel geographically constricted: Lake Tai is so vast; it always seemed to me that simply by plying its waters I could reach anywhere I wished. In the North we have been penned in by the dimensions of our courtyard.

I wonder how everyone at home is faring. What will Father do with the time he normally spends overseeing my training? Will Murong find himself suddenly starting his martial arts tutelage? And who will help Auntie Xia with threading needles and picking out grit from dried beans?

"Has it been difficult for you, leaving home?" asks the princeling quietly.

It is discomfiting how well he reads me while he himself remains a complete enigma. "I don't want my family to miss me too much—but I also don't want them not to miss me at all."

"I'm sure they miss you just the right amount," he says, rising.

I stand up too.

"Eat more," he instructs. "Sleep early. I'm going out for a walk."

I envy him the kind of pass that lets him roam abroad at this hour, unconcerned with the wrath of night watchmen. But I'm also thrilled at the prospect of some privacy. After I finish my dinner, I visit the commode in our part of the inn, which actually has a door. Then I ask for hot water to be delivered to our room, which comes quickly.

Not knowing when the princeling might return, I don't dare disrobe, but wash only my face and feet. When I'm done, I collapse onto my cot and am instantly asleep.

I don't know how much time passes, but suddenly I'm awake, my heart pounding. The princeling stands at the foot of the cot, studying me in the light of a lantern, his gaze intent yet unreadable.

I grip Heart Sea's hilt, my motion unthinking, instinctive, my breaths reverberating in the silent room.

"Still awake?" he murmurs. "We ride at dawn."

Then he walks away to his own bed. The light goes out. He lies down and seems to fall asleep immediately.

But my heart goes on pounding for a long time.

5

We cover more than two hundred li the next day. The ride, like the previous day's, is largely silent, though Captain Helou proves himself an amiable companion at our midday meal. From time to time I get the sensation that the princeling intends to say something to me, but he never does.

We have barely spoken at all since I awakened to find him standing at the foot of my cot, pinning me in place with his gaze. In my mind I have gone over that moment again and again. The jolt of awareness that made my heart race and my breaths shallow—that wasn't only alarm, but also a lightning-like branching of heat that left my finger-tips tingling and my entire body tense. Even now, as I think back, those sensations spark and spread, threatening to tilt into chaos.

But what bothers me isn't that I feel those things. It's that I felt a similar, perhaps identical, unrest the last time I fought

Yuan Kai. Am I that inconstant, or am I still convinced, deep down, that he *is* Yuan Kai?

My instinct is to look in the princeling's direction. Instead, I bury my face in my noodle bowl.

After lunch, we stop at a saddlery shop. To my surprise, after a brief consultation with the princeling, the saddler comes and fits a padded cover on my saddle.

My backside *has* been feeling tender—I've never ridden so much. But though I might have winced now and then, mounting and dismounting, I haven't said anything to anyone about my discomfort.

"Try it, young xiong-di," says the saddler. "It should feel nicer now."

This time I do not forget my manners. I sink to one knee before the princeling. "This humble conscript thanks His Highness for his boundless kindness and hopes a lifetime is enough to repay it."

My eyes are on his boots, but I feel his gaze as he replies, "Our country is in peril and more than ever depends on the valor of her sons. Be brave, Hua xiong-di, and you will have repaid me a thousand times."

✦ ✦ ✦

Late in the afternoon, we arrive at Pingcheng, the capital of the North.

When I was nine, I visited Jiankang, the Southern capital, a grand place—opulent, even, in certain parts. But it is an opulence marbled with a seediness so unmistakable that as young as I was, I recognized it and felt uneasy the entire time I was there.

Pingcheng is nothing like that. In fact, if I hadn't been told, I might not have guessed that it is an imperial seat. Set it down in the South and it would have been considered a middling city—acceptable, but without anything special to recommend it.

But that it is a well-laid-out, well-constructed, and bustling place is remarkable in and of itself: Less than a hundred years ago, Pingcheng, which literally means "city of peace," was sacked in war, and almost everything has been rebuilt since.

It is also quite northerly, fewer than three hundred li from the Wall. But it sits in a basin surrounded by mountains on three sides—north, east, and west—and that natural defense must have been considered a significant advantage in the choosing of a capital in uncertain times.

I'm not sure what I expect to see inside the gates. A Xianbei stronghold, perhaps, where everyone dresses in nomad garments and speaks Xianbei. Where I will feel like a complete foreigner.

The prevailing fashion does seem somewhat impractical—the sleeves on men's robes practically sweep the ground—but overall, the residents are not dressed all that differently from what I have seen elsewhere in the North. And while the accent takes some getting used to, I understand everything that is being said around me.

To my Southern ear, Northern words are like fists. When I first arrived in the North, every time I passed by a market-place, I thought fights would erupt. But what I took to be loud, nasty exchanges were often nothing more than neighbors and acquaintances asking after one another's latest meals. It is the same here. Flights of staccato, sometimes explosive-sounding syllables accompany friendly smiles and affectionate demeanors. Hawkers and stall-keepers throng the streets. Men joke and brag from the balconies of wine houses. Old women haggle while exchanging tips on how best to deal with arthritic shoulders.

And everybody speaks Chinese.

Where are the Xianbei people in the capital of this Xianbei dynasty?

We leave the busy thoroughfares and arrive in a quieter district, where streets are paved with slabs of granite and homes are hidden behind high walls topped with green glazed tiles.

At last we come to a long blind alley with only one set of doors opening onto it. The doors are large and red-lacquered, spangled with dozens of bronze ornamental studs. As we dismount, two black-clad servants rush out.

"Your Highness! Your Highness has returned safely!" chirps one of them, taking charge of the princeling's horse. "*Fu-ren* is waiting. She's impatient to see you."

Fu-ren—her ladyship. His mother?

The princeling's expression tenses. "She's back from her retreat?"

"Yes, Your Highness," says the servant, oblivious to his reaction. "His Grace sent word about the war and she returned with the messenger—got in just before the city gates closed last night."

The princeling glances at me, then at the front doors standing open to welcome him home, and hesitates, as if he is no longer sure he has come to the right place.

The servant, confused by this delay, asks, "Does Your Highness have any other instructions for this lowly lackey?"

His Highness frowns, shakes his head, and marches into the ducal residence, Captain Helou and me in tow. The first courtyard inside is a rather bare, utilitarian space. Here the lackeys lead our horses away, and a more important servant comes to offer his greetings.

"This young xiong-di is Master Hua, who is a rare hero despite his tender age," says the princeling, though his age can't be much less tender than mine. "Hua xiong-di, this is Master Yu, our majordomo."

"Welcome, Master Hua," said Yu.

"Thank you, Master Yu. I can only hope that my presence here will not add too greatly to Master Yu's duties."

"Of course not, Master Hua. It is our honor to host young heroes such as yourself."

I reply with more florid language about my gratitude. Then the princeling says, "Master Yu, will you show the captain to his lodgings? Hua xiong-di will come with me."

That the princeling wishes to keep me by his side both alarms and flusters me, but somehow doesn't surprise me as much as it should. I interest him—that I know by now. But I'm not sure whether that's due entirely to my skills.

The royal duke's residence is sizable but not magnificent, at least not by Southern standards. We walk past a reception hall, then a small warren of alleys bordered by self-contained courtyards of different sizes. One is large and entirely set aside as a garden. But the year is young yet, and the capital, more than four hundred li north of where I was yesterday morning, is much, much colder. The pond at the center of the courtyard seems to have barely thawed from the winter, its waters still and deep green. Beside it, boulders have been worked and arranged together so that they resemble a precipitous miniature hill; the small pines that grow in the crevices of this rockery make me think of winter, of snow falling off clusters of shivering needles.

The princeling's private quarters are in a medium-size court-yard immediately beyond the garden, with two suites of rooms, one set facing south, the other facing east. The most important resident of a courtyard always has the south-facing rooms—they are warm in winter and cool in summer.

The princeling walks into the south-facing suite. The first room is an elegantly simple reception room, where a young male attendant, no more than eleven or twelve, is laying out tea and refreshment. The princeling calls the boy Xiao Yi and asks after his parents, then instructs him to make ready a room in the east-facing suite for me.

My heart leaps. If I'm to have a room of my own, in a

separate suite, then I might be able to wash tonight.

When the boy has left, the princeling turns to me. "I need to offer my greetings around the residence. Hua xiong-di, please help yourself to the refreshments."

"Thank you, Your Highness."

He is a son of the family coming home. Of course he needs to call on his elders to inquire into their well-being and let them know of his safe return. He disappears into a room deeper in the suite. When he reemerges, gone are his simple travel clothes. In their place, he wears an amber brocade overrobe trimmed in dark green, with long, loose sleeves that are almost two hand-spans wide at the cuffs. A green-enameled gold band encircles the knot of his hair.

I try not to stare. And I'm glad that he, like the rest of us, has never seen an accurate reflection of himself. It would turn him vain. It certainly would turn *me* vain, if I looked like that.

Our eyes meet. He stills, then resumes pinning a braided jade ornament onto the silk sash at his waist. "Hua xiong-di, please remain in this courtyard. I will be back before too long."

Odd that he issued me such a reminder, as if I were a nosy child. Then again, after he leaves, I'm terribly tempted to be exactly that and peek into his private rooms.

Fortunately the boy, Xiao Yi, returns to lead me to the east-facing suite. As I enter, I let out a gasp of delight: Two entire walls are covered with *books*. And not only paper volumes, but antique silk scrolls and even-more-antique bamboo strips, strung together and carefully rolled up.

Summer months in the South are too warm for vigorous activities after lunch. Father and I sometimes took a covered punt and a stack of books from his collection and let ourselves drift on the lake until sunset. Part of my dissatisfaction with the North has to do with the lack of books in our new life—we had to leave most of Father's collection behind when we fled the South.

Xiao Yi brings more tea and refreshments and lights the lamps—it's getting dark outside. Then he absents himself and I fall upon the princeling's books. The Four Books and Five Classics, the *Records of the Grand Historian*, the essential commentaries—all the titles considered indispensable in the library of a well-educated person. A well-educated man, that is; a woman reading so much would make people uneasy—not that it has stopped me.

There are also collections of poetry, and treatises on philosophy, medicine, horticulture, and every other subject under the sun. I choose a volume titled *The Arithmetical Classic of the Gnomon and the Circular Paths of Heaven*—I don't remember ever seeing books about mathematics or computation in Father's collection.

The room is obviously a study. But it is perhaps also where the princeling was instructed in the classics. Certainly there are places for a tutor and two pupils: The head of the room has a raised platform on which sits a low table; below, across an aisle from each other, two more tables, smaller and less ornate than the first.

I unfasten my sword, gather a plate of delicate, round *bing*, and sit down at one of the smaller tables with my book. Three lines into the second page, I hear footsteps approaching. Very, very light footsteps, followed closely by two sets of much heavier ones. The party of three arrives in the courtyard. I can't see them through the paper-thin panes of mother-of-pearl on the window, but I hear Xiao Yi come running to greet them.

"Fu-ren! This humble lackey didn't know fu-ren would be here. This way please, fu-ren. I'll also bring tea and a brazier immediately."

"I don't need tea or a brazier. Where is my nephew?" rings a clear and clearly cross voice.

Not his mother, then, but his aunt. And the term she uses for "nephew" indicates that the princeling is her sister's son.

"His Highness went to offer his greetings to His Grace," Xiao Yi says. "And then he was going to call on your ladyship right away. He must have been detained by His Grace."

The woman sighs. "You are right. I'm still too impatient. He's probably already at my—"

She stops. I imagine her frowning.

"Why is there a light on in that room? Is someone in there?"

"His Highness brought back a young hero, Master Hua."

"Oh? This is the first time he's invited anyone to stay in his own rooms. Go knock on the door for me. I want to meet this Master Hua."

Hastily I rise and straighten my clothes—my blue overrobe

is dusty and wrinkled after two days in the saddle. The knock comes. I open the door.

Beyond the threshold stands a beautiful woman of about Father's age. Behind her are a pair of maids, each holding a lantern covered in pale yellow silk. The princeling's aunt opens her mouth to say something, only to gape at me, her expression a complicated snarl underpinned by shock, dismay, anger, and finally a great grimness.

I grow alarmed. Surely my clothes are not *that* offensively rumpled.

"Master Hua, is it?" she says stiffly.

All at once, her speech sounds strongly of the South. Why does the princeling's aunt have a Southern accent?

I bow. "This humble conscript greets fu-ren. Fu-ren, please forgive my intrusion. His Highness has seen some use in this humble conscript and has treated me with every undeserved kindness. Will fu-ren please come in?"

She stalks into the room, leaving her maids outside. "You are from the Lake Tai region."

"Yes, fu-ren. Fu-ren has keen ears."

"And your father is Hua Manlou?"

I blink. This is not something she can glean merely from my accent. Then I notice how she phrased her question. There are different ways to refer to someone else's father. Her words convey little respect but much disdain.

My eyes narrow. "Fu-ren is acquainted with my father?"

My tone is still deferential, but I take a step toward Heart

Sea. It is easy for a swordsman to make enemies, and Auntie Xia has at times alluded to Father's wild youth.

Footsteps. Someone is running in our direction at a flat-out sprint.

"Oh, yes, I am acquainted with your father," says her ladyship, her tone caustic. "And you are Hua Muyang?"

As I debate whether to correct her, the princeling bursts into the room and skids to a stop. Breathing hard, he looks at his aunt, at me, then at his aunt again. But his first words are to the servants. "You three, don't stand around in the courtyard. Go to your other duties."

When they have dispersed, he closes the door and salutes her ladyship formally. "Auntie, my apologies. Father has several lords and ministers in his study and didn't want me to miss his discussion with them. I left as soon as I could and stopped by your courtyard, only to learn you already came here."

He sounds calm enough, other than his still-irregular breaths. Yet I hear a rising desperation in his words. I think back to his reaction when he learned that her ladyship had returned unexpectedly. He glanced at me then, outside the front doors he was suddenly reluctant to enter.

Did he know, somehow, that she would take one look at me and know my exact lineage? And does that mean—my head spins—that he too knows exactly who I am?

When her ladyship says nothing, he exhales and puts on a placating smile. "Has Auntie been well? I understand you arrived back only last night. I hope the trip was not too taxing." Belatedly I notice that when he speaks to her, he takes on a Southern accent that is similar to hers but much less noticeable.

She still says nothing, her expression dark as a storm. The princeling looks at me again. My heart lurches. He isn't just desperate; he's in a state of panic.

When he speaks again, however, his voice holds steady. "I see Auntie has already met Hua xiong-di."

She slaps him, an explosive *thwack*. I gasp. Her ladyship has struck the son of a royal duke in front of his subordinate. I can't think of what he could have done to merit such harsh, humiliating treatment.

The next moment a different kind of shock rolls over me. The slap happened so fast that I can't be sure I would have been able to leap aside—or parry it—in time. Perhaps he knew the smack was coming and decided to take it. Still, it is clear: The princeling's aunt is a master martial artist.

What did he say when I asked why he didn't visit pleasure houses? *My master would have my hide if I frequented such places.* He could have been speaking of either a man or a woman. I assumed it was a man, as I have never met, or even heard of, a female master. But I of all people should know that there is nothing impossible about it—and that I cannot be the only woman under the sky trained in these skills.

"How dare you?" Her ladyship's voice is knife-cold, knife-sharp. "How dare you bring that man's son into this household? How dare you dishonor your mother's memory?"

The princeling's hand clenches, but his reply is soft and respectful. "Auntie, let us please speak of this elsewhere."

"Why? Why should we hide the truth?" She turns to me. "I see by your expression that you know nothing. Of course your father would be such a coward."

My father, a *coward*?

"Your ladyship is elevated in rank and age," I answer slowly and with as much control as I can muster, "but I cannot allow your ladyship to speak ill of my esteemed sire, who is the very embodiment of honor and forbearance."

She laughs. "The very embodiment of what? Has he not told you anything at all? He is a breaker of oaths and a murderer."

My ears ring. None of this is happening. I am not standing in a Xianbei royal duke's residence. There is no beautiful mad-woman pouring scorn and loathing upon Father. And Father, my dignified and much too self-contained father, he could never, ever have done anything to merit such relentless slander.

"Auntie—"

"Who permitted you to speak?" roars her ladyship at her nephew. "Go fetch your sword."

My veins scald. Is she going to make him fight me, *right now*, for what she thinks Father did ages ago? And is he going to do it?

The princeling pales, but he bows and leaves. I stare at his retreating back. Her ladyship sits down at the head of the room. She does not deign to look at me, but the force of her anger chokes all the air from my lungs. I can barely breathe.

The princeling returns with a shiny, black-lacquered case. He sets it down and lifts the lid.

Heart Sea!

No, not Heart Sea.

This sword is of the same dimensions as Heart Sea, its pommel decorated with the same fish-scale pattern. But instead of magnolia blossoms, the carving on its scabbard is of chrysanthemums.

Not until my fingers wrap around the handle do I realize that I have crossed the room. I have not asked for permission to unsheathe the sword, but I take the princeling's silence as assent and draw out the blade.

The same unmistakable chill of menace; the same intricate checkerboard pattern. But instead of *A Heart as Limitless as the Sea*, its inscription reads

A BLADE THAT PIERCES THE SKY

This is Sky Blade, Heart Sea's mate, which badly notched my practice sword half a month ago.

I look up at the princeling's carefully blank expression. From the very beginning my instincts have drawn parallels between him and Yuan Kai. Each time, I've scoffed at myself, because sons of Xianbei royal dukes have no cause to be involved in such a hereditary duel.

"Now do you know who we are?" demands her ladyship.

Slowly I sheathe the sword and turn around to face her. "You are the Peng family."

The Pengs and the Huas, rivals for far too many generations.

"The Peng family is no more," she says coldly. "My father had neither brothers nor sons. He hoped to end the duels by uniting our two families. Your grandfather agreed to the match."

I did not think I could be shocked again this day. "A match between . . ."

"Your father and myself."

This woman could have been my *mother*? I quake at the thought.

"But your grandfather died before the match could take place, and your father reneged on the promise."

I blink. Was *that* what Auntie Xia referred to as Father's wild youth? His decision to break a matrimonial contract would have been considered a major breach of faith, and rightly so.

Her ladyship continues. "My father was already gravely ill. The news so angered him that he passed away two days later. No more wedding, but now there was once again a duel to fight. I would have faced your father, but a few days before the appointed date, I fell ill with a high fever that refused to come down. The physicians feared I would die. I thought the duel would be postponed, but without my knowledge, my sister took my place."

This . . . seems possible. I always assumed that Father fought a man, but he never specified the gender of his opponent.

"My sister defeated him." Her ladyship stares at me. "She *defeated* him."

I thought that there was no clear winner—but I dare not

correct this woman. "My father is paralyzed, your ladyship. I see that defeat every day of my life."

"But do you know what he did to *her*?"

My gut tightens. Father's opponent walked away unscathed, didn't she?

It dawns on me that we are speaking of the princeling's mother. I glance in his direction. He stands with his head bowed, his eyes on the floor, the imprint of his aunt's hand vivid on his cheek. He is so tense that it's a wonder he doesn't break apart.

"I see Master Hua is looking at the son she left behind," says fu-ren scathingly. "She died two days after the duel, not because your father was ever able to scratch her with his sword, but because he used hidden weapons."

I recoil. Hidden weapons are not allowed in the duel, which is strictly a contest of swordsmanship. For Father to have deployed them would have been worse than dishonorable. It would have been appalling.

"The Huas weren't satisfied merely to be great swordsmen. They wanted to learn about hidden weapons and the art of healing as well. Do you know what all that interest in herbs and substances led to?"

I see Father's old library in my mind's eye. In a hidden corner, there were scores of manuscripts dealing with . . .

"Poisons," her ladyship continues inexorably, each word a kick to my temple. "The Huas were famous—and feared—not only for their swordsmanship but for their poisoned bronze lilies."

My hands clench into fists. The only hidden weapons I have ever practiced with are all spherical in shape, without an edge anywhere. But long ago, in a silk pouch of such harmless metal balls, I found an intricate little device that looked like a miniature water lily, each paper-thin petal sharp as a knife's edge. In my delight of discovery, I showed it to Father.

His alarm was so extreme he nearly toppled over. With shaking hands, he grabbed mine and examined them in minute detail while asking again and again whether the little metal flower had broken any skin. When he was at last reassured that I hadn't been lacerated by the beautiful device, he whisked it away and warned me that if I ever came across one again, I was not to touch it.

I was never able to get any explanation from him as to why.

"Two bronze lilies struck my beloved sister, and she—" Her ladyship's voice breaks. She inhales shakily. "And she died in extreme agony because your father possessed no honor. How perfidious can a man be, to break a matrimonial agreement—and then kill the woman who would have been his sister-in-law?"

It's not true. None of it. It can't be!

But the screams in my head are nothing compared to the pain etched across the face of the woman before me. The loss of her sister is still raw, her hatred of my father still seething.

She has no reason to tell lies about the broken engagement—one of the most humiliating misfortunes that can befall a woman. And would she really make up stories in front of her nephew about how his mother died?

Whatever happened, she believes deeply that she is telling the truth.

I have no idea what to believe anymore.

For a moment no one speaks. Her ladyship's harsh breaths reverberate. Mine too, I realize dimly—I'm panting as if I have just pitted myself against a deadly foe.

"Auntie," says the princeling quietly, "I didn't get the chance to tell you, but Father has invited his esteemed visitors to stay for dinner. The heroes present will also attend. And he has asked that you please grace the gathering, as many of us will depart tomorrow morning."

Her brows draw together. "Not you too. You're leaving again so soon?"

"Yes, Auntie. My apologies."

"But you've only just returned!" She grimaces and waves a hand. "No need to remind me that it is a time of war. I know."

He bows. "May I accompany you to your courtyard, Auntie?"

No doubt her ladyship must appear at the farewell dinner. But I'm sure the princeling's greater purpose is to put some distance between her and me. I'm thankful that he will lead her away, but he should have never brought me here in the first place.

And never exposed me to this horrifying past that I cannot unhear or unlearn.

Her ladyship glares at me. "Remember, both swords should be in the hands of the winner. It was when my sister went to disarm your father that he ambushed her with hidden weapons.

If you possessed any honor at all, you would surrender Heart Sea this moment."

The hairs on the back of my neck rise. Is she going to forcibly seize my sword?

But she seems to have had all she can take of me. She turns back to her nephew, and for the first time I see a glimmer of tenderness in her eyes. "Let's go."

6

It isn't until Xiao Yi timidly informs me that he is to conduct me to the banquet that I realize I am one of the "heroes" expected to take part.

He guides me to the middle hall, probably the grandest portion of the ducal residence, a standalone structure that can accommodate a hundred for New Year celebrations or other major occasions. I am placed at a table with several strangers, one of whom appears vaguely familiar. A long moment passes before I recognize Captain Helou.

It feels as if I last saw him a decade ago.

Everything has changed. Everything has shattered.

Captain Helou slaps me on the back. "Hua xiong-di, where have you been? Here, meet the brothers I'm setting out with tomorrow. You should come too—we can always use skills as marvelous as yours!"

He introduces me to a Han Chinese man in his midtwenties

named Bai, who recently entered the royal duke's service. The other man, Kedan, is a distant relative to Captain Helou.

"You two grew up together, then?" asks Bai.

"Alas, I wasn't so fortunate," answers Kedan with an easy smile. "It would have made me a better man to have grown up alongside a true hero like Captain Helou."

He goes on to explain how exactly they are related. I don't hear much of what he says. It barely registers even when he mentions that though his clan belongs to the Xianbei now, they were originally Xiongnu.

Xiongnu, the Huns, were the great enemy of the Han Dynasty. I grew up listening to tales of their bloodthirstiness— Auntie Xia's particular favorite concerned a Xiongnu prince who made a cup out of the skull of a conquered king. As a power, the Xiongnu have vanished, but the mere mention of them still sends a shiver up the collective spines of the Han Chinese.

Had I met Kedan at lunch, I would have responded to his ancestry with a clench of apprehension, if not a recoil of alarm. Now I feel almost nothing, my head too full of pandemonium to care about anything besides what happened on the day of that fateful duel.

In recent years, Father and I have not spent much time together outside my training routines. But once upon a time, it was different. We played games of go on the terrace overhanging Lake Tai. I punted him onto the lake at sunset to watch the sky turn pink and lilac. He recounted to me all the folktales he had heard during his youthful travels, and I listened to them again and again, basking in his knowledge of the world at large.

And all that time—my entire life—he has held back the truth, an omission as enormous as Lake Tai itself.

A commotion startles me: The royal duke and his family have arrived on the low dais at the front of the hall. The princeling seems to have two younger siblings, a sister and a brother. Next to the royal duke stands her ladyship. My skin scalds at her appearance, even as I grow cold inside.

The gathering rises. The guests salute the hosts. The royal duke, a broader, more rough-hewn version of his eldest son, thanks all the heroes present—is every man who can pick up a stick and fight a hero these days?—and introduces the guests of honor who will sit at the head table with his family. The men's names and positions enter my hearing and leave immediately.

The royal duke speaks some more. *Honor. Duty. Courage. Loyalty. Heaven. Earth. Gratitude.*

Words. Just words.

The princeling glances at me, his face pale, his expression uncertain. Anger burns my throat: If it weren't for him, I wouldn't be crushed under the weight of all these revelations. But almost as quickly, my anger evaporates, leaving behind only a corrosive shame. Is my father really the kind of man her ladyship described? If so, then what am I, who have always yearned to make him proud?

The royal duke finishes his speech to thunderous applause. We all sit down. Food arrives within moments, platters upon heaped platters. Grain wine flows freely. I eye the amber fluid, tempted to drink myself into a stupor. But I am a woman in the midst of many men. As such, I don't even have the luxury of behaving recklessly.

I almost change my mind when the entertainment begins. A troupe of musicians, singers, and dancers has been engaged to mark the occasion. Judging by the reactions of others in the hall, they offer a welcome diversion. But I see only chaos; I hear only cacophony.

Too many people, too much talking, too many rumbles of laughter. My head is in danger of cracking in two. My cheeks hurt from the effort of maintaining an interested half smile while the three men at my table chatter on and on.

Kedan, to hear his cousin-by-marriage Captain Helou tell it, is a famed hunter in the Greater Khingan, a mountain range far more northerly than any I've ever visited. Bai, to hear himself tell it, has led a life of exemplary uneventfulness and hopes to at last experience some excitement in this war.

Captain Helou gives an exaggerated account of my skills catching arrows. I have no choice but to return a similarly embellished version of his fight with the young soldier who didn't know his place. Kedan knocks his cousin on the arm, his gaze full of admiration.

An eternity later, Captain Helou rises to use the facilities. Kedan wastes no time refilling everyone's wine bowl, urging me to drink more.

"I've never been north of the Wall. I've never even been

anywhere *near* the Wall," says Bai, who doesn't seem to have drunk any more than me, but already sounds a little tipsy.

Kedan, on the other hand, has been guzzling. But he is so alert and unaffected that he might as well have been tipping back tea all this while. "Nothing changes drastically at the Wall. It's the same landscape, the same vegetation, the same climate whether you are north or south of it."

"But a different country," muses Bai. Then he waves his hand, as if there's a fly buzzing before his face. "Eh, what does it matter what country I'm in? As long as I'm the kind of man with his feet on the ground and his shoulders against the sky."

"Hear, hear!" cries Kedan.

I've had enough. I've been waiting for Captain Helou to return so I could use my bladder as an excuse to leave the banquet. Now I decide it doesn't matter whether he's back or not. I mutter something and exit the hall.

Outside, the sharp teeth of the night air make me hiss, but my head throbs a little less.

As I near the first alley that branches out of the path from the middle hall, I hear Captain Helou's voice. ". . . my life or my death I can serve my people, then I will not have lived or fought in vain."

I want to roll my eyes but can't. In fact, I'm filled with a searing envy for his conviction. I don't know that I believe in anything anymore.

"We who remain in the capital are grateful, Captain," says an unfamiliar voice. "The days ahead will be difficult."

The war. Nothing about it seems remotely real or important at the moment.

Two men turn from the alley onto the path: Captain Helou and one of the duke's honored guests, who is wearing some sort of ornament that jangles as he walks. I groan inwardly. I don't want to speak to anyone else tonight, especially any elevated personage before whom I must act humble and reverential.

But I have no choice except to bow and salute. "*Da-ren*. Captain."

I don't remember the honored guest's name or rank, but da-ren—important person—is a suitable catchall honorific.

"Hua xiong-di, I didn't see you drink that much. You headed to the outhouse?" Captain Helou laughs a little. "Need me to show you where it is?"

"I'm just going to bed," I answer, too worn-out to lie. "It's been a long day and I can feel a headache coming on."

"Sleep well, then, Hua xiong-di," says Captain Helou. "Your headache will be gone by morning."

"Thank you, Captain." I salute again. "Da-ren, Captain, please take care."

I remain in place until they walk off.

Back at the princeling's courtyard, Xiao Yi rushes out. When he sees that it's only me, he remains just as courteous, lighting the lamps in the east-facing suite, assuring me everything is in readiness for my rest, and begging me to please let him know if I need anything else.

When I'm finally alone, I slump down and clutch at my head.

My solitude does not last long: The princeling's footsteps come into the courtyard. He knocks on my door. When I do not reply, he walks in. I continue to sit with my elbows on my knees, my face in my hands.

"Captain Helou told me you might not be feeling well," he says quietly.

And Captain Helou is correct!

I wish now that I'd become roaring drunk at the banquet. I wish the princeling's aunt had not returned from her mountain retreat to see her nephew. I wish—

"Is it all true, what your aunt said?"

I hear him sit down across the room. "When I was in the South, I called on the referees who oversaw the duel between your father and my mother."

Auntie Xia told me there is always a crowd of spectators at every duel. Most simply get wind of it and show up, drawn by the intrigue and excitement of a fierce contest. But a few are invited as observers and referees.

"The version of events my aunt had always related to me had been told to her by a referee named Master Zhuang. He said that when my mother went to take Heart Sea, the reward for her victory, your father, whom everyone believed to be already incapacitated, fired two bronze lilies at her in gross violation of the rules. But by the time of my sojourn in the South, Master Zhuang was already dead.

"The second of the three referees was still alive, but reluctant to say anything. But the third one, a Master Lu, said that he did not believe Master Zhuang had it entirely correct. Master Lu had been seated exactly opposite my mother as she approached your father, and he feared that instead of merely taking his sword, she meant to kill him. He was convinced that your father used hidden weapons out of self-preservation, not treachery."

I wish he hadn't told me this. Without corroborating evidence, I could still hope to deny everything. But now, even if this Master Lu's account clears Father of murderous intent, it still confirms his killing of the princeling's mother.

"Why did you visit the referees?" I manage after a while.

"For most of my life I believed my aunt to be an eyewitness at the duel. From time to time, the details of her story changed. I would ask her why that was so, and she would always tell me that I was the one who remembered wrong. And then one day, when I was fourteen, I learned that she hadn't been there at all. That she had been at home, deliriously ill."

Did that shock him as much as what I learned today shocked—and still shocks—me?

"Did you . . . did you tell your aunt what Master Lu said?"

"No." He is quiet for some time. "Master Lu told me that he spoke to her shortly after she recovered from her illness. If she chose not to believe him then, my repeating his version of events wouldn't make any difference."

I breathe hard, my head still in my hands. I'm unsure whether the sensation coursing through me is relief—or fright for what I might yet learn.

"I'm sorry for what happened this evening. I thought you wanted to leave the muster, and I thought my aunt was far from home."

I shake my head. I actively campaigned to get out of the encampment—he's blameless in that. As for what I learned today, I could not have been spared forever. At our actual duel, with his aunt and my father both in attendance, my blissful ignorance would have gone up in flames.

"Anyway," he carries on after a while, "I've come to ask whether you plan to continue with us. Captain Helou, Kedan, Bai, and I will head out in the morning. Master Yu will accompany us."

I vaguely recall meeting Yu, the majordomo.

"To the lands beyond the Wall?" That was what Bai and Kedan were discussing at dinner, wasn't it?

"Yes."

"Why?"

"To scout the movements of the Rouran."

I look up at last, expecting to see him seated formally—knees on the mat, legs folded under, back perfectly straight. But he has one knee on the mat before him, the other raised to the side, his hand on that knee. I've forgotten that he is in not just his own home, but his own rooms.

"No, I mean, why is your father sending you on a dangerous mission?"

"We are in a time of war."

"I know that. Why hasn't he pulled some strings for you?

Shouldn't you be looking after the ledgers at the central granary, or another safe place?"

He frowns, a sharp crease between his brows. "I'm a trained fighter. How can my father deploy thousands of other people's sons while hiding me in the back of the central granary?"

The South is filled with officials who would do just that. I look at my hands.

"I see," he murmurs. "You thought that I would be stowed somewhere away from danger. And that if you were assigned to me, you would also be safe."

I sigh over my great error, but do not feel remotely ashamed that I have no desire to risk my life in this war. "What if I don't continue with you?"

"You can stay here and see if my father has other tasks for you. If you don't want to stay here, then someone must escort you back to the encampment."

I grimace. I absolutely do not want to remain at the ducal residence—not with his aunt in the same compound. And I have just as little desire to return to the encampment and its sanitation trenches. There I would not be able to keep my secret for long. And when I am discovered . . .

I'd like to think that my deception would be looked upon kindly—after all, honoring one's father is all that is good and proper. But I dare not trust in that hope. Worse, after I am punished, the sub-prefect's men will still clap a heavy fine on my family, then drag Dabao off to fill my slot.

"Now that I think about it, I can see a third alternative," says the princeling slowly. "We will stop at a border garrison before we go into Rouran territory. If you pretend to fall sick or something of the sort, I can cite our haste and leave you behind."

A garrison won't have thousands upon thousands of men, but it could very well house hundreds. I might not fare any better there than I would at the encampment. And wasn't I trying to avoid going anywhere near the border in the first place?

The urge comes over me to throw myself to the ground and beg for a pass home. Surely his father can manage it—an act of mercy toward one lowly, utterly insignificant conscript. But how can I demand such a favor of the royal duke when he is sending his own son into danger? When my father was responsible for the death of his wife?

I drop my face back into my hands. "I guess I can try my luck at the border garrison."

The princeling sighs. "I'll let you rest, then. It'll be an early start."

I hear him rise and walk toward the door. "Wait!"

He stops. "Yes?"

A few heartbeats pass before I can ask my question. "Why don't you want to kill my father—or me—to avenge your mother?"

"I have seen your father and I do not wish to inflict any more suffering on him. As for you . . ." He exhales. "I've said it before: We did not choose this rivalry; we were born into it, that's all. Had we met under different circumstances, we could have been friends."

All at once I'm perilously close to tears.

The door shuts behind him. I wrap my arms around my knees, as if I could make a fortress of myself, as if that would make me feel less lost, or the room not so echoingly empty.

7

I don't remember falling asleep, but in the morning I shudder awake from a dream in which I am forcibly evicted from the ducal residence, not by the princeling or even his aunt, but by the royal duke himself, tossing me bodily out of the front doors.

After I stop shaking and get up, I learn from Xiao Yi that the princeling will take his leave of his family in private. I'm glad that I won't see his aunt again, yet I can't help wondering whether her ladyship is as enraged this morning—and as disconsolate—as she was the night before.

Whether that has been her state of being for almost the entire time I've been alive.

The men of the company and I gather in the first courtyard of the residence. My stomach drops when I spy the royal duke and his son approaching together. Surely, His Grace will have learned by now whose daughter I am.

I brace myself for the worst. Still, I almost flinch when His

Grace's gaze settles on me. But there is no bitterness in his eyes, only contemplation and . . . sympathy.

My shame burns all the more for my confusion.

The royal duke salutes us and bids us a safe journey. The princeling, again in dark, simple garments, kneels before him in farewell. As he rises, he glances at me. I look away, not wanting to meet his eyes.

It occurs to me that I don't even know his name anymore—his surname cannot possibly be Yuan, for one thing, because that is a Han Chinese name and he is Xianbei. And since a lowly conscript like me is never allowed to address someone of his station by name, I also have no excuse to ask anyone about it.

We mount and set out in two columns: the princeling and Captain Helou in front, Kedan and me in the middle, Yu and Bai at the rear. The city is waking up. Smoke rises from chimneys; young wives sweep outside their front doors; enticing aromas billow out of bing shops and noodle places, luring in their first customers of the day.

The city gate opens as we draw near. The city walls are the height of six men, their crenellated top wide enough for eight guards to march abreast. But here at the gate the walls widen even further to accommodate a set of three impressive guard towers on top.

"Do you ever wonder, Hua xiong-di," says Kedan, the Xiongnu descendant, "whether there are places in the world where cities do not have walls? Where peace has reigned for so long that when the walls crumble, people do not bother to build them again?"

What kind of question is that? "I have not seen much of the world," I tell him, hoping to end the conversation.

He glances at me. Last night I took him to be around twenty-seven. Now, with the sky turning a fish-belly white, I see that although he is weather-browned, he is much younger than I supposed—at most twenty-one or twenty-two, with an impish face and dimples when he grins.

He looks wistful. "Me neither—or at least I think the world must be far larger and greater than what I've seen so far. But have you ever imagined such a durable peace, such easy times?"

I shake my head. Despite my preoccupation, I feel a twinge of regret for not having shared his lofty imagination.

We are just through the gate when a young man of about Kedan's age, sitting by the side of the road, leaps up and waves his arms. "There you are!"

The princeling signals us to halt. He dismounts and greets the man affectionately. "Tuxi xiong, we thought we'd have to go without you!"

I note the surname, a Xianbei one.

"I arrived after the gate closed last night," says the man. "Thank Heaven for enterprising folks who keep inns for stragglers like me. I thought if I could get up early enough, I'd catch you on your way out."

"And you were right." The princeling turns around. "Let's acquaint you with everyone."

Tuxi is a big man, taller than the princeling and Captain Helou by a hand-width, and robust—almost chubby—in build, with a round face, thoughtful eyes, and surprisingly light, graceful movements. His horse is of a commensurate size, a handsome black beast with neat white socks.

The princeling tells us that Tuxi is the son of an aide to his father, and sets him to ride between Kedan and me. After a while I realize why: Tuxi, despite his air of general friendliness, is actually rather shy. But Kedan is warm and outgoing, and soon puts Tuxi at ease.

I listen to them getting to know each other with half an ear. From time to time Captain Helou also turns around and briefly joins the conversation. The rest of the men—and I—are quiet.

We do not ride as fast as we did on our way to the capital, as we begin our climb through the mountains not long after leaving the city behind. The roads I have been traveling on since I left home were all built during the Han Dynasty. They are wide and smooth, engineered to last. Even cutting through the mountains, two riders can proceed comfortably side by side; and where there are steps, they have been made as shallow and even as the shape of the ground allows.

For our midday meal, we eat at a pavilion that overhangs a sharp ridge and boasts a commanding view. A statue of a sitting Buddha shares that view with us.

In the South, Father regularly sent me, dressed as a man, to climb a mountain not far from our home. On the flank of the peak sat a small Buddhist monastery, led by an abbot who maintained a correspondence with Father—my trips there were as much to deliver Father's letters as to test my stamina. In the beginning I was wary that the abbot might preach to me. He never did. And here in the North, I have missed his kindly eyes and quiet demeanor far more than I thought I would.

As the rest of the company concentrate on their food, Yu makes his way to everyone, offering delicacies. I note his perfect carriage and efficient motion. It's ridiculous to bring a majordomo where there won't be a large household to manage, but maybe not as ridiculous if that majordomo is also a skilled martial artist.

Yu stops by me. "Her ladyship is from the South, and she enjoys buns made with lotus seed paste. I understand Hua xiong-di is also from the South. Would Hua xiong-di care to have one?"

I probably shouldn't take anything prepared with her ladyship in mind. But lotus seed paste is hard to come by in the North, and who knows when—or if—I'll ever have the chance to taste it again? I accept the pastry and thank Yu with a profusion of words.

He doesn't leave my side immediately, but bites into a dried apricot. Together we contemplate the pitched green and orange roofs of the capital, now in the distance. After a while, I can't help but ask, "Is Master Yu, by some chance, experienced in warfare?"

He shakes his head. "I am just here to serve His Highness."

Someone less important than he can look after the princeling. But since he doesn't seem interested in talking about himself, I shift the subject.

"Her ladyship must have been sad to see His Highness leave."

"Undoubtedly. But she would not have burdened His Highness with tears. She is no ordinary woman, and her husband is a soldier."

So she *is* married to the royal duke—I wondered last night when I saw that she sat next to him at the banquet. I exhale. I have heard horror stories about broken matches and the women who never get another chance.

"The royal duke's younger children—they are hers, then?" Children who are both siblings and cousins sometimes happen in grander households, where the master's concubines might be sisters.

"No, His Grace married again after the death of His Highness's mother—a strategic alliance arranged by the court. That lady gave birth to His Grace's younger children. She passed away four years ago. Her ladyship married His Grace only last spring."

"Has she been in the North long?"

"Oh, yes. She has been a member of the household since His Highness's mother died. She raised him as her own."

"And he—he reveres her as his own mother too, I imagine?"

"Very much so. He is devoted to her."

Kedan calls out something. Yu excuses himself and rushes over. I eat the lotus seed paste bun, lightly sweet and delicious, and wallow in a rush of memories. Fishing with Murong on a terrace, one such pastry in hand; Auntie Xia setting down a plate of them before me, complaining that Father worked me too hard; me busy eating one while Mother combed my hair, her fingers gentle and sure, the jade bangles on her wrists clinking softly.

But these memories can never again be as sweet and pure as they once were.

While I soaked up the care and affection Mother lavished upon me, a boy grew up motherless because of Father's poisoned bronze lilies. And the woman he abandoned to marry my mother spent the rest of her youth as a poor relation in the royal duke's household, raising her nephew. That she is now married to the duke does not negate those years, which must have been lonely and difficult.

Worse, I can't help but wonder now why exactly Father decided to break the match that his father had arranged. The idealistic answer is love for my mother—a love so grand and passionate that it could not be denied. But I no longer know whether my father has ever been that kind of man.

One time I asked Auntie Xia how it was possible that Father was paralyzed in the duel. I couldn't imagine anyone getting the better of him. Auntie Xia sniffed and said that the Pengs were so poor that all they had were their swords, and the only thing they ever did was training at swordsmanship.

Was there an element of snobbery in Father's repudiation of the princeling's aunt? And did he not want to be married to a woman who was a greater sword master than he?

I wish I could spread wings and fly south to ask him all these questions.

And I wonder whether I would ever receive any answers, even if I managed to safely return home.

✦ ✦ ✦

When we leave, I pass the Buddha statue again. Someone has laid a tiny blossom, the first I've seen this year, in its upturned palm. I pick up the pale pink flower and hold it under my nose. It gives no fragrance but that of the freshness of growing things. I put it back and walk on.

That evening we lodge at a village nestled in a small valley, which has a larger inn than I expected. Tuxi explains that we are on one of the main roads from the capital to the Wall. As it is typically a two-day journey for a party with fast horses, this settlement, near the midpoint between the capital and the garrison at the end of the road, is where many travelers choose to spend the night.

I like Tuxi. There is an air of gentleness to him—the only person in the company I can say that about. Captain Helou is, of course, fierce despite his amiability. Kedan, just as genial, gives off a sense of great mischief barely held back. Bai I'm not sure about: He acts convivial, yet I'm under the impression that he is in fact completely guarded. Yu is unfailingly solicitous of everyone in the party, but he does not bother with joining conversations or forming camaraderie. Instead he watches over the princeling with a perceptible anxiety.

The princeling conducts himself as he always does in public, with great propriety and even more silence. I find myself thinking back to our dinner, the day we first met, during which he not only spoke a fair bit, but even cracked a joke.

All the while knowing that my father is the reason he grew up motherless.

Was it a strategic choice? In *The Art of War*, Sunzi says, *If you know the enemy and know yourself, you need not fear the result of a hundred battles.* Was he getting to know me so he can better vanquish me?

Or is it truly as he said—that under different circumstances, we could have been friends?

He was speaking of Hua Muyang, of course. He and *I* could never have been friends. Confucian principles forbid fraternization between members of the opposite sex once past age seven.

Yet of everyone under the sky, I might be the only person who understands, viscerally, the life he has led. My father compelled me with fear; his aunt drove him with her need for retribution. We have each spent countless hours perfecting a single move, because every single move is judged by a relentless standard. And we have lived in each other's shadow since we were old enough to understand that we too might not leave this duel unscathed.

But we can never truly be friends. Too much enmity lies between our families, too much blood spilled.

After our simple dinner, I go for a walk. All of us have been put into one room, with a platform bed that is said to accommodate ten, but which will be a tight squeeze even for seven—and

I don't want to spend my evening cooped up with so many men in such a small space.

The wind bites with fangs like a wolf's. My behind is quite frozen when I've done what I needed to do. And I itch in places where I don't want to be seen scratching.

At the ducal residence, after my conversation with the princeling, twice his attendant sidled up to my door to inquire whether I needed anything. Wanting to be left alone, I sent him away each time. Stupidly: Nobody's heartache has ever been eased by also being dirty. No matter how distressed I was, I could still have asked for some hot water!

When I return it's fully dark, but I can make out the princeling and Yu standing some distance from the inn, speaking too softly for me to hear. Inside our room, Kedan is holding court, telling Tuxi and Bai the history of his friendship with Captain Helou. Alas, they have been separated by a great deal of distance and time, and have met once a year at most, at weddings or other occasions that gather far-flung relatives under one roof.

"This is the first time we'll be doing something other than sitting at a table and drinking together," declares Kedan, clearly relishing the prospect. Then he points a playfully accusatory finger at Captain Helou. "By the way, my brother, you did not recommend me when the royal duke wanted a tracker."

Captain Helou throws both hands up in a placating gesture. "He wanted one urgently and I thought you were a thousand li away, deep in the mountains, your location known to no one except yourself."

"Well, that happens often," admits Kedan. "So it's lucky for everyone that when I went to the ducal residence to visit you, Master Yu recognized what a prize I am. And by the way, you would know my location better if you replied more regularly to my letters!"

"I'm away so much. If I come back and there are three letters from you, I can't reply three times!" answers Captain Helou, laughing.

He has been leaning against the wall. Now he straightens and brushes away brick dust from his sleeve. It's a little odd for me to see him in civilian clothes—he seems made for uniforms. But we are trying to pass ourselves off as a party that has nothing to do with the imperial government. When the innkeeper asked, Master Yu told him that we are a band of hired swords, traveling to the border to escort a commander's family to safer surroundings farther south.

"It's getting late," says Captain Helou. "I'm going for a walk to stretch my legs. You lot had better get ready for bed. It will be another early start tomorrow."

Kedan, who is sitting on the platform bed, jumps off. "I'll come with you."

"Didn't you say you need a letter written? There'll be less and less time for that in the future. Better get on with it. Tuxi xiong-di here can help you."

"I do carry the four treasures of the study with me," says Tuxi as Captain Helou marches out.

Kedan slumps back down at having been left behind,

but he rallies himself and pats Tuxi on the arm. "We'll do it tomorrow—I don't have any letters that are *that* urgent. Why don't you tell me something of your travels, Tuxi xiong, the things you've seen?"

Yu comes into the room at that moment. "Ah, Master Hua, just the person I want to see. You will sleep against this wall."

The platform bed stretches from one end of the room to the other. I was hoping I might get a wall so I wouldn't be wedged between two of my traveling companions. I waste no time taking the spot as Tuxi tells Kedan that he was a sickly child who never did much except read.

Yu leaves the room then. Kedan lowers his voice and asks, "Tuxi xiong, I'm under the impression that His Highness is the one leading our crew. Why him and not Captain Helou, or even this Master Yu?"

Tuxi raises a brow. "You doubt His Highness?"

"No, no, of course not. But he's awfully young, isn't he? I think only Hua xiong-di is younger. Is it because he's a royal duke's son?"

Tuxi chuckles a little. "I see you probably haven't spent much time with His Highness."

"Met him for the first time before the banquet last night, after he and Captain Helou came back from their trip."

"Well, first, he's the best martial artist I've ever seen. Second, and this may be more important, he is both the calmest and bravest man I've ever met."

"Are you saying he's a greater and more courageous fighter

than Captain Helou?" Kedan is clearly incredulous.

"I don't know Captain Helou that well," answers Tuxi. "I'm only saying that, knowing His Highness, I have no problem serving under him."

I don't care whether Kedan prefers a different leader or how the rapport between members of this crew might develop. Tomorrow we will reach the garrison, and that will mark the end of the road for me.

My eyes close and oblivion comes. I have no idea when the spot next to me fills. But at some point I wake up slightly and know, just know, that it is the princeling beside me.

When I fall back asleep, I dream of the terrace of my old home in the South, a thousand water lily blossoms floating on the lake beyond. Standing on the terrace are the princeling and I, facing each other, swords drawn, blood dripping from both Heart Sea and Sky Blade.

✦ ✦ ✦

"Word is that nearer the border, there are Rouran spies along the imperial road, and we don't want them to get wind of our party," says Yu the next morning as we swing into our saddles. "It has been decided that we will take a less-traveled route. On this detour, we might encounter bandits. So be alert, be careful, and do not stray from the group."

We pass through one last guard post before veering onto a narrow but well-trod trail. I don't need to ask why the trail is so well-trod when the imperial road is both fast and smooth: There are always those who do not want to travel in the open.

We wend halfway up a rocky hill, descend to a small, clear brook, then climb up the next hill. From that point on, neither the scenery nor our route seems to change. One hill after another, one valley after another, sometimes with a stream at the bottom, most often without. If it weren't for the occasional glimpse of a tiny village, or a hermit's hut, or a footbridge across a stream constructed from fallen trees, I'd be convinced that we are circling the same hills over and over again. Even with the minor variations, I have to tell myself that we—most probably—aren't.

We ride in single file and no one speaks. Even nature itself is mute. Birds barely sing. Squirrels do not leap from branch to branch. And not once does a hare dart across our path.

I almost long for outlaws to charge down the slopes—they would make for a welcome distraction from the noise and disruption in my head. It is only the second day after her ladyship's revelations invalidated everything I thought I knew about my life. My dismay has not lessened, but now there is also a sense of despair—that I will always live in the long shadow of Father's choices.

I almost bump into Tuxi, who has reined to a stop. In fact, the entire company has halted. The silence, which earlier was only tedious, has turned heavy. Oppressive.

We are in a shallow valley, along the center of which lies a long streak of dried mud. A rivulet probably flows here in wetter months, but now there is only the empty streambed, dotted with small boulders. I glance behind me. Bai, Kedan, and Yu all look grim. In front, Tuxi's broad back blocks the view to Captain Helou and the princeling. But Tuxi is flexing and unflexing his free hand. And when he clenches those fingers into a fist, his knuckles turn white.

His horse, perhaps sensing his tension, steps to the side, and I finally see what made everyone stop: a three-tiered pyramid of heads.

The bottom ones are grinning skulls, but the head on the very top is only partially rotted. Its eyes, cheeks, and much of its nose are gone, but its hair is still tied more or less neatly in a topknot. The blood that remains at the severed neck has turned black. The lips peel back, baring teeth like a snarling monkey.

As I stare in revulsion, a centipede as long as my forearm crawls out of an eye socket, only to disappear into the mouth.

My stupefaction is the only thing that prevents me from vomiting.

"Hua xiong-di," comes the princeling's soft voice. "Do you hear anything?"

Forcing my agitated breaths to calm, I listen. There is no rustling of leaves or snapping of branches to indicate anyone approaching. I shake my head, my stomach lurching with the motion.

The princeling wheels his horse around. He confers briefly with Captain Helou, during which Captain Helou does most of the whispering. Then the princeling stops opposite me, in the exact middle of our single-file procession, and everyone else pulls in close.

"Such warning signs are usually not meant for potential marks—no need to scare those away," says the princeling. "We have likely stepped into a territorial dispute between rival gangs of bandits. But we have sixty more li of these hills and no choice but to press on.

"Our current formation will do. Captain Helou has cavalry experience and will continue on in second place. Master Yu will bring up the rear. Be vigilant. A volley of arrows could be loosed upon us before we see or hear anyone."

We ride faster, not at a gallop—that would tire the horses after a few li—but at a sustained trot. On the imperial road, this would be fine. But here on paths that twist, turn, and change elevation—sometimes all three at once—our speed feels nerve-rackingly swift.

I am a decent rider on flat surfaces, able to keep my seat securely. But this pace on this terrain tests my equestrian skills. I concentrate on breathing, on moving up and down in rhythm with my horse's gait, so as not to allow fear a chance to take hold.

The length of a meal passes. The scenery becomes more forbidding—we are making our way through a ravine hemmed in by cliffs to either side. The muscles of my back and abdomen ache from holding to the pace without bouncing in the saddle. I am both hungry and too tense to eat, my mind excruciatingly alert yet increasingly tired.

My hands too are tired. I've been holding the reins in one hand and a trio of hidden weapons in the other. Iron lightning, they are called—a fancy name for metal spheres a bit smaller than walnuts, mostly hollow but still hefty enough for a multitude of purposes.

The end of the ravine comes into sight. I exhale. *The Art of War* advises against being the second on the scene in narrow passes. The sooner we are out of this bottleneck, the better.

The air hisses. The hidden weapons leave my hand and meet three arrows. A fourth arrow barely misses Captain Helou as he ducks low in the saddle.

"Faster!" commands the princeling.

We break into a gallop, another volley of arrows striking the ground in our wake.

Bandits block the ravine's exit. They brace themselves as we approach. My heart, already pounding, lurches when I see why they don't fear being mowed down by a company of riders: They have strung a rope across the mouth of the ravine at withers height. If the princeling plows into it, his horse will instantly lose its footing and throw him.

The princeling veers left. Through the space he vacates, Captain Helou hurls a short-handled axe. The axe embeds itself in the forehead of the first man beyond the rope. He collapses before a scream leaves my throat.

We are on a downhill slope, our progress thunderous. But the princeling accelerates even further, his sword in hand.

"Careful!" My cry echoes on bare cliffs.

His horse leaps over the rope, an astonishingly beautiful feat. At the height of the horse's trajectory, the princeling leans to the side, almost hanging off his saddle, and slices the rope in two.

Our roars of approval meet a din of dismay from the bandits. As Captain Helou clears the canyon, he throws himself nearly out of his saddle and yanks his axe from the head of its victim. I'm too busy keeping up with my companions—and keeping my seat—to be nauseated by the sight.

The princeling whistles sharply. All the horses immediately slow—I almost plow nose-first into my horse's mane. What's the matter? Why aren't we making our escape as fast as possible?

As I emerge from the ravine, I see why. Bandits stand three deep in a semicircle, each holding a long bamboo pole with a pointed end. Bamboo is light, flexible, but extremely hardy. Properly sharpened, a bamboo spear can easily pierce skin and sinew, equine as well as human.

Fear grips me by the windpipe. My heart thuds, each beat a hammer strike against my rib cage. Kedan nudges me—we seven are to form a circle, facing out.

"Leave your horses and you may go," shouts a bandit, presumably the chief.

I swallow. Even a three-year-old would not be taken in by that promise.

"Lay down your weapons and we will suffer you to live," replies the princeling, not raising his voice.

The bandit chief guffaws and spits. "The brat is tired of living. Let's give him what he wants."

The men with their knife-sharp bamboo spears step forward, shrinking the radius of the semicircle.

The princeling sheathes his sword and dismounts. The rest of his men follow. After a moment of hesitation, I join them on the ground—and sway. I knew my midsection ached from the strain of riding; I didn't realize the muscles of my thighs were also exhausted.

"Everyone grab a bamboo spear," commands the princeling, his voice still soft.

Before he has uttered the final syllable, he has already yanked a spear from the bandit closest to him. The rest of the company needs no further urging—except me. I have never been trained to take another's weapon with my bare hands.

Kedan takes two spears and tosses one at me. I catch it gratefully. The bamboo spears are long, almost half again as tall as me, and Heart Sea's reach would be too short to offer me much defense.

The bandits rush in, shouting, their faces contorted with battle lust. All six men on my side swing their bamboo spears wide, pushing the enemies back. But I only stare, not moving at all.

I have never been in a situation where anyone actually wants to harm me, let alone scores and scores of hardened, ferocious men looking to kill me as fast as they can.

Patience. Concentrat—

I could die here! Pinned to the ground, writhing in agony, and bleeding to death, while everyone else fights on.

My companions succeed in widening the semicircle, but that only leaves more room for bandits to rush in and surround each of us. Three bandits hurtle toward me, their bamboo spears pointed at my throat. I open my mouth to scream but all my muscles have seized, and only a weak bleat emerges.

"Hua xiong-di!" Kedan cries. "Watch out!"

Somehow I swing my bamboo spear and knock those of the three bandits away from me. But the bandits immediately attack again. This time, instead of three sharp points coming at my throat, I have one aimed at my belly, another at my chest, and yet another at my shoulder.

My mind stutters. I have also never trained against multiple opponents. What do I do?

Kedan leaps in front of me and, with one diagonal slash of his bamboo spear, followed by several quick jabs, forces my attackers back several steps.

"Fight, Hua Mulan!" The princeling's voice comes from twenty paces away. "Fight, and your training will take over."

But my mind is completely blank. My palms sweat. And my feet—my usually quick, agile feet—are stuck to the ground as if they have grown roots.

Kedan returns to combatting his own share of bandits. Mine press in again. The desire not to be pierced through makes me raise my bamboo spear and counter two bandits' strikes. The third jabs his spear toward my foot and I jump back—clumsily and off balance, but at least I'm moving.

Another bandit joins the fray, this one not holding any

weapon, his meaty hands immediately reaching for the shaft of my bamboo spear. I retreat again.

"No!" shouts Kedan, from somewhere to my left. "Don't give ground. Push *out*."

I understand what he is trying to tell me: Our goal in engaging the bandits is to drive them back and put them in enough disarray for us to rush to our steeds and break out of this siege. All the same, the bandits before me are so hideously murderous that I give way again. What happens when they trap me against my horse? What do I do then?

I step backward yet again, barely doing enough to hold my attackers at bay. From my other side, Yu comes to my assistance, repelling the bandits off me.

Another sharp whistle. A horse whinnies. I hear someone leaping into a saddle. "Time to go!" commands the princeling.

Yu runs to his steed. I want to do the same. But I'm already too close to my horse, and my three bandits are on me again.

"Go, Hua Mulan. Go!"

The princeling, two bamboo spears in hand, bears down on my attackers. I clamber onto my horse, shaking all over. Out of the corner of my eye, I see him launch the spears against the nearest bandits.

I wheel my mount around and urge it after the others. Two bandits reach for their bows. Now that I'm out of immediate danger, my training does take over. I stick my hands into my saddlebag, seeking more hidden weapons. What I find is an extra pair of lotus paste buns that Yu gave me yesterday.

Swearing, I let the two buns fly, hitting one bandit on the hand and the other on the temple. They probably don't hurt much, but they startle the bandits enough that both drop the arrows they were about to nock. The princeling comes through safely and gains on me as I gain on Bai, the next person ahead.

We gallop alongside a tranquil, shallow-looking river. The valley is wider and flatter than any we've seen since we left the imperial road, the banks smooth and grassy. The shouts and curses of the bandits fade. The sun is even shining overhead.

I see no beauty and I know no relief. All I feel is a burning, abrasive shame: At my first real test, I've proved myself completely useless.

Worse, I am a coward.

Bright blue sky, spotless clouds, rolling grassland dotted here and there with herds of sheep and horses, and, at the edge of the horizon, blue-violet hills that are almost unearthly in their beauty.

We stop, even though we intended to forge ahead. No one speaks, but the breeze that meanders past sounds like a collective sigh. And the air has a subtle sweetness. Spring—it smells of spring. Not the Southern spring of soft rain and apricot blossoms, or the Northern spring of high wind and yellow dust, but a spring that has no beginning and no end. A spring that does not quite belong to this world.

Even with the upheaval in my head, I can't help feeling a little inebriated by the silence and purity of this place. In stories Auntie Xia used to tell me, gods and goddesses always lived in inaccessible mountains or on hidden islands far into the ocean. If those deities had any sense, they would claim this place, ride their phoenixes and giant cranes across this diamond-clear sky, and set their feast of longevity peaches and immortality elixirs on this soft, fragrant carpet.

I sigh. If only this heavenly peace was the sum total of my life.

But already I sense my companions' attention. When I look back, they hastily glance away. Still I glimpse Bai's disapproval, Captain Helou's confusion, and Kedan's bewildered concern.

My cheeks singe. I can only be thankful that the princeling has not turned around to study me. If I were to see any disdain from him—or worse, pity . . .

He urges his horse forward. The rest of the company follows suit.

"Where *are* we?" Kedan asks, almost as if speaking to himself.

"About thirty li south of the Wall," answers Captain Helou, from ahead.

So we haven't stumbled upon some earthly paradise far removed from the current strife. Quite the opposite: Should the Rouran swarm past our defenses, this beautiful grassland will be one of the first places they'll trample underfoot.

I ride on, trying not to think of anything at all.

◆ ◆ ◆

At dusk we reach our destination, a large border garrison commanded by a man who once served under the princeling's father.

A chain of mountains looms north of the grassy plain, a natural barrier. But obviously that wasn't considered enough protection against invaders, as the Wall snakes across the foot-hills of this range. And the garrison, squat and foursquare, built of stone and mud bricks on an abrupt rise, oversees this stretch of the Wall.

The commander, excited to welcome the princeling, takes him aside for a private chat. The rest of us are shown into a barrack room.

Yu assigns everyone tasks. After four days in the saddle, my entire body aches. But no one else seems worn out. I grit my teeth, help Yu beat comforters and blankets, then crawl along-side Kedan to examine the sleeping platform inch by inch for fleas—all while drowning in my own thoughts.

I am useless. I am hopeless. I have humiliated myself beyond redemption. I am not worthy of Heart Sea and I have wasted all the years Father has spent on me.

Is it because I'm a girl? Is it because of some innate weakness that despite all my training, I turned into a block of wood when I most needed to bring that training to bear?

At dinner, the princeling and Captain Helou are seated with the commander. I plow through my food and, with Yu's per-mission, leave the canteen while everyone else is still eating. When I've had a spell of privacy at the facilities, I go back to the barracks and sit in the dark, barely able to understand everything that's happened since I first passed through the gates of the capital.

I arrived at the royal duke's residence feeling as pleased as was possible under the circumstances. Not only had I done my duty to my family, but I'd extricated myself from the encampment and entered the service of an important scion. It seemed highly reasonable to assume that I would return home in safety *and* honor at the end of the war.

The naïve girl I was two days ago would have been dismayed and flabbergasted to learn that in so little time she would find herself on the northern border. Yet I barely care about my precarious location: Not only can I no longer trust my father, I cannot even trust myself.

I prized the strength, agility, and power that resulted from my training. I treasured the thought that I would never be at the mercy of any man. That I needed no father or brother to shield me. That I was my own shield.

I am my own very, very shoddy shield, which cracked as soon as it was struck.

The sound I make is that of an injured animal, cowering in the dark.

My companions return. They fall silent outside the door and whisper about the unlit interior.

"I'm not asleep," I am obliged to call out. "And the lamps are right here."

Two lamps flare to life, illuminating my companions— everyone but the princeling, who has been given a separate room. It's the first time since the bandit fight that we are thrown together without some other task at hand, not even a duty as

123

undemanding as eating. Tuxi and Kedan look both concerned and sheepish. Captain Helou appears embarrassed. Bai seems more suspicious than anything else, and Yu's face is, as usual, completely opaque.

I wish the lamps would go out and darkness would swallow me again. What do I say to a group of men who have witnessed my utter incompetence?

"Everybody ate well?" I might as well fall back on platitudes.

"You left too early, Hua xiong-di," Kedan tells me. "His Highness sent dishes from his table to ours. Our group is now the envy of the entire garrison."

"I think that was his way of telling the commander that he shouldn't have assigned us a barrack room that we needed to clean ourselves," says Tuxi. "Some commanders are like that. He probably thought that since he gave His Highness nice quarters of his own, His Highness wouldn't care what happens to the men he brought."

"Careful what you say about a commander in his own garrison, Tuxi xiong-di—sometimes walls have ears," cautions Yu.

Tuxi's eyes widen in surprise at the warning, but he inclines his head. "Master Yu is right and I thank him. I have been too free with my tongue."

Yu nods in return. "Tomorrow a messenger heads south from the fort. If any of you wish to send letters home, this is the time. Make sure, however, that you do not mention where you are, who you are with, or what you are going to do."

I rub my throbbing temples. A letter.

Dear Father, all was well on my grand adventure as a male conscript until I met the last member of the Peng family—the woman whom you scorned, and whose sister you later killed, for reasons that may or may not be nefarious. Things took a sharp turn for the worse when I discovered that I am no asset to anyone in a fight, not even to myself. I wish I could fly home and ask you face-to-face why you never told me the truth. But I am a thousand li away and can only founder in doubt and unhappiness.

Tuxi climbs onto the sleeping platform next to me and sets a low table before himself. From his bag he removes a carefully wrapped package, which contains paper, a brush pen, an ink stick, and a small ink stone: the four treasures of the study, as he mentioned last night.

He pours a few drops of water into the depression on the ink stone, then grinds the ink stick against the stone in a gentle, circular motion. At the other end of the platform, Bai sits cross-legged, mending a pair of trousers. The room is quiet, except for Kedan dictating a letter to Captain Helou. From time to time, Tuxi glances at Kedan, as if wishing he could be the one writing Kedan's letter.

I spread open a piece of paper myself, but I only stare at it, no words coming to mind. Or perhaps too many words coming to mind, but none that can be set down in a respectful missive to one's parent.

"Hua xiong-di, do you want to use my pen and ink?" asks Tuxi. "I'm already done."

I glance up and can't believe my eyes: He writes a remarkably lovely script, each stroke perfectly controlled. I stare at his giant hands, then at the tiny, immaculate characters—and close my mouth when I realize that I'm agape. "Exceptional penmanship."

"Thank you." He grins, exposing a small gap between his front teeth. "I was beaten a lot until I wrote better."

At least his handwriting is indisputably superb. What do I have to show for all my aches and bruises?

I grind ink for myself, dip in Tuxi's brush pen, and hesitate some more, staring at the paper.

Esteemed Father,

Your humble son sends heartfelt greetings and begs your indulgence for being so far away, when he should be faithfully attending to your needs at home.

I almost write *daughter* but catch myself.

I have traveled much in the past few days. The soldiers have been kindly and helpful. I have been given decent food and a better horse. One might say I need and want for nothing.

Except the truth from your own lips, Father. And for me to be a different person altogether, one who isn't immobilized by the least hint of danger.

*Greetings also to my virtuous brother, Murong, to
venerable Auntie Xia, and to much-respected Dabao.
May every day bring you blessings and good fortune.*

In kneeling supplication,

Mulan

Leaving the letter to dry, Tuxi and I go outside with a scoop of water to wash his brush pen and ink stone. We're shaking everything out when he says, "Hua xiong-di, don't be too concerned."

At the kindness of his voice, tears rush into my eyes. I blink them away. "It's difficult not to be concerned."

"His Highness told me you've never been in a battle—or even in danger. Let me tell you, Hua xiong-di, the first time is unpredictable. Some throw themselves into it. Others don't react as well. My father has seen grown men soil themselves on battlefields before the fighting even started."

At the mention of the princeling, my face burns. I could handle the other men thinking me a burden if only he hadn't also witnessed my utter ineptitude. "So that my trousers remained clean is a point in my favor?"

"Yes, I'd say so," Tuxi answers with great sincerity. "Tomorrow we rest here at the garrison. If you want, we can train you as if it's real combat. You just need to get used to it."

I doubt that any training will help; actual danger cannot be simulated. "Your kindness I will never forget, Tuxi xiong."

He nudges me with his shoulder. "Eh, don't be so formal. We look out for one another."

I sigh. "Then I hope someday to look out for you too."

◆ ◆ ◆

"Hua xiong-di, have mercy!" shouts Kedan, laughing.

I stop. The four soldiers who have been recruited by Tuxi and Kedan to attack me cling to their poles to catch their breath. I wipe a sleeve across my forehead, but despite the bright sunshine, it's fiercely cold in the fort's bailey and I've barely broken a sweat.

"Hua xiong-di is exceptionally accomplished with a pole," says Tuxi, trying not to sound surprised and not succeeding.

I wasn't altogether correct about the usefulness of the training: I do benefit from practice against multiple attackers. We started with two, quickly progressed to three, and soon after added a fourth. Everyone chose poles—spear shafts without the metal points attached—because in war one is more likely to encounter longer weapons.

As I picked up a spear shaft and tested its weight and balance, almost without thinking, I took a two-handed stance. And that's when I became angry at myself.

I lack experience with spears, but in my panic yesterday, I completely forgot that I am well acquainted with poles. *Before you can beat others, you must learn how to get beaten* is a fundamental tenet of martial arts. And a pole is a good weapon for learning that, as it usually leaves a novice with nothing worse than bruises. Much of my footwork training took place while fighting with poles. And although I haven't used one in years, all my old skills are still here.

I could have handled the bamboo spear as a pole and I would have been all right. I could have yanked out Heart Sea and decapitated the sharp points from the bandits' bamboo spears. I could have taken out a few eyes with hidden weapons and ensured that no one came near me again.

So many things I could have done, and I did none of them. I only flailed like a tortoise set upside down.

That frustration makes me fight with a seething intensity today, my pole a blur of wide slashes and fast jabs. I've hit each of the soldiers multiple times in the arms and calves, with two struck directly in the chest—I had to pull back on the forcefulness of my moves at the last second to avoid breaking their ribs. Instead of the soldiers intimidating me, they are the ones bent over panting, probably hoping that I am done with them.

"You could take on Captain Helou, Hua xiong-di," says Kedan softly, shaking his head.

As if conjured by those words, Captain Helou rides through the fort's gate with the garrison commander—and the princeling. At the sight of him, my face once again blisters with humiliation. He dismounts and climbs up to the gallery that overhangs three sides of the bailey. By all appearances he never glances in my direction, but my mortification refuses to fade.

Kedan runs off to greet Captain Helou, sparing me the necessity of responding to his compliment. He can probably give no higher praise than to compare me to his hero, but I don't want it.

I only wish I could go back in time and acquit myself passably the day before.

To have never become someone I need to be ashamed of.

9

After the midday meal, a number of soldiers leave the fort to work in fields that have been cleared in the grassland. Others herd sheep out to graze. Their commander is aiming for a certain level of self-sufficiency, possibly as a result of an imperial directive—and maybe also a more varied diet for his men.

When my own company rides out for exercise, I see that still more soldiers are walking around scanning the ground, occasionally bending down to pick something up.

"What are they collecting?" I ask Kedan.

His brows waggle. "Droppings."

"To fertilize the fields?"

Manure plays a greater role in Northern agriculture; in the South, farmers raise fish in their paddy fields, and fish excreta usually suffice as fertilizer.

"For fuel, I'd say." Kedan grins. "Wasn't our sleeping platform nice and toasty last night?"

"It was," I say slowly.

I awoke when the barrack room was still near pitch-dark, everyone else sound asleep. Something jolted through me when I realized that the man on my left was the princeling, lying with his back to me. What was he doing, sharing our bed? Hadn't he been given his own quarters?

I got up and tiptoed out—I've been rising before the men to secure a little privacy. At the door, however, I whipped around, an instinctive reaction to the weight of another person's attention. But only stillness and somnolence greeted me.

"An enviable life, isn't it?" Kedan says, yanking me back to the present. He makes a sweeping gesture with his riding crop, encompassing the wide-open grassland ringed by hazy blue mountains. "Almost, that is."

"Almost," I reply—if one doesn't consider the inherent danger of being on the front line in turbulent times. I nod toward the soldiers in the field. "Aren't we at war? Don't they worry that the crops they're planting might never see a harvest?"

"Well, according to Captain Helou, the Wall is in excellent repair—it isn't *that* easy for enemies to swarm over. Not to mention, of the two large-scale Rouran attacks that have taken place recently, one was about fifteen hundred li east of here, and the other a thousand li west. This may be the safest spot on the entire frontier."

With Captain Helou and Kedan as tutors, our group trains in equestrian skills. Being back in the saddle exacerbates my muscle aches, but I don't mind the discomfort. I am as competent here as I was earlier in the bailey of the fort: Whether urging my horse into various leaps or deploying bow and arrow while galloping, I do well and bring no shame upon myself.

Which, of course, makes me want to howl with frustration. Why couldn't I have fought properly when it counted?

"Let's go see the Wall and the beacon tower," proposes Kedan at the end of the session.

Everyone agrees, even Captain Helou, who already inspected the defensive works this morning.

Some big forts are built right up against the Wall itself, especially if they are guarding important passes. Here, however, the Wall traipses over hills too steep for any sizable edifice, and the fort is located one li south.

We approach on a well-maintained path. The Wall, up close, is grander than I imagined—almost twice my height, all solid brick and stone. We climb a flight of access steps to reach the top, which is the width of two of my wingspans and as well paved as an imperial road.

Crenellations inset with observation ports and firing holes face north. On the south-facing side, no such defensive measures exist—only a waist-high parapet to prevent soldiers from falling off. Captain Helou calls our attention to the drainage ports, which pour out only on the friendly side: Any plant growth to the north might give cover to incoming enemies.

The nearest beacon tower also sits apart from the Wall: It is located on an outcrop a few paces to the south, surrounded by its own defensive walls—almost like a miniature fort. Within the walls are barracks for a small unit of men, a kitchen, and a stable. The tower itself, about four times as high as the walls around it, is rectangular at the base and narrows gradually toward the top. Inside the tower, which houses a storage room with large water drums, we climb up on rope ladders, another defensive measure: Should enemies overrun the tiny courtyard below, soldiers on the top can pull up the ladders and hold out for reinforcements.

And reinforcements, of course, would be summoned with fires at night and columns of smoke during the day—I've heard it called "wolf smoke." Beacon towers are roughly ten li apart, and news of an invasion would travel along the length of the Wall at breakneck speed.

The rope ladders take us up to a crenellated platform. From the ground, the Wall impresses with its height and bulk. But from the top of the beacon tower, seeing the well-built, well-manned barrier snake across a line of hills stretching east and west, knowing that it continues beyond the limits of my sight, east to the sea and west to the edges of the legendary Takla Makan Desert, more than ten thousand li in total length—I can only shake my head at its utter scale and magnificence.

And yet . . .

I know from my reading that during the Han Dynasty, the Xiongnu broke through the Wall multiple times—either by finding a section in disrepair or by simply taking control of one of the main gates. And even before a comprehensive wall was built against the . . .

I find that I have trouble using the word *barbarians*, as the Xianbei I've met so far are no more barbarian than anyone else I've ever known.

Well, then, long before a comprehensive wall was built against the nomadic tribes, substantial stretches of lesser walls already existed, erected by the Warring States to keep out one another's invading armies. And none of them prevented the first emperor of Qin from conquering those states on his path to unification.

"You guarded the Wall for a while, didn't you, on a beacon tower?" Kedan asks Captain Helou.

"I did. Not too far from here. The commander I served under is still there, last I heard."

"How was it?"

"Tough. Tedious. And surprisingly hot in summer, for all that it freezes your stones off the rest of the year."

Yu meanders to the opposite corner from where everyone else stands. I join him. He seems surprised but says courteously, "What does Hua xiong-di think of the scenery?"

"The scenery is excellent." Then I lower my voice. "Master Yu, the Wall looks mighty, but how useful is it?"

Yu glances about to make sure we can't be overheard. "Beyond these mountains lies a great desert. If an army has marched past the desert and through the mountains, a wall will not make them turn back."

"But if the Wall kept proving itself useless, why did more of it get built?"

Yu's voice dips even lower. "Because it seemed an obvious solution. It made both the emperor and the people think something was being done. And we have all, at some point, confused doing something—anything—with actually solving the problem."

◆ ◆ ◆

That evening, I slip out of the garrison. This is no mean feat, as the gates are already shut and I have to climb down from a parapet, timing it so that I don't get caught by either the two sets of patrols on the parapet or the two sets on the ground.

My destination: the beacon tower. She who was too foolish to request a hot wash at the ducal residence must make do with a cold one at the Wall, because in the crowded garrison men wash in groups of thirty or more, and she can't find any other place that provides both water and privacy.

The tower has a crew of nine. Four are on watch duty at any given point—two atop the guard tower, two on the low walls that surround it—plus one extra man who cooks, fetches supplies, and looks after the animals.

I have the advantage of approaching from the south; the wall guards look toward the north, the beacon guards east and west. I scale the wall at the foot of the tower on the southwest side, away from the barracks.

Once inside the enclosure, I slide along the bottom of the tower until I reach the entrance. It should be barred from the inside, but I guessed it wouldn't be. The guards at the top of the tower need their food brought up by the cook, who has to return to retrieve the bowls and utensils later, and perhaps deliver some hot beverage to help the guards stay warm at night. If the door were barred, then any time the cook came, one of the guards would need to climb down to let him in, which would quickly become tiresome.

I dart into the tower, bar the door, and dash to the storage room I toured earlier in the day. Inside it is pitch-dark, but I remember where the water drums are, lined up along the wall to my right. Above them hangs a pair of shallow buckets. I feel about until I locate one bucket and lift it off its hook. Then I explore lower and encounter the smooth, woven lid that covers a water drum. My fingers rummage around until I find the gourd scoop placed on the lid. I pick up the lid and reach in with the scoop, but this drum is empty. The next drum is still half-full. I fill the bucket and carry it to a corner of the room, where I spied a drain hole.

I listen. An occasional bark of laughter comes from the barracks. Overhead, one of the guards stomps his feet, the sound reverberating softly in the underside of the tower. And somewhere in the distance, a wolf howls, a forlorn yet menacing baying, as plaintive as a spring night in the far North, and just as cold.

I am about to experience exactly how cold a spring night can be. But I feel as if I must get clean, before the grime of travel and fighting becomes permanently encrusted on my skin.

I strip, begrudging the amount of time it takes to unwind

my binding cloth. Sidling over to the bucket, shivering a little, I soak one of the washcloths that I've brought. Then I wring it out, grit my teeth, and apply it to my skin.

So cold. So heart-freezingly icy. Oh, how I long for a bucket of steaming water and a roaring stove an arm's length away. But the thought only makes the pitiless washcloth drag across my body like a glacier, my goose bumps the size of grains of rice.

As quickly as possible, I clean myself. With another washcloth, I go over my surfaces again. I am about to rinse out the cloth and perform one more iteration—who knows when another opportunity to wash will come along?—when a guard cries from above, "I saw someone! I saw someone come over the wall into the courtyard! Where did he go?"

"Did he go into the tower?" hollers another guard. This one must have been on wall duty.

I swear. I need to get out of the storeroom immediately. With shaking hands, I pour the rest of the water down the drain hole and rush to the empty drum, on the lid of which I stowed my clothes.

"Why is the tower door locked?" someone shouts indignantly.

"I didn't lock the door!" his comrade retorts just as righteously.

My washcloths! I dropped them in the bucket. Swearing again, I run and grab them, almost kicking over the bucket in my hurry. From above, a guard descends with alarming speed. I won't have time to put my clothes on before he reaches the bottom and pulls the bar from the tower door.

I clamber into the empty water drum, my clothes and boots

in a bundle in my arms, and barely manage to swallow a shriek. The drum is not entirely empty. There are still three fingers of ice-cold water at the bottom.

The guard from the top opens the tower door.

"If you didn't push the bar into place, then the intruder must have," says the guard who walks in. "We'll need to search everywhere."

Given a few more moments, I could rearrange my position and get my feet out of the freezing water. But there is no time to do anything except pull the drum lid over my head.

"The rope ladders were all up before I came down, so he can only be down here."

"I'll check the storeroom."

I hold my breath.

The door opens slowly. Light seeps in from the space between the lid and the drum. A man steps in cautiously.

My pulse races. Have I left the bucket by the drain hole? I have, haven't I? I want to bang the back of my head against the side of the drum. Why rush back for the washcloths and not grab the bucket too? I can only hope the man's lantern is too dim for him to discover that irregularity—or that he has never paid attention to where the buckets should be.

"Old Guo! Old Guo!" An urgent whisper comes from above. "Get back up here. Lieutenant An is coming."

The guard who climbed down from the top mutters an imprecation. "Young Shen, get back to your post. I can't bar the door until you leave."

"What about the intruder?"

"If he's here, he'll still be here when Lieutenant An arrives."

"But—oh my mother, the idiots in the barracks are gambling."

Young Shen runs out. Old Guo, still muttering, hauls himself back up the rope ladder to his post. I struggle to free myself—it's easier getting into the drum than out. Once my feet are on the floor of the storeroom, I dress with trembling gratitude.

After returning the bucket to its hook on the wall, I slip out of the storeroom. Footsteps sound in the enclosure outside—if I leave the tower now, I will be seen. I wait behind a support pillar. A knock comes and Old Guo descends again to open the door.

An age of the world passes as the lieutenant inspects the storeroom and climbs up to check the readiness of the beacons. He is not a tall man; in height and build he and I could almost pass for each other. Given the darkness of the night—the moon is behind clouds—I decide to simply walk out of the tower and then out of the enclosure. Young Shen will keep his gaze fixed where he is supposed to look, rather than stare at a superior who might stare back.

Heart pounding, barely daring to breathe, I do exactly that. The backs of my knees tingle with the certainty of impending disaster. But I leave the beacon tower behind without any mishaps, and the incredulity that wells up inside me at this turn of good fortune is almost as wild and choking as my earlier fear.

My teeth chattering, my feet so cold I almost can't feel my toes, I march at top speed toward the fort, vowing again and again that I'll let myself get dirty as a pig before I take any more risks for something as minor as cleanliness.

The moon emerges from behind the clouds. Not much of a moon, but I curse at the sight of it—I still have to scale the fort's wall and avoid four sets of patrols.

And then something far brighter than the moon illuminates the sky.

I spin around.

The beacon tower has become a giant torch, burning against the night.

10

Shouts erupt from the fort and the beacon tower. Before a single thought can penetrate my brain, two dots of light flare in the distance, one to the east, one to the west. Cries from the fort intensify. Horses neigh. Shod hooves strike ground, a reverberation I feel in my spine.

The beacon has been lit. And now towers up and down the Wall are lighting theirs to pass on the news. But is there an attack in progress? I was mere steps from the Wall and stood listening for a bit after I left the tower enclosure. I should have heard something if there was an advancing force. And if there is no enemy storming the Wall, if this is just a prank, then the moment the chaos dies down, everyone will need to account for their whereabouts.

I get off the path just before riders gallop past, followed by sprinting soldiers. Running in a half crouch to remain out of sight, I scramble toward the fort, hoping for a scene of general disarray so I can slip in undetected.

My luck holds. At the gate, two lieutenants argue: One wants to take another group of men to the Wall; the other advocates for patience until the already-deployed group reports back. Some of the first lieutenant's soldiers try to push forward, while others hold them in place.

Sticking close to the outer wall of the fort, I slip past the soldiers and through the gate. The bailey is packed. The commander comes running, his clothes askew, still putting up his damp-looking hair. At least I'm not the only one caught washing at an inconvenient time. I sidle along the edge of the bailey and pray that none of my companions see me.

Something makes me turn my head sharply to the right.

The princeling stands three steps away. He closes the distance between us. "You entered the fort just now. Where were you?"

I feel like a tree felled by lightning—fine one moment, the next a smoldering ruin. How do I answer his question? How can I convince anyone that even though I was outside the fort, I had nothing to do with the flames lighting up the night sky?

"I went for a wash—at the beacon tower," I hear myself say. "There is water in the storeroom."

No man, not even one with an abnormal love of washing, would need to secret himself in the beacon tower to do it. By revealing where I was and the length I'm willing to go to avoid being seen unclothed, I have informed him of the truth of my gender, almost as plainly as if I paraded before him with jade combs and pearl pins in my hair.

It's an instinctive decision—and an appeal for aid. He is the last person I want to burden with my problems, but if he doesn't help me, then one way or the other I must confess my deception tonight. The consequences of that—disgrace and expulsion—will still be less severe than the punishments meted out to someone who deliberately causes trouble on the Wall during a time of war.

But I haven't come all this way for disgrace and expulsion. And I need him to both hold my secret and absolve me of any wrongdoing tonight.

He is silent. In the flickering light of a nearby torch, his profile is sharp, his expression severe.

"Who else was there?" he says at last.

I nearly give in to a fit of nervous laughter. What a question. "For the wash, only myself. But the guard Young Shen saw someone approach the tower, shortly before Lieutenant An arrived for an unannounced inspection."

"When did you leave?"

"Ahead of Lieutenant An. I was almost back at the garrison when the beacon was lit."

He is silent again. In the distance, a rider is returning. The commander has restored order outside the gate. As men clear out of the center of the bailey, I see the others from our group on the opposite side. Kedan waves at us, his hand above his head.

"Follow me," says the princeling.

Will he keep my secret? My Old Heaven, what if he didn't even understand what I meant to convey when I told him the truth?

My heart thumping, we cut across to our companions. The princeling looks at each one in turn. Yu looks closely at me. I clench my hands together behind my back, praying that my agitation doesn't come across as guilt.

"Your Highness, should we not go and help at the Wall?" asks Bai, sounding frustrated that we aren't doing just that.

"We are at the disposal of the commander," answers the princeling coolly. "He will let us know what he needs."

The rider, a messenger, gallops through the gate almost before the princeling finishes speaking. He steps away to hear the messenger's report to the commander. Dismissing the messenger, the two men confer softly for some time. The bailey is silent. My nails scrape the centers of my palms. My heart thumps harder. Then the commander calls for his lieutenants. The princeling returns and leads us into our barrack room.

He studies each man again—each man, but not me. "There is no sign of an invading force. The two guards atop the tower were incapacitated by a single masked intruder, who then lit the beacon. Interestingly enough, according to the guards, the intruder reached the top of the tower not from the inside, but by climbing the exterior wall. Not many people can do that. And in this garrison, everyone who is capable of it is in this room."

The pounding of my heart echoes in the back of my head. Even among this group of seven, not everyone is capable of such a feat. Not Tuxi, I don't think. And probably not Kedan either. Which leaves only five of us. And if anyone besides the princeling saw me going in or out of the fort . . .

Tuxi is visibly shocked. Kedan's eyes, as always, go to Captain Helou, who appears more vexed than anything else. Bai and Yu both look impassive. So for the moment, at least, no one is paying attention to me.

"Master Yu?" says the princeling.

"Yes, Your Highness?"

"Please take care of the matter."

What? Is the princeling abandoning me to the wolves? But I don't dare look at him. I can only hope that my face isn't awash in fear and perspiration.

"Yes, Your Highness." Yu bows and turns to the rest of us. "Captain Helou, Kedan xiong-di, Tuxi xiong-di, please come here."

The three men go to him.

"The four of us left the mess hall together, returned to the barracks, and did not leave again until we heard the commotion. I hold us innocent of this crime."

I would be more surprised that the princeling hasn't been declared innocent by virtue of who he is if my distress weren't pitching headlong into panic.

"Hua xiong-di, you left the company first, before the end of supper. Your Highness, you were next, departing from the commander's table. Bai xiong-di, you came back to the barracks with us, but went out soon thereafter. I didn't see any of you until well after the beacon was lit. Each of you needs to give an account of your whereabouts."

"I was in the privy," Bai answers immediately. "Travel makes me constipated. So I was there some time."

If he is telling the truth, then I can't also claim to have been there.

My stomach roils. I can barely speak. "I was attending His Highness."

"And I was writing letters while Hua xiong-di attended me," he says half-dismissively, as if it's something so ordinary it's barely worth mentioning.

My knees nearly buckle under a sudden avalanche of relief. I exhale and hold absolutely still. Kedan raises a brow at what the princeling said, but his is the only such reaction.

Yu steps forward and lowers himself to one knee. "If you would, Your Highness, your hands."

The princeling holds them out.

Yu takes a sniff. "Ink." He rises. "Hua xiong-di, yours."

I extend my hands out and up.

"Cold water," declares Yu after a moment. "Bai xiong-di, your turn."

Bai chuckles. "Master Yu, you'll embarrass me. You'll say you smell my bowels."

Yu also smiles. "I'm not looking forward to it, but that will be good for you. Shall we?"

Bai raises his hands. Yu leans in. Then Bai, lightning-fast, pokes at Yu's eyes. Yu must have been prepared for that, because he catches Bai's wrist and twists it. Bai grunts in pain but slashes down with his other hand at Yu's neck.

Yu lets go of his wrist and aims a kick squarely at Bai's solar plexus. Bai flies backward and lands on the platform. Captain

Helou and the princeling rush forward and hold him down. Yu grabs his hand and at last has a sniff.

"Fire," he pronounces.

"Tie him up and take him to my room," commands the princeling. "I will need to question him."

Yu and Captain Helou truss up Bai and escort him out, the princeling following close behind. This sequence of events takes place so fast that Tuxi, Kedan, and I remain in place and stare at one another for some time.

"So . . . what will happen to Bai?" I ask when I recover my power of speech.

Tuxi slashes his palm toward the back of his neck. "He must be a Rouran agent, setting off a false alarm like that. Imagine if it happens again and again. Then no one will care in the least when a beacon is lit for a real invasion."

I sit down on the edge of the sleeping platform, my knees giving out after all. "So how do we tell garrisons along the Wall that this is a false alarm?"

Tuxi shakes his head. "Riders and pigeons, I suppose. I hope this isn't a strategy to empty out a nearby garrison and attack it."

It feels like a lifetime since I left home—a lifetime in which everything I once knew has been upended. And I have been so wrapped up in my own turmoil that the war, the reason I left home in the first place, receded to a distant non-concern.

But now it is taking over my life again.

Kedan slaps Tuxi's arm. "Why so much truth, Tuxi xiong?

Hua xiong-di is still young. Go easy on him." He nudges my boot with his own, reminding me that my feet are still frozen inside. "Tell us about yourself and His Highness."

Tuxi returns a slap on Kedan's chest. "Don't be so nosy. Why are you asking after His Highness's business?"

Kedan is undeterred. "His Highness picked Hua xiong-di out from a crowd of thousands. He's been sleeping next to Hua xiong-di during our travels. And just now he had Hua xiong-di attend him in his room. Don't you think he harbors some special affection for you, Hua xiong-di?"

A sharp pain pulses in my heart. What I have felt for my opponent, in both his incarnations, I have felt for no one else. But that he does not despise me is miraculous enough. There can never be special affection, just as there can never be different circumstances. "Kedan xiong is approaching this from the wrong angle. His Highness is younger than everyone here except me. I'm the one he can treat however he likes without being accused of disrespecting his elders. So of course when he wants someone to pour tea or grind ink, the chore falls to me."

As an excuse, that is . . . not bad.

Kedan shakes his head. "Maybe Hua xiong-di is too young to understand such things."

I wave a hand. "Not so young I can't tell the difference between 'You, come here and serve me' and"—I speak in a slow, flirtatious tone—"'You, come here and serve me.'"

Kedan whistles and laughs. "All right, all right. I guess we don't have to worry about you being too innocent."

Tuxi shakes his head, but he doesn't seem annoyed, only slightly exasperated. He brings out a small cloth bundle from his bag and extracts a paper chessboard and equally thin game pieces made of bamboo bark. "I'll bet none of us can sleep now. But it isn't wise to leave this room either. Let's play a few matches."

I wish we could speak more of the events of the night. I hardly know Bai. But I am staggered that someone so close to me—at least in physical proximity for the past few days—has done so much to undermine the usefulness of the Wall. What about the potential consequences to the princeling? Will he not be held responsible for the actions of one of his men? And what will that mean for our little group?

Specifically, will I still be welcome to stay here when everyone else leaves?

"All right, let's play," I say.

✦ ✦ ✦

We finish three games before Captain Helou returns. But he doesn't have any real intelligence to impart—he was not invited to witness the interrogation. All he can tell us is that the soldiers have scoured the area inside and outside the Wall and found no evidence of any Rouran military presence.

Another match is played, which lasts longer than the previous three combined—Captain Helou is a more deliberate player. Then Yu enters and requests that we go to sleep. He might be a servant, but he has such innate authority that we

150

obey immediately, and no one dares to demand of *him* what he knows, not even Kedan.

The lamps are out for quite some time before one last person climbs onto the platform beside me. The princeling. Has he extracted any answers from Bai? Has Bai already been executed? Will we never mention him again?

I fear that I might dream of Bai being beheaded. But when I bolt upright, breathing hard, it is from a dream of a huge centipede crawling out of Bai's eye socket.

Next to me, a dark silhouette also sits up. Have I awakened the princeling, or has he not fallen asleep yet? He does not move, nor does he speak. But sitting in his silent company, listening to his soft, slow breaths, I begin to feel less unsettled. After some more time, I yawn and lie back down.

◆ ◆ ◆

In the morning, I'm relieved not to see Bai's severed head hanging from the parapet.

The princeling, Yu, and Captain Helou are not at breakfast. Kedan becomes restless for news, so I ask him and Tuxi to train with me. We stop as soon as we spy the princeling and Captain Helou emerging into the bailey.

Almost immediately Captain Helou bows to the princeling, who inclines his head and murmurs a few words. Then Captain Helou straightens, spins on his heels, and heads in the direction of the stables. Kedan rushes after him.

The princeling is stopped by one of the garrison commander's lieutenants. By the time he joins Tuxi and me, Kedan is also back, looking crestfallen.

"Tuxi xiong, Kedan xiong, please make ready to leave," says the princeling. "Hua xiong-di, let's take a walk."

Kedan, despite his dejectedness, manages to waggle his brows at me. I roll my eyes, but something in me shifts as I recall the solace I derived from the princeling's silent company during the night.

The solace that he *offered* me, I now realize.

We walk out of the front gate of the fort.

"Bai is my uncle's man," says the princeling.

A chill crawls down my spine. Is he telling me what I think he is?

"My uncle holds a command near the southern border. Bai arrived at my father's place with a letter bearing my uncle's seal. I have convinced the garrison commander to have Bai transported back to my father. But en route there will be an opportunity for him to escape."

He wants to see which way Bai runs. Or more importantly, to whom.

"Master Yu will follow him—he's skillful enough to do that without being detected and canny enough to handle just about any situation. Captain Helou I've tasked with carrying the news to my father. He'll need men like Captain Helou at his side if my worst suspicions come to pass."

My stomach flips. "What are your worst suspicions, Your Highness?"

He passes a finger over the faded scar on his forehead, an absent gesture. "You don't need to worry about that, Hua xiong-di. The commander has heard glowing reports of your martial prowess, and I have vouched for your loyalty and trustworthiness. He is happy to have you stay here and be an asset to the garrison, as you planned to do in the first place."

"I—I see." I remember my manners. "My unending gratitude to Your Highness."

"Hua xiong-di may not thank me in the end." He is silent for some time. "Do you remember asking me why my father would send me on a dangerous mission outside the Wall?"

I nod.

"My father has never admitted it, but I believe that by deploying me here, a thousand li from the nearest Rouran attack, he probably *did* think he was doing something akin to stowing me at the central granary. But the events of last night have shown this to be a hollow assumption. I no longer believe that this stretch of the Wall is any safer than its counterparts farther east and west. In fact—" He stops abruptly and takes a breath. "I shouldn't speculate too much. Just be careful, Hua xiong-di."

I bite the inside of my cheek. "You too, Your Highness."

He smiles briefly. "Perhaps we will meet again. If I recall correctly, after the war, we have an appointment to keep."

I knew before we set out from the capital that this is where we would part ways. But now that it is happening, I'm suddenly stunned, as if I learned of his departure just this moment and had no time to prepare myself.

I bow low and salute, not wanting him to see how difficult I find this farewell. "I wish Your Highness many successes on this expedition. May your return be as swift as your departure."

"Take care, Hua xiong-di."

He sets a hand on my shoulder, a fleeting touch, and walks away.

I remain in the same spot. Below me, the grassland undulates, green and beautiful under brilliant sunlight. Yet in the blink of an eye, it could be overrun with men and gears of war, marching south.

A cold dread falls drop by drop into my heart.

Perhaps we will meet again, he said.

But most likely we won't.

11

"What's the meaning of this, Hua xiong-di? Why are you not coming with us?"

Kedan.

When I first heard his footsteps, my heart leaped wildly. In that too-brief moment, I believed that the princeling had come back. That he had changed his mind and would remain at the fort. That even if the fort was no longer the haven we first thought it to be, we'd still be safe here. Together.

Until I realized that the gait was too heavy and impatient to be his.

"I was only ever going to travel this far and no farther," I tell Kedan.

He doesn't look angry, only befuddled. "His Highness said that. But we are brothers, aren't we, all of us?"

I blink. What can I say to this kind of naïve sincerity? *One of us proved himself a traitor only last night. And I am nobody's brother, ever.*

"Tuxi xiong speaks many tongues and I am an exceptional tracker, if I do say so myself. But we are not fighters of your caliber, Hua xiong-di. And this is a time that calls for fighters."

I scoff bitterly. "You've seen what happens to me when I'm faced with real danger."

"That means nothing. The first time I came face-to-face with a full-grown tiger, I fainted. My relatives make fun of me over that to this day. And then they have to admit that I've become a much better hunter and tracker than they have ever been."

I only shake my head.

"But you are so good, Hua xiong-di. What greater joy can a man have than to put his hard-honed skills to use? Here you will be buried, a knife in the dirt. But out there you will be like a dragon that descends from the clouds, all power and invincibility."

I shake my head some more.

Kedan looks at me as if I am a child who refuses to listen to reason, his natural affection mingled with both frustration and disappointment. "Aren't you concerned for His Highness? He's barely older than you, but the burden he carries is as heavy as mountains."

"I met His Highness only six days ago."

"And he has treated Hua xiong-di with the greatest courtesy—not to mention that day he put himself at risk so that you could get to your horse in time."

I clench my hand into a fist. Will Kedan now remind me that

he too leaped in to save me from the bandits? That I also owe him my life?

But he only sighs at my continued silence, looking as dispirited as he did at Captain Helou's departure. "If Hua xiong-di's mind is made up, then let me not talk on and on. Hua xiong-di, take care. Perhaps someday we will meet again."

◆ ◆ ◆

The sun shines. The grassland sways in the restless wind from the north. In the fort, soldiers practice their fighting formations, stamping their feet and shouting "Forward!" in unison. Out here, I am hunched over, my hands tucked inside my sleeves, alone with the cold, hard weight of my decisions.

I have chosen well. Indisputably, I have chosen well. Before I left home, I made three separate promises that I would return. Heading north of the Wall would break all those promises.

But I do not feel the satisfaction of having chosen well. Instead I feel pricked by a thousand needles.

I did not lie about the fort being my final destination. I never pledged that I would continue beyond this point. Although I do owe Kedan and the princeling a debt of gratitude for coming to my aid with the bandits, I owe my family a far greater obligation—to keep myself away from danger.

Why, then, am I ashamed again? Why am I more frustrated and disappointed than Kedan? Why do I feel as if I've damaged some wholly indispensable part of myself?

I pace back and forth. The wind flogs my ears and threatens to undo my topknot, but I barely feel anything except the stinging sensation in my heart.

I have been trained in the art of violence, long considered the domain of men. I have experience in dressing and moving like a man. But otherwise I have been raised as a woman, taught to do as I am told and leave all the greater decisions in life, all the larger concerns under the sky, to those who know better.

To men.

Father never instructed me in *yiqi*, the code of honor and brotherhood that governs righteous conduct for men. A woman is not expected to be righteous. She is expected to serve her father, then her husband. And to bear children, the more sons the better, in the hope that someday, one of her sons will achieve such worldly stature that he—or his wife, more likely—will be able to care for her as she deserves to be cared for, after a lifetime of seeing to the needs of others.

A woman's conduct is judged almost entirely on her chastity, obedience, and self-effacement. By these standards, I have done well. Other than my own blood relations, and until I left home on this journey, I have rarely interacted with members of the opposite sex. I have undertaken years of arduous training because my father wished it. And while I desperately want to win the duel so that Father will see me as me, and not as the replacement he tries to pass off as his son, I have asked for no special recognition for years of sweat, tears, and toil.

These narrow standards for women, however, do not apply

at all to my current situation. Nor can I judge myself as a man, since I am not one. But what if I look at myself as a . . . person, a person with skills that some consider helpful, even if I myself have deemed those skills less than reliable?

The thing is, I do not need to be taught yiqi. Brotherhood might be unique to men, but loyalty, devotion to friends, and a sense of fairness are not. They are the precise reasons I became a conscript in Dabao's place. I could never have been at peace with myself knowing that it was within my power to do something for Auntie Xia and Dabao and not to have done it. Even Father did not argue with that.

It's strange to think of men as my friends, but that is what Tuxi and Kedan have become. As for the princeling, I owe him much—too much, when I consider the blood debt between our families.

Everything Tuxi said about Bai's trickery implied a danger that was close and imminent. What the princeling said, and chose not to say, confirmed it. Kedan's dismay that I am abandoning the company only further underscores the truth behind his words: This is a time that calls for fighters.

And I can no more bid them farewell here than I could have stood by and watched as Auntie Xia walked Dabao to his conscription.

Fear grips me as I understand what I am about to do. But at least the needle-pricking of my conscience stops. I look south and send a silent apology in the direction of my family.

My fate will be decided by Heaven, but I have chosen my own path.

I break into a run as my three companions walk out of the gate with their horses, the commander and his lieutenants in tow.

The princeling's expression does not change at my approach. "Hua xiong-di, you have come to see us off."

I skid to a stop. "Your Highness, with your permission, I have come to join you."

Kedan gasps. "I knew you would, Hua xiong-di! I knew you were a true brother!"

The princeling's face remains carefully blank. "Is Hua xiong-di certain? Outside the Wall, danger lurks everywhere, and I cannot guarantee anyone's safety."

I take a deep breath. "My gratitude for Your Highness's kind concern. But the fate of the realm is the responsibility of every man. And I have no better means of repaying Heaven and Earth than to defend my country from grave peril."

"Well said," exclaim the commander and Tuxi at the same time. The commander continues, "Your Highness is fortunate in having followers devoted to duty and principle. I would have gladly made a place for this young xiong-di at the garrison, but Your Highness has the greater need."

"Commander, you are correct as usual," says the princeling. He turns back to me. Something flickers in his gaze, but it's gone before I can take it in. "Since Hua xiong-di has decided, we will wait for you to gather your things."

A delighted Kedan accompanies me to our barrack room and points with no small amount of pride at the bundle that's been left beside my saddlebag. "Four such bundles were prepared for us. His Highness would have sent yours back, but I insisted that it remain here. I knew you'd change your mind."

The bundle consists of a bedroll, a sheepskin cape, and some miscellaneous items wrapped inside. Kedan hoists it to his shoulder. "I'll secure this to your saddle."

When he's gone, I sit down for a moment on the sleeping platform, at last overwhelmed by my decision. And more than a little disappointed that the princeling isn't more elated that I am rejoining him. In fact, it almost feels as if he would prefer me to remain here.

Was he as repelled by my paralysis before the bandits as I was? Has he lost all faith that I'll be able to fight when the time comes? Is he convinced that I will be a burden, instead of an asset, to the company?

Well, it's too late to change my mind again. I will simply have to prove to myself, and to him, that just because I was a coward once doesn't mean I'll be a coward always. Or ever again.

I grab my saddlebag, rise to my feet, and go out to meet the great unknown.

12

North of the Wall, a single long, narrow valley takes us almost thirty li on a well-trod path that runs alongside a small but lively river. We ride single file, without speaking. My eyes dart from the occasional clumps of trees that cling to rocky slopes to the ridgelines of farther hilltops, constantly expecting a Rouran presence, since we are now in Rouran territory.

But the morning passes without incident and I begin to relax a little. Midday we stop and eat bing that have been made fresh this morning and stuffed with thin slices of broiled mutton.

"I'm going to gather some firewood," says Kedan, flicking crumbs off his fingers.

"Are we going to make a fire?" I ask.

I thought we were about to continue on our way, but I wouldn't mind some tea so hot that it burns my lips. At the bottom of the valley it isn't too windy, but even just past high noon, the day is still steadily cold, and the contents of my water-skin are as chilled as the air I breathe.

"Not now," answers Kedan. "But we may not stop again until nightfall, and we may not find firewood so easily beyond these hills."

Tuxi, who is always happy to go where Kedan does, stands up. "I'll come with you."

They amble off toward a nearby copse of trees, while I wonder again about my suitability for scouting beyond the Wall. I wouldn't have known to prepare for not finding fire-wood later. I don't know anything about how to live outdoors.

"Don't worry," says the princeling. "Tuxi xiong isn't any more knowledgeable than you about surviving in the wilderness. His greatest skill as a traveler is his ability to gauge the quality of inns—scarcely applicable where we are going."

I glance at him, surprised not so much that he is speaking to me, but at the good humor evident in his words. He is seated on a small outcrop overhung by a scraggly pine tree, one booted foot on the rock, looking more relaxed than he has been at any point since he learned, upon arriving home, of his aunt's unexpected return.

"What about you, Your Highness? Are your skills as a traveler any better suited to the wilds?" I hear myself ask, tilting my chin toward the bow and arrows that he now carries on his back.

"My father wanted me to retain some of the skills of his nomadic ancestors. If necessary, I can hunt and start a fire—but

I'd be embarrassed to do either before Kedan xiong. And I've been on some minor campaigns with my father, sleeping under the stars. So at least I know what to expect on that front. I suppose Hua xiong-di has always had a roof over his head?"

He speaks to me in the same courteous, formal tone he has always used. His entire demeanor remains unaltered, as if our tense conversation of the night before, during which I divulged my gender, never took place. Did he help me without understanding what I said? Or did my revelation make no difference because I was telling him something he already knew? Throughout our travels together, in his unobtrusive way, he has created more space for me and made it easier for me to slip aside for privacy.

"The closest I've come to sleeping outside is when I opened all my windows during Southern summers," I say.

He smiles a little and I am warm all over. Perhaps he doesn't care that I'm a woman, but I can't help but be aware that he is a lithe, handsome man. "Does her ladyship not begrudge it when you go away with His Grace? Doesn't that interfere with your training?"

In safer times or surroundings, I would have been more hesitant to bring up his aunt. But we are headed deeper into enemy territory with every step, and I no longer care as much about staying away from fraught subjects.

He doesn't seem to mind. "She does begrudge it when I'm away for more than half a month. But she also knows that with my father being who he is, my life cannot be only about the duel, as hers was once upon a time."

His answer only further encourages me. "Your Highness, if you don't mind my curiosity, how was your parents' marriage arranged?"

The question has been at the back of my head for days. How in the world did a young female martial artist from the South marry a Xianbei nobleman of the North?

He smiles again. "The old-fashioned way, actually. My father did some sightseeing in the South while his father was envoy to the Southern court. He passed through the village where my mother's family lived and came upon her training outside their cottage.

"According to my aunt, he took a room in the village and came to watch my mother practice every day. After seven days of this, my aunt told him he had better either never come back or return with a proper proposal of marriage, backed by parental approval and a respectful bride price. Ten days later, my father returned with his father and trunks of gifts."

My eyes widen. "How did he get his father to agree?"

"At the time he had several older brothers, so it wasn't as important whom he married. Also, the Northern court has never frowned upon marriage between Xianbei nobles and Han Chinese. Preferably the marriages result in useful political and economic alliances, but occasionally a love match falls through the cracks."

"And her family—they didn't have objections?"

I don't need to mention the deep-seated Southern fear of the nomadic tribes. He has been in the South. He knows.

"They didn't realize at first that he was Xianbei. They thought him merely Northern, a point in his favor, since the Pengs were originally from the North. When they learned his true identity, they had second thoughts, but my mother reminded everyone that they required only parental approval and a good bride price. Nothing had been said about whether he had to be Han Chinese. Eventually they relented and agreed to the marriage."

Is it my imagination or does he glance my way at the word "marriage"? My heart thuds. If, instead of a duel, we had prepared since childhood for a marital arrangement, would either of us have objected?

"I guess your aunt doesn't mind anymore that your father is Xianbei," I say, "since she married him herself."

To my surprise a shadow crosses his face. And when he replies, he speaks slowly, as if he is choosing words with care. "My aunt would tell you that she *never* minded that her sister married a Xianbei man; she simply didn't want to deal with what others would say if they learned. She has also never told anyone she knew from the South, or anyone who might be a referee at our duel, that I am half-Xianbei. She says she doesn't want me to be disadvantaged, because all the referees will be Han Chinese. But sometimes I wonder . . ."

His voice trails off. Kedan and Tuxi are back, each with an armful of branches, which Kedan quickly chops and splits. He chooses only a few pieces, wraps them in rough cloth, then sticks them inside the bundles that are secured to the backs of our saddles.

"Let's go," says the princeling, rising. "We've a long way yet."

As we head out, my mind lingers on his unfinished answer. Does he wonder whether his aunt, however much she loves him and his father, still feels a reflexive shame at her personal closeness to the Xianbei, especially in front of her Han Chinese connections from the South?

Of course, it may not be that at all. It may be exactly as her ladyship claims: that she simply does not want to disadvantage him by broadcasting before the duel—which has always been an exclusively Han Chinese event—that one of the combatants is in fact half-Xianbei.

But her nephew has had to use a different name to write to us—a name that sounds more Han Chinese. What conclusion would *he* draw from all this?

Probably the same one I did, from having been required to pass as my dead twin all these years: that there is something about me that does not measure up, that will never measure up, no matter what I achieve.

But I'm still trying.

Is he?

◆ ◆ ◆

The second half of our journey is arduous, the trail winding upward a great deal more than it slopes down.

Near sunset we breach the last pass. I expected a long, steep descent. But the mountains we've climbed are barely hills on this side. Looking back, it's as if the range serves as a giant staircase up to a plateau.

I also thought we would be ankle deep in sand the moment we crossed the mountains. But what awaits us is more grassland. The grass is shorter than that south of the range, and more yellow than green, but come summer, no doubt it will also be a wide, verdant expanse.

We stop near a lake ringed with tall, swaying reeds. Kedan says that we are close enough to the mountains for there to be snowmelt streams, sometimes underground, to feed a small body of water.

He and the princeling go off to hunt in the fading dusk. Tuxi and I split one small log of firewood into kindling with Kedan's short-handled axe. When the hunters return, they each hold a blob of mud, which they claim are a pair of already gutted waterfowl. We bury the muddy blobs in a shallow hole, fill the hole, and start our fire on the spot.

Kedan arranges the logs so that they can hold up a small pot. I again think of tea. But as it turns out, the hunters have also brought back some tender reed stems, which go into the pot, along with bones and innards from the birds, to make a soup.

The mud-baked waterfowl are surprisingly decent—perfectly de-feathered too—and the reed stem soup is downright excellent. I drink more of the soup than is strictly prudent, its heat a necessary antidote against the increasingly merciless night. My fingers have turned icy from doing nothing more than sticking out of my sleeves. The meat, almost too hot to touch on the birds themselves, loses all warmth the moment I tear it off the bone and move it to my mouth.

The wind grows more teeth. I shiver in spite of my new sheepskin cape. The fire warms only my front; the rest of me is at the mercy of the oncoming night, which howls madly.

"Wish I had some wine to warm my insides," mumbles Kedan.

"Funny you should ask," says the princeling. He reaches into his saddlebag, brings out a wineskin, and hands it to Kedan.

Kedan's eyes widen as he takes a sip. "This is grape wine, isn't it?"

The princeling nods. "From beyond Jiayu Pass."

The westernmost terminus of the Wall.

Tuxi sighs when it's his turn to imbibe. I half expect the wine to taste like raisins, but I should know better: Sorghum wine, for example, doesn't taste remotely of sorghum. And this wine, nowhere near as sweet as raisins, is crisper, more nuanced, and more interesting.

The princeling lets everyone have another sip. "They say wine elicits truth. I don't know whether there is enough wine here for that, but I have a confession to make."

"Please don't tell us that *you* set off the beacon last night," says Kedan, a note of real apprehension underlying his playful words.

"No, I was in my room writing letters." After a pause, the princeling adds, "As Hua xiong-di can attest. He ground ink for me."

"Next time let me grind ink for you," declares Tuxi in all seriousness. He turns to me. "Not to embarrass you, Hua xiong-di, but your ink-grinding technique could use some improvement. The angle at which you hold the ink stick and the—"

Kedan taps him on the shoulder. "You think Hua xiong-di was really there grinding ink?"

"Oh, I was most certainly grinding ink," I counter. Kedan didn't say much at either lunch or supper—Captain Helou's absence weighs heavily on him. But I'm glad to see that a bit of his old mischief seems to have returned. "Tuxi xiong, tell us more about your technique. I need to learn from the best."

Tuxi chuckles, squirming a little. "We'll get to that later, Hua xiong-di. Your Highness, before our rude interruption, you were saying?"

His Highness tosses another log onto the fire. "As you know, the first large-scale Rouran attacks came nearer the two ends of the Wall. My father assigned me here in the middle because he believed his more experienced scouts were needed elsewhere—that the Rouran will come down east and west like a pincer grip. But after what Bai did, I'm beginning to wonder otherwise."

My stomach tightens. This must be what he refrained from saying in the morning.

Kedan frowns. "But surely the Rouran aren't going to attack in the center, not after Bai brought official attention to that particular stretch of the Wall."

"Did he?" murmurs the princeling.

Kedan looks at Tuxi, then at me.

"His Highness can explain this better," I say slowly, only beginning to see what the princeling is implying, "but I'm not sure the truth of Bai's guilt will be reported up the chain of command. Bai came with us because he had a recommendation from the royal duke's brother. To state that connection plainly would be to implicate His Grace's family members.

"On the other hand, if Bai's betrayal isn't stated clearly in a report, the fault for the false alarm might fall on the commander of the garrison. He is caught between a brick to the face and a knife in the ribs. He doesn't want to appear to blame His Grace, His Grace's brother, or His Highness, but he also doesn't want his own head to depart his neck. I'd guess that he said it was an accident and those responsible have already been dealt with—the exact same thing he would have said had Bai not been caught."

Kedan glances at the princeling, who nods.

"The commander's superiors would only know that they have some idiots manning the Wall," I continue. "Preparations proceed apace to meet the Rouran east and west. In fact, I would be surprised if the lighting of the beacon didn't coincide with some incursion a thousand li from here, to make the generals think that the beacon was but a diversionary tactic."

I hold out my hands to the fire. "Tuxi xiong said to me, the night Bai was caught, imagine if it happens again and again. Then no one would care in the least when the beacon is lit at the beginning of a real invasion. But that isn't the only danger here. The real danger is that . . ."

This time I am the one who glances at the princeling, because what I am about to say is so unthinkable I don't want to put it into words. Our eyes meet. In the firelight, his expression is grim, but he nods again.

I exhale. "The real danger is that we might hollow out our defenses by deploying troops east and west, leaving the center undermanned."

"The capital!" Kedan gasps. "The capital is only three hundred li southeast of the garrison, as the crow flies. There is a fair bit of rough terrain in between, but only *three hundred li*. Light cavalry can cover that in two days."

No one says anything.

"Wait!" Kedan sits straighter. "You did send Captain Helou to your father, Your Highness. Which means at least one person in the capital will know the truth—two, if we count Captain Helou."

"But my father's hands are tied until he finds out who is directing Bai's movements. And depending on how wily and alert Bai is, that could prove a difficult task, even for Master Yu." The princeling tosses another piece of wood onto the fire. "I did ask my father not to deploy his forces from the capital until he hears from me again. But should the emperor order him to take his men and march east or west, he would have no choice but to obey."

The wineskin is back in my hands, but I only hold it. "You

advised His Grace to stay put until he hears from you again, Your Highness. What is it that you hope to find out in the meanwhile?"

He looks at the fire. "The Rouran don't have a centralized power structure. But they do have a khan who is recognized by all the allied clans as their leader. Periodically the clans gather to negotiate trade, arrange marriages, discuss important matters—and reaffirm the legitimacy of the khan. It's long been rumored that one of the locations used for the gatherings is not too far east of here. And—"

And if I were mounting an invasion and needed to hold a muster, that's where I would gather my troops!

It takes me a moment to realize I have not just thought that but spoken it aloud. "Forgive my interruption, Your Highness."

"You said what I was going to, Hua xiong-di." He holds his hands out to the fire. "Our task beyond the Wall is dangerous, but fairly straightforward. The most difficult mission belongs to Master Yu. I hope he can discover the identity of Bai's true master—in time."

"I can't help but think that the man is highly placed: He seemed to know where and how to strike to cause maximum disturbance," says Tuxi.

"That is also my thinking—and my fear." The princeling looks at each of us in turn. "But there is nothing we can do about that from here. Let's focus on finding the Rouran meeting ground and leave the unmasking of traitors to our allies in the capital."

◆ ◆ ◆

We divide the night into four watches. The princeling assigns the first watch to Tuxi, the second to Kedan, the third to himself, and the last to me.

Lying in my bedroll, it immediately becomes clear that I am not going to enjoy my first night outdoors. The ground is unrelentingly hard. The cold penetrates all my defenses. The fire burns down to smoke and ember, a tepid mirage. I wrap myself as tightly and thoroughly as possible in my sheepskin cape. But I can't get any warmer, as if I, like the fire, have also run out of fuel.

Just sleep, I tell myself. *You are covered enough. And the sooner you sleep, the sooner your watch—and morning—will come.*

But the more I want the oblivion of slumber, the more elusive it becomes. I shiver. My muscles become so stiff I might never unfurl from my current curled-up position. My toes ache, a dull, blue pain. I try to recall all the summers of my life, the sun shining bright on Lake Tai, the green foliage heavy in the breezeless heat, the long afternoons of soft perspiration and warm lethargy.

But summer does not exist anymore. Even memories of summer have been erased by the bitter rawness of these Rouran lands. There is only the wind, the cold, and the distant howling of wolves.

I jerk awake.

Was I asleep? How long has it been? And why are my eyes suddenly wide open, my blood pulsing with alarm?

The fire has gone out completely. The grassland is dark except for the faint glimmer of starlight. The smell in the air is deep, musty, animal.

Our horses snort nervously. There comes the soft tap of claws on hard earth. A black shape advances. No, several.

My heart jams in my larynx: The wolf in the lead is almost upon the princeling. He is sitting up, scooting backward, his sword in hand, still sheathed. The wind dies and the night echoes with his rapid breaths.

His *panicked* breaths.

Why not unsheathe his sword? Why isn't he getting up to fight?

My hand searches along the edge of my bedroll. Earlier I moved several small rocks to make a smoother spot for myself. My fingers close over one.

The rock sails through the air and hits the lead wolf between the eyes. It yelps, shudders, and stumbles a few steps back. Before it can growl, I hit it with another rock. The wolf turns and runs. Its packmates hesitate. I strike the next nearest wolf under its ear. It yowls and takes off too. The rest of the wolves follow suit.

"What's going on?" asks Kedan sleepily, up on one elbow. "Is everything all right?"

"Nothing is the matter," says the princeling, his voice surprisingly steady. "Go back to sleep."

Kedan mumbles something and lies down. I listen. When his breaths become deep and regular again, I get up and go to the princeling.

"Are you hurt?" I whisper, sinking to one knee.

He shakes his head.

I reach out and grip the scabbard of his sword. It trembles—from the trembling of his hand.

Did my hands shake during the bandit attack? I can't remember—most of the episode has been blurred by shame and self-recrimination. Only certain details remain. Kedan jumping in front of me. The princeling shouting for me to fight. The princeling charging toward the bandits, a pair of bamboo spears in hand.

I hold the scabbard steady. "The wolves are gone."

He doesn't say anything. I wonder if I'm dreaming. He should have been able to take on any number of wolves and emerge victorious. Tuxi called him the calmest and bravest man he has ever met. But there is no denying that he is still shaking. Less than before, but the tremors have not completely subsided.

"Are you afraid of wolves?" I can't believe the words coming out of my mouth.

"I—I'm afraid of many things."

I stare at him. Murong is afraid of many things—but he is still a child. Dabao is afraid of many things too, but he is, in essence, also a child. The young man before me has fought me three times and led us past a horde of bandits whole and unharmed.

"Are you also afraid of the dark?" That would explain why he came down to sleep with us in the barracks.

"No, but I'm afraid of being in a dark room by myself."

He has an entire courtyard to himself at home. How did he manage there?

"Sleep," I tell him—the same thing I would have told Murong if he crawled into my bed in the middle of a thunderstorm. "It's time for my watch anyway."

"I won't be able to sleep now. You sleep. I'll take your watch."

But what if the wolves return? I can't believe I'm doubting the princeling's valor. But he would probably take the same precaution with me if bandits were roaming about. "We can both keep watch."

He hesitates. "Bring your bedroll here. We can sit back-to-back."

I do not hesitate nearly as long before I pick up my bedroll and join him. We wear our capes backward so that they form a tent. Underneath, we are separated by enough fabric and hide to make a real tent. Still, it is his back against mine, and I can sense the contours of his body and detect his smallest movements.

My heart beats faster as his warmth begins to seep into me. The muscles of my back and shoulders, made rigid by the cold, unclench one by one.

"So, how did you sleep all these years, in a courtyard by yourself?" I ask, more because I don't want him to hear the thudding of my heart than anything else.

"When I was younger I had a nursemaid in the next room. Later, an attendant. And if I'm alone for some reason, I keep a lamp burning." He sighs. "I guess you are not afraid of the dark."

"No."

"Or wolves."

"No."

"I don't think you fear bandits either—it was just jitters," he murmurs. "Is there anything you *are* afraid of?"

Yes. I'm afraid of never escaping the long shadow of my twin's death—of never existing except as his inferior replacement.

"Your aunt," I tell him. "I'm deathly afraid of your aunt."

We both laugh at that. I love not only hearing the sound of his laughter, but also feeling those small convulsions of mirth against his back.

And speaking of his aunt, I suddenly remember something. "When I asked you why you don't wish to kill my father to avenge your mother, you said you have seen my father. When? Does your aunt know?"

"I toured the Lake Tai region during my sojourn in the South, before I met with any of the referees. My goal was to speak to your father. And no, my aunt doesn't know. I made a point of not asking for her permission."

"But you never did pay my father a visit. Or—did you?"

I met with the princeling three times and never said anything to Father. Father could very well have met him and never said anything to me.

"I hired a pleasure craft. It glided by your house. Your father sat on the terrace, drinking tea and reading a book. It was such an idyllic scene—and I became as angry as I'd ever been in my life. My aunt was right: He was an unrepentant killer.

"Just then, a large manservant came and lifted him bodily to take him inside. The sight shook me—I'd had no idea he was paralyzed. I didn't know what to think. Had it happened at my mother's hand? Did my aunt know? And did I see something he wouldn't have wanted me to see?"

"Most likely. He is very proud, my father. And his paralysis has been difficult for him," I say, in reply to his last question. "Was that what changed your mind, knowing that he too has suffered? Was that what made you no longer want to kill him?"

"What?" His surprise sounds a little woolly, as if he is sleepy. "No, I never wanted to kill your father."

"Really? But your aunt . . ."

If the duel didn't have rules against reprisals, there's no telling what her ladyship would have done.

"My aunt isn't the only one who raised me." His speech is becoming slower and less precise. "She isn't even the only one who raised me with cause to hate your father. But my father taught me that the first thing a general does after he ends a rebellion is to make sure that agricultural production goes back to normal. He does not burn the fields or punish the civilians. He does not make things worse.

"What would I have done, by killing your father, except make things worse for his family? And what would I have done, by *wanting* to kill him, except make things worse for *me*?"

I think of the royal duke looking at me with sympathy, just before our company left the ducal residence. At the time I couldn't understand it—couldn't even see not hating me on sight as a possibility for him. But like his son, he does not despise me. And he *was* sorry that my illusions were shattered, that the old enmity has once again created so much pain.

"Your father is wise," I say, with more envy than I intended.

"My aunt thinks he might be too soft. She thinks I'm definitely too soft."

His last few words are barely audible.

Sitting back-to-back does not seem to have the same invigorating effect on him as it does on me. I listen to his quiet, even breaths and look up at a magnificently starry sky, such as I haven't seen since my last summer in the South.

"Wait," I wonder aloud. "When you were gliding around on Lake Tai in that hired pleasure boat, did you see me too?"

He does not answer. After some time, his head drops onto my shoulder.

◆ ◆ ◆

Kedan is smug: He was the first one up in the morning, so he saw the princeling leaning against me.

"I'm never wrong about special affection," he declares for my ears alone, with much satisfaction.

"There were wolves at night, my brother," I correct him.

"His Highness's and my watches overlapped. It was too cold to sit apart, so we sat together."

The news of wolves sobers him a bit, but only a bit. "Nothing forges special affection like facing down wolves together."

I shake my head and get on with my preparations for the day's ride. But when Kedan isn't looking, I glance toward the princeling, standing by his horse, checking the contents of his saddlebag. *That* much contact between us—under normal circumstances, a formal proposal of marriage had better be on its way. But by now it's clear that where we are concerned, there are no normal circumstances.

And I still haven't seen any unmistakable indication that he even knows I am a woman.

He looks up. Our eyes meet. Heat ricochets through me, but I do not look away. Neither does he, until Tuxi calls to him for something.

At noon we stop to rest our horses.

Thus far Rouran country has been thinly populated. We passed two bands of nomads, each about fifteen to twenty in number, traveling with their livestock, horses, and all their belongings. We also passed a few huddles of yurts—felt-and-fur-covered tents that can be easily taken apart and put together again—where other such small bands took up temporary residence.

Tuxi, our linguist, spoke to some of them but didn't recoup any useful information. Admittedly he didn't ask any direct or probing questions, as we don't want word to get out that a group of travelers is suspiciously interested in the Rouran meeting ground.

"Shall we spar a little?" I propose to Tuxi and Kedan, before taking a sip from my waterskin. "We'll be able to see anyone coming from several li away."

The narrow, hilly terrain we traversed the day before wasn't suitable for training exercises. But today is all gentle rolling surfaces, and I don't want to just sit while our horses graze.

The two men look at each other. Kedan puts on an exaggeratedly pained expression. "Only if you promise to have mercy on us."

"I'll take your place, Kedan xiong," says the princeling. "Then Hua xiong-di won't have to worry about having mercy."

I almost choke on the water I'm drinking.

Since morning I've been stealing surreptitious looks at him. He doesn't seem any different: calm, graceful, yet with an inner ferocity that belies his unassuming demeanor. Nobody would believe me if I told them how terrified he was in the night.

This is a man afraid of wolves and being alone in dark rooms—can I make him afraid of *me*?

"You can take my place too, Your Highness," says Tuxi. "I'll just be in your way."

Unhurriedly, the princeling unsheathes Sky Blade. "Shall we, Hua xiong-di?"

I take Heart Sea off my back and toss the scabbard aside. Both Tuxi and Kedan suck in a breath as they realize that we are holding highly unusual yet practically identical swords.

Looking at the princeling now, I see no trace of the trembling boy, but only the inexorable rival who has always loomed large in both my imagination and my reality. What does he see when he looks at me? The conscript who needed to be rescued from bandits? Or the equal who will never cede him the duel?

Our swords clash, an impact that jolts my arm. But I welcome the discomfort because I'm not paralyzed by fear. We break apart, clash, and break apart again. I aim directly at his throat. He parries and kicks toward my solar plexus. I duck under the sweeping kick and thrust my sword where he is most vulnerable. He leaps sideways, pivots around, and slashes at my shoulder.

My mind is blank again, but it is a rewarding blank. No thoughts, only seeing. Sometimes I can predict what he will do, and I get there just a fraction of a moment earlier and take the upper hand. Other times he is too wily and canny, and I find myself under-rotated or overbalanced. Then I have to fight like a tiger not to face sudden defeat.

The grassland clangs with the metallic crash-and-scrape of our priceless blades jarring together again and again. Dimly it occurs to me that I want more of this sparring. Not strictly to win, but because it is exhilarating.

And beautiful.

Almost as soon as the thought happens, we leap apart and start circling each other. Now I see what the predawn darkness of our previous meetings obscured: the singular purpose in his eyes, a will to win that makes me quake somewhere in the depths of my heart.

I glare at him. No one is going to rob me of my courage again—not bandits, not Rouran soldiers, and especially not a boy scared of wolves and sleeping by himself.

I leap toward him. He meets me halfway. Again our swords clash.

"Stop!" cries Kedan. "Listen!"

The princeling and I break apart, both breathing hard. But I hear it now: horses in the distance, closing in fast.

The princeling sheathes Sky Blade. "Tuxi xiong and I will wrestle. Hua xiong-di, you get busy."

We discussed this the night before. As much as possible, we will pretend to be a group of revelers, headed to a wedding at the foot of the Greater Khingan Range, far to the east. Tuxi will speak for us. Kedan and the princeling are his friends. I, who don't know any of the tongues used beyond the Wall, am their mute servant.

I run to the horses and pretend to look after them. When the incoming riders stop a short distance from our group, Tuxi and the princeling are braced together. Kedan has plenty of opinions on the prowess of the wrestlers—or at least that's what I assume he's offering, since I can't understand a word he's saying.

They don't drop the act until after the riders have had a good look at this trio of carefree, frolicking youths. Tuxi lets go of the princeling and hails the riders in an open, friendly manner. The riders are nowhere as amiable. None dismount; their leader asks Tuxi question after question.

Tuxi gestures at Kedan and the princeling, then at me. I stand with my mouth half-open in what I hope is a credible performance of bumpkin-ish naïveté. Tuxi then points to the east in an exaggerated fashion, indicating how far we still have to travel.

The lead rider isn't satisfied. His next question has Tuxi clearly affronted. But the other riders close in and Tuxi smiles in supplication. He shouts something at me. After a moment of staring inaction, I jump to do his bidding, making sure to almost trip in the process.

I rummage through two different saddlebags before coming up with the item Tuxi wants—also agreed on the night before. Running to him, I make my strides heavy and clumsy, and put in another near-fall for good measure.

Tuxi clucks his tongue at me and shakes his head, but takes what I've brought and shows it to the riders. Salt, a solid rock, a most presentable wedding gift for friends in remote reaches.

A few more exchanges back and forth. The lead rider's tone becomes friendlier. Tuxi waves over Kedan, who uses his small axe to chip off a palm-size chunk of salt. This handsome gift is wrapped in a piece of cloth and offered to the lead rider, who has the courtesy to come off his horse to receive it. Kedan gives him a friendly slap on the chest as he hands over the salt.

After the riders finally leave, tearing across the grasslands, I sidle up to Tuxi. "Rouran scouts?"

"Rouran scouts."

They are headed east, in the direction of the rumored secret Rouran meeting ground. "Are they going to . . ."

The princeling is already marching toward his mount. "Let's find out."

13

At first I'm concerned that we might give ourselves away and the Rouran scouts will realize they're being followed. But we ride at a leisurely pace, and after a while I start to worry about the opposite: that we'll lose the Rouran party's trail.

"No fear of that," says Kedan, chewing on a piece of dried mutton. "Look at the ground. I can make out those hoofprints for days."

I remember that he is a highly regarded hunter and tracker. "I guess I'm the only one who doesn't possess any useful skills for life outside the Wall."

Kedan laughs. "Hua xiong-di, don't worry. Idiots live outside the Wall too—I've met my share. If you're willing to learn, skills will come."

"Can you teach me to read those trails?"

Kedan looks toward the princeling, who says, "When we come across the spot where they stopped to rest their horses, we'll do the same. There you'll have plenty of trails to show Hua xiong-di."

It's a long time before we stop. And when we do, the trails on the ground are too many: Rouran hoofprints, Rouran footprints, our hoofprints, our footprints, and prints belonging to animals and nomads that passed this way earlier.

Hoofprints I can make out by the indentations they leave. But the soil is hard and I am sure that I myself leave no marks.

"Granted, you walk very lightly, Hua xiong-di. But I see your prints."

With his sheathed dagger, Kedan draws an outline around one of my prints. I have to put my face very near to the ground and squint to see the faint impression left behind by my boot. And even then I'm only half-confident that I am in fact seeing and not imagining it.

Kedan points. "This other footprint of yours lies on top of the Rouran scout leader's and—"

"How do you know it's his?"

"He was the only one who came off his horse earlier, to receive the salt from us. Also, he is the only one in leather boots. The others with him have footwear made of cloth, and they walk more gingerly on the ground."

"You have a remarkable eye!"

"Trust me, Hua xiong-di. I possess no skill as remarkable as that of knocking three arrows at once out of midair while riding at a fair clip. This is just the result of practice."

"I could say the same about knocking multiple objects out of midair—just the result of practice."

We grin at each other. I slap him on the shoulder in brotherly appreciation.

"Tell me what you observed of the Rouran riders," he says. "You must have noticed different things than I did."

"I think the rider at the rear is the best fighter. And he is left-handed, which would make him a difficult opponent for me—if, that is, I don't fall into a dead faint should he come at me. What did you notice?"

"I was looking at the condition of the horses, wondering how much distance they've already covered today. What about you, Tuxi xiong?"

Tuxi rubs his chin. "To me the man's accent didn't sound as if he hails from this region, or areas farther east. I wouldn't be surprised if his origins are far, far west of here."

"I can't comment on the man's origins," says the princeling. "But the horses—they are of the breed for which Emperor Wu of Han waged two different campaigns against the kingdom of Dayuan."

Dayuan lies beyond the Takla Makan Desert, even beyond the Heavenly Mountains, which I have always considered impossibly far. There are, of course, realms even farther away, including the eminent yet mysterious empire that produces a luminous glassware much prized in wealthy households.

But those lands and their peoples have been no more real to me than the immortals who dwell in the Nine Heavens. And the campaigns the princeling refers to, waged with sixty thousand soldiers, took place five hundred years ago.

"Dayuan horses are said to sweat blood, aren't they?" I ask the princeling. Or a reddish perspiration, to be more precise, from the shoulders.

He nods. "When the scout leader dismounted, his sleeve brushed his horse at the withers. His cuff was stained a light reddish color."

"*Those* were the divine horses?" Kedan exclaims in disbelief. "They were ugly!"

The Rouran horses did have a lean, scrappy, almost hungry look, with their elongated bodies and prominent rib cages.

"They weren't prized for their appearance," I say, recalling what I've read of the breed in the *Records of the Grand Historian*. "But they were said to possess extraordinary stamina, able to cover a thousand li in a day."

"Really?" marvels Tuxi. "At that speed, we could cover the length of the Wall in ten days."

"I don't think that was ever true," says the princeling. "But such horses haven't been seen for a long time in the Central Plain. The bloodline brought back by Emperor Wu's campaigns has thinned to complete uselessness. And later raids by the Han Dynasty captured good but not exceptional horses."

This gives me pause. The *Records of the Grand Historian* mentions those later raids, and I thought nothing of them. The Han Dynasty territories didn't produce the best horses for war, so of course better horses had to be procured somehow.

But now I wonder. Much has been made of nomadic raids on Han land, and I've always thought those tribes unreasonably aggressive. But were they any more aggressive than the supremely civilized Han Dynasty going out to steal horses?

Kedan pats his chest, as if he's looking for something inside his clothes. His eyes widen. The next moment, he sucks in a breath.

The princeling glances at him. "What is it?"

"I . . . ah . . ."

"Looking for this?" I open my hand. On my palm is an object that resembles a miniature *zongzi*, a package of glutinous rice wrapped in bamboo leaves.

Kedan stares at me. I waggle my brows. He should have taken it as a warning when I told him I observed the Rouran in the rear as the best fighter: My gaze is drawn to movement and my mind to the analysis of movement. I recognized Kedan's parting slap on the Rouran leader's chest as more than a friendly gesture, and I imitated it.

It wasn't difficult to lift the package from him, given all the dexterity exercises I've had to do to deploy and catch hidden weapons. But I haven't had time to examine the object until now. I glance down. I know my bamboo leaves, and this thing is not wrapped in a bamboo leaf.

"That's a grape leaf!" exclaims Tuxi. Then to the princeling, "Isn't it?"

"It is." The princeling's gaze lands on Kedan. "You took this from the Rouran?"

Kedan has the grace to look abashed. "He was an ass."

"For suspecting you of being a Xianbei spy?" murmurs the princeling. "How dare he."

I have to suppress a smile.

"Well, what's inside?" asks Tuxi.

I open the grape leaf, which is the size of my hand with all fingers spread. At the center of the leaf is a small pile of golden raisins.

"Taste one, Tuxi xiong," instructs His Highness.

Tuxi does. "Grown in the Turpan oasis, no doubt about it."

The Turpan oasis must be two thousand li west of where we are. And the grape leaf in my palm can't have been separated from its vine more than seven days ago.

A shiver darts down my spine. We look at one another in silence. Are the men we are chasing really scouts if they have come from that far away, in such a great haste?

But if they aren't scouts, then what are they?

◆ ◆ ◆

That night, we seek shelter with a band of nomads. I again play the part of the mute servant. Tuxi makes a gift to our hosts of a thumb-sized chunk of salt, which is received with much delight and gratitude.

After dinner, despite the cold, I bundle up and take a walk with Tuxi, in the hope of unknotting muscles made stiff by yet another day in the saddle. During the walk I ask him to teach me some useful words in Rouran.

Tuxi takes to the task with relish. He is a good teacher, patient and interested, and tells me that Rouran isn't that different a language from Xianbei. But since I don't know any Xianbei, that doesn't help me.

"Will I need to learn to read?" I ask after some time. The *Records of the Grand Historian* mentions that the nomads possessed a script, which has nothing in common with Chinese.

He shakes his head. "That wouldn't be terribly useful. Occasionally a written message might be sent, but by and large, in a nomadic life, there isn't much use for text."

"I find it almost impossible to envision a society without reading and writing," I muse.

We walk in silence for some time before he says, "I think writing must have first arisen for record keeping. South of the Wall, with all the fertile land, the population has long been enormous. So many people living so closely together gave rise to a strong government, which required contributions from everyone to build roads, administer laws, and defend the borders. That in turn necessitated detailed accounts of lands, crop yields, births, and deaths.

"But look around us . . ."

In the deepening dusk, such an endless open expanse surrounds us that I almost cannot remember the unbroken swaths of cultivation and the teeming towns and cities south of the Wall.

"The nomadic life results in a much lower population," Tuxi continues. "Herds of sheep and horses require great areas to graze. The distances involved lead to leagues and confederations, rather than all-powerful kingships. From time to time, a strong leader emerges and the other tribes acknowledge him with gifts and answer his calls to arms. But I'm sure you can see why there has never been the same need for record keeping, or for a sophisticated written language."

The mythology around the invention of Han Chinese characters echoes what Tuxi has said about the demand for record keeping. But it never occurred to me that other peoples, living in other places, had no such demands to answer.

"I too am boggled that my ancestors got by without the written word," says Tuxi, "especially since I can't remember not being able to read. Sometimes I tell myself that we Xianbei weren't a literate people because there was no need for us to be. And other times I wonder, because I grew up south of the Wall, where literacy is so deeply venerated, and where Han Chinese literary traditions are often flaunted as a sign of superiority . . . I wonder whether it's true: that we were an inferior people."

I hardly know where to look. I have held the exact same view of the Xianbei, a casual yet ingrained contempt that I never questioned until a few days ago. Until then I wasn't even aware of my prejudice, let alone that it might be wrong.

"You shouldn't think like that," I say weakly.

"I don't think like that very often." Tuxi is silent for a few heartbeats. "But there is something regrettable about our lack of literary traditions: We haven't written our own history. The nomads have been on this earth for as long as the Han Chinese, but the only records that exist of us are what the Han

Chinese have chosen to put down, usually because we were at war.

"Have you ever talked to two people who just had an argument? You come away with two completely different versions of events." He sighs. "My ancestors' voices have been lost to time; I will only ever know what their opponents thought of them."

◆ ◆ ◆

Perhaps because of the precious gift of salt, our hosts vacate an entire yurt for us to sleep in. I lie down in the same thin bedroll and sheepskin cape, but this time around I have a carpet underneath me and blankets above. Still, I won't be as warm as I was in the small hours of last night, sitting back to back with the princeling.

"Don't think we'll need to worry about wolves tonight," the princeling murmurs.

Surprised that he has brought up the subject again, I open my eyes. It's pitch-dark inside, yet I feel the weight of his gaze from across the yurt. I ought to say something, but what, I'm not sure.

I clear my throat. "The smoke lit by the beacon towers—I've heard it called wolf smoke. People say it's because it's lit with wolf dung. How do you suppose they collect enough of it? There are hundreds if not thousands of beacon towers along the Wall. And to make a big column of smoke, each tower must keep a few *dou*, perhaps a whole *shi*, of wolf dung on hand."

Silence. Then raucous laughter, not only from the princeling, but also Tuxi and Kedan.

"No, no," says Kedan, gasping for breath. "They're not burning wolf dung. There aren't enough wolves for that! Or at least there aren't enough guards to forage for it in such quantities, dropping by dropping."

Tuxi, through fits of giggles, adds, "They burn ordinary dung for the daytime smoke columns. You know, what they collect from the livestock they keep on hand."

"Then why—" I start.

"Our nomadic brethren, especially the Xiongnu, carried wolf banners," says the princeling. "At the sight of those banners, Han Dynasty soldiers rushed to light their beacons. That is a more likely reason the smoke columns are called wolf smoke."

Kedan is still cackling. "Oh, Hua xiong-di, you are such a Southerner."

"I was told this in the North," I protest.

Kedan does not miss a beat. "North or South, the truth gets lost everywhere."

Tuxi sighs softly. Is he thinking again of the long-lost history of the nomadic tribes?

And how strange it is, now that I think about it, that books such as the *Records of the Grand Historian* are accepted as accurate for events spanning hundreds of years, involving dozens of major players and tens of millions of people—when two conflicting accounts exist for the death of the princeling's mother at my father's hands, which took place less than a generation ago.

◆ ◆ ◆

"We're falling farther behind," pronounces Kedan.

It's the next day and all four of us are on the ground, studying the tracks left behind by the Dayuan horses. Kedan deems that the tracks are older than the previous set we examined, which implies that the distance between us and our quarry has increased. I don't see anything different in the tracks, but my well-trained ears pick up something.

I set one ear squarely to the ground and listen. The princeling, seeing me, does the same. A moment later he leaps to his feet. "On your horses. Now."

We mount quickly but ride at only a moderate pace. The time of a stick of incense later, a party of riders sped past us, returning only curt nods to Kedan's friendly waves.

They are on Dayuan horses.

We ride late into the evening, using makeshift torches to check the ground for tracks. When we stop for the night, I'm so tired that I fall asleep as soon as I crawl into my bedroll, and only realize the next morning how cold I am.

Midmorning, I've warmed up only a little when Tuxi shouts excitedly, "Do you sense the change? The wind is coming from the south!"

Even this far north, spring is arriving. I turn my face southward, half hoping to feel the sultry warmth of my ancestral home, thousands of li away.

The princeling, however, does not seem pleased. Kedan's

expression is even darker. "It had better not rain."

Late in the afternoon, rain pours down for the time of a meal. We huddle under a piece of fur felt, Kedan muttering unhappily all the while. His words are lost in the din of rumbling thunder and hard rain striking our makeshift cover.

By the time the sky clears, the tracks left by the Dayuan horses have washed away.

"The first riders were already more than half a day ahead of us," says Kedan, kicking the ground in frustration. "They could have turned in any direction during that time."

"They've been headed east for a while," I say. "Let's continue on the same course. We might come across their trails again before they make any significant turns."

"That's the only thing we can do now," the princeling concurs. "Let's get on."

But we do not pick up their trails.

The weather, after a half day of warmth, turns cold again. The next night we huddle silently around a smoky fire—what fuel we can gather is all damp. I cover my face to shield myself from the sooty air as the wind changes directions capriciously.

Dinner revives our spirits somewhat: Kedan shot down a wild goose. The migratory birds are returning to their northern home, even though winter squats on in these lands, refusing to be fully evicted.

"Should we split into two teams?" asks Tuxi when we have finished eating.

It's not the first time the question has been raised—we can cover more territory that way and be less likely to miss the Rouran trails. The problem is, once we separate, we are unlikely to reunite except by chance.

"Not yet," answers the princeling. "But ask me again tomorrow."

I move closer to Tuxi. "Better teach me some more Rouran."

It isn't the group splitting into two that worries me, but that the duo I find myself in might need to split again. I can only get so far pretending to be dumb and mute.

But learning a language, even a language that doesn't require me to read, is no minor undertaking. The more time I spend at it, the bigger the task becomes. It complicates matters that we don't know which phrases will be most useful for me to tackle. Tuxi decides that beyond basic greetings, I should know how to say, *I'm looking for riders on western territory horses*. But when it comes to the answers I might be given, again we face difficulties. Words for cardinal directions are easy to learn—the nomads might even simply point—but what if they have more information to share?

The princeling doesn't help when he says that instead of attempting to teach me enough to understand answers, it might be more useful that I be able to lie convincingly about who I am, should there be hostile questions.

Tuxi clutches at his head. I rub my temples.

"Have some." Kedan passes us the raisins he stole. "You two have been working too hard. Rest your brains for a bit."

I eat glumly, barely appreciating the sweetness of the costly delicacy in my mouth. Tuxi and the princeling both look grim. Kedan is the only one who doesn't seem overly affected—yet— by our fruitless search for the Rouran.

I take another raisin from him. "How are you still cheerful?"

"I've spent longer than this sniffing out lost tracks."

He grins and I find myself smiling back, glad for his stalwart heart, and secretly relieved that I didn't choose to keep my distance when I first learned of his Xiongnu origins.

Which reminds me . . . "By the way, Kedan xiong, how did your family go from Xiongnu to Xianbei?"

He shakes his head a little. "I'm not sure, exactly. Even my grandfather wasn't sure. But it has been passed down that our clan was forced to flee to this plateau, when the first emperor of Qin struck against the Xiongnu in the Ordos region."

The Ordos region is enclosed by a large rectangular loop in the Yellow River, the cradle of Han Chinese civilization. I am reminded that other peoples have always been here, living in lands we Han Chinese prefer to consider exclusively our own.

"First emperor of Qin," I muse. "Almost seven hundred years ago." That predates the legendary enmity between the Xiongnu and the Han Dynasty, which came after the Qin Dynasty.

Kedan nods. "Long enough for us to become Xianbei and then migrate sou—"

The princeling and I lift our hands at the exact same moment to signal for silence. Distantly, so distantly I can't be sure I'm not imagining it, there rises the howl of a wolf.

My eyes dart to the princeling. Did he hear it? Will he freeze in terror?

But he is in complete possession of himself, his face without even a shadow of fear. And both Tuxi and Kedan are looking at *me*, since I'm probably the one who seems more worried.

Another howl rises. Not close, but noticeably nearer than the first.

After several more howls back and forth, the princeling says, "They are not wolves."

I blink.

"His Highness is correct," confirms Kedan.

I almost ask what the howling animals are, until I realize that they must be people imitating wolves. "Who are they?"

But even as I pose the question, I already know the answer.

They are those who fly the wolf banner.

14

We ride all night, but at a pace that is almost doddering. The princeling is adamant that we not make the kind of ruckus that can be heard from twenty li away by an attentive ear on the ground.

At some point during the day and a half since the rain washed away the trails, we must have shot past where the Rouran scouts changed course. We are headed west-southwest now, toward the hills that ring the plateau on its southern edge.

Every so often, we dismount and listen. On one of those occasions, I happen to be next to the princeling. As we rise to our feet, I ask, "How did you know the wolves weren't real?"

To me the howls sounded just like the ones I heard that night at the beacon tower. Or were those not real either?

He hesitates. "Because I wasn't struck by fear."

Not a bad method of detection, as such things go.

"Do you think they use wolf howls because the party that is on the move doesn't know exactly where the other one is?"

"Could be. Or it might be a way to gauge how much distance remains between them."

A little after dawn, Kedan locates fresh trails. They do not belong to either of the groups of Dayuan horses that we saw before, but Kedan decrees that the trails have been made during the night, when most nomads do not travel, and we should follow them.

We heed his advice. As the sun rises, however, the princeling leads us into the hills. We find a place to sleep and set out again shortly after noon, keeping close to the hills so we can hide should we hear riders approaching. And we do hide, twice, first from a small group, and second from what Kedan estimates to be about five hundred riders.

"We must be getting close to the Rouran muster," says Tuxi after the regiment of riders passes.

"There'll be sentries soon," replies the princeling. "We shouldn't use the main route anymore. Let's make our way in the hills."

Our plan calls for us to penetrate a li or so south into the hills before turning sharply west. We are looking for a large valley and a major encampment. Theoretically, that shouldn't be difficult to find. But the hills stretch on endlessly, and they split into so many spurs and ridges that I become cross-eyed from all the ascents and descents.

The landscape is stony, the greenery sparse. Paths are few and narrow. But by midafternoon I hear what we seek, the muffled sounds of many, many pairs of feet and almost as many hooves. Kedan goes ahead to scout a safe path for us.

"There is one thing I don't understand," I say to Tuxi as we wait. "Suppose—suppose that it's true there is at least one highly placed traitor at court. Why has the traitor chosen this moment to ally with the Rouran?"

The history of these lands is littered with rebellions great and small. But rebellions usually foment under conditions of great adversity. A tyrannical ruler isn't sufficient cause by himself. More often than not, it has to be tyranny wedded to incompetence, with perhaps a natural disaster in the mix too, before anyone opts for an uprising as the least terrible option.

At the moment, however, things are not so dire. The Xianbei emperor seems conscientious enough. The people of the North are growing more prosperous. Taxes are not heavy, historically speaking. Even the weather has been fairly calm of late, and the Yellow River on tolerable behavior. Not a time I would have picked, if I had the toppling of dynasties in mind.

Tuxi glances at the princeling, who says, "There has been . . . tension at court. Internal divisions."

Now that's a different matter altogether. "About what?"

"There are those who want to implement a complete ban of Xianbei speech and customs and have everyone of Xianbei descent change their surnames to Han Chinese ones. And there are those who are opposed, naturally. Since the emperor seems receptive to the ban, I would imagine the traitor to be a member of the opposing camp."

My mouth opens and closes a few times before I can utter,

"But why ban everything Xianbei? Did *Xianbei* courtiers propose such measures? And how in the world do so many people take on new surnames all at once?"

"A list of substitutions has existed for a while," says the princeling. "The Han Chinese surname that the imperial Tuoba clan would adopt, if the ban comes to pass, is Yuan."

So at least his aunt didn't pick a random surname to make him seem fully Han Chinese.

"And yes, Xianbei courtiers and ministers proposed these measures. As for why—" The princeling glances at Tuxi. "We are a minority dynasty, and most such dynasties haven't lasted very long. Some would rather not have the fact that we are Xianbei held against us by the Han Chinese, who greatly outnumber us."

"Do you agree with that—with the banning of everything Xianbei?" I ask.

"No. I'm not convinced that the benefits, if there are any, would outweigh the turmoil and dissension it would cause. But the last thing I would do is put the Rouran on the throne because I am displeased about a possible imperial edict that can be reversed any time the emperor changes his mind. It would be like cutting off my own head because I don't like that a fly has landed on my hair."

I look at Tuxi, who mourns the lack of a literary tradition in the Xianbei language. "And you too would be against this ban?"

To my surprise, Tuxi grimaces. "I don't know. I can't make up my mind on this matter."

"Why not?"

"Because every time a dynasty falls, it's the people who suffer. Sometimes the suffering seems worth it—the end of the Qin Dynasty ushered in the Han Dynasty, and with it four hundred years of peace and prosperity. But it's been more than two hundred years since the Han Dynasty collapsed, and the North is still recovering from all the ensuing chaos.

"If the decision fell to me, and if the Xianbei becoming completely Chinese would make the people of the North accept us as their own, I would consider it. I am not so proud that I would cling to my surname if changing it would mean another fifty years of peace. And the banning of Xianbei speech is only meant for official purposes, not for private use at home.

"Not that it's even spoken widely among the Xianbei in private—we've been south of the Wall for many generations. Of the Xianbei in our group that set out from the capital, everyone speaks Chinese better, including me—and some might not speak any Xianbei at all."

This might explain why I heard only Chinese spoken in the capital.

"But would being Han Chinese make our dynasty more long-lived?" asks the princeling, half shaking his head.

"That's where the difficulty lies, isn't it?" answers Tuxi. "How do we know whether the seeds we sow today will grow into mighty oaks—or barely even germinate?"

"I would be happy if the emperor gave half so much thought to these questions as you do, Tuxi xiong," I say.

"That may or may not matter in the end," says the princeling darkly. "Because whoever is orchestrating this may not even be interested in saving Xianbei ways south of the Wall. They might just be exploiting resentments to further their own ends."

We sit silently for some time, then Tuxi walks to his horse to get some walnuts for us to share. When he is out of earshot, I murmur, "Your Highness has a suspicious mind."

"Perhaps I do," he answers solemnly. "But I trust you, Hua xiong-di. In matters having to do with the survival of the state, I trust you completely."

◆ ◆ ◆

Before I can react to this astonishing statement, Kedan returns. He doesn't speak but signals us to come on foot. We secure our horses and hurry after him.

The next valley is a ravine, for all intents and purposes. We half climb, half slip down to the bottom, then grimacing and straining, scale the rise. At last we come to a narrow gap between two enormous rocks and squeeze through the passage, Tuxi barely avoiding getting stuck. On the other side, a few outcrops shield us from view.

Beyond lies an enormous valley, as shallow and even as its neighbor is narrow and steep. A stream leaps down from the opposite hills to flow along its western edge. Yurts by the hundreds have been erected at the center of the valley in concentric circles. Horses are congregated in large pens.

New arrivals pour in from the mouth of the valley to the north, even though there must already be thousands of horses and tens of thousands of men on hand. In the fading light of the day, more yurts are being assembled and more pens built, as horses are exercised around the rim of the valley to keep them swift and fit.

I knew to expect a large-scale muster. I have heard, as we climbed up the ravine, the din of horses and men. Still I find myself having to swallow a gasp when faced with the actual sight of our enemies, preparing for war.

"I'm almost sure there are more horses and men in the next valley. And livestock—I've heard bleating that can't otherwise be accounted for," whispers Kedan, in case what we are seeing isn't alarming enough.

It's getting late. I'm about to remind the princeling that we had better return to our horses soon—the idea of negotiating the ravine in the dark is terrifying—when he says, "Tuxi xiong, Kedan xiong, you two head back. Hua xiong-di and I will stay here and observe."

"Will you be able to see much at night?" asks Tuxi.

"We'll manage," says the princeling.

At the tone of his voice, my stomach drops. After Tuxi and Kedan leave, I say to the princeling, "You mean for us to go down there after dark, don't you?"

"If one does not enter a tiger's lair, how can one hope to retrieve the tiger cub?" he answers, seemingly unperturbed.

"I've never understood that proverb," I grumble. "Who wants a tiger cub?"

He laughs softly. Of course it has never been a literal saying. During the reign of Emperor Ming of Han, he sent an emissary named Ban Chao to the king of Shanshan, a small realm beyond the western terminus of the Wall. Ban Chao was at first warmly received, but the king's attitude soon cooled considerably. Ban Chao learned that the Xiongnu also sent an emissary, and the king was now wavering between alliances.

Ban Chao was warned that the situation had become volatile and possibly dangerous. *If one does not enter into a tiger's lair, how can one hope to retrieve the tiger cub?* he famously said in reply. And that night, he and his entourage killed the Xiongnu emissary and more than a hundred of his followers.

A period of friendly relations with some fifty different kingdoms in the region followed, and the story has always appeared to me as a fine example of shrewdness and audacity. But those Xiongnu deaths were murders, weren't they? Committed in the name of empire and emperor, but murders nevertheless. It disturbs me now that I wasn't remotely disturbed by that before, when I read the anecdote the first, second, or third time.

And of course there is no record of the Xiongnu version of these events.

I'm sure the princeling didn't use the saying to make me think of the Han Dynasty's dealings with the nomads. But sometimes, as I'm beginning to realize, language *is* history.

"We won't be going down for at least the time of a meal," he says, perhaps misunderstanding my silence.

"What exactly are we going to do down there?"

"Learn what we can, without getting caught."

I swallow. "What if we do get caught?"

He only says, "Better use this time to study the layout of the yurts and the movements of the guards." Then, after a minute, "And maybe see if you can deduce where the rations are kept. Let's swipe some for ourselves, if we can."

✦ ✦ ✦

Feeling more than a little ill, I scan the slope nearest us and search for a good way down. Several huge yurts, almost three times the size of regular ones, dominate the center of the valley. Each of these palatial yurts flies a different banner. The designs incorporate not only wolves, but horses, rams, and geometric patterns.

The encampment doesn't appear to be tightly patrolled. Guards walk in pairs along the peripheries and the main thoroughfares, but they are not spaced closely and seem to treat their task as a leisurely bore. I suppose they have reason to be somewhat lax. The valley is hidden and difficult to find, and they probably don't think that anyone is looking for it.

When darkness falls, the encampment does not illuminate. There are no outdoor fires and only the five largest central yurts leak any light at the seams. The patrols do become more frequent, judging by the number of lanterns circulating the grounds. But it's hard to tell, given the unhurried movements of those lanterns, whether the night guards are being more careful and alert or still simply going through the motions.

Eventually my gaze returns to my companion. We have been peering out from behind a boulder almost as tall as we are, but now he sits down, a darker shadow in the night, and signals for me to join him. We drink from our waterskins and he offers me some walnut pieces.

"Why have you picked me?" I ask him. "Wouldn't it be better to go with someone who understands the language?"

Part of me—maybe most of me—yearns for the safety of the other valley, where Kedan and Tuxi will be spending the night. Another part of me—maybe also most of me—is thrilled that the princeling chose me over everyone else.

"You are faster and quieter on foot. And you can fell men in the dark, at a distance, without making much noise," he answers. "We must not be discovered. There are too many soldiers down there for anyone to fight their way out. Our safety lies in stealth, and only in stealth."

"Why not go by yourself, then? One person is stealthier than two."

"I'm afraid to go by myself."

I laugh softly before I realize that he isn't joking.

I—I'm afraid of many things, he said the other night. I didn't believe him entirely, and I still don't. He is so self-possessed in his demeanor, so calm and decisive—it's easier to think that I might have been mistaken about his hands shaking than to imagine that he carries within him near-debilitating fears.

Impulsively, I reach out and take one of his hands.

It shakes. Just perceptibly.

I let go. "Why are you afraid of wolves?"

But he takes my hand again. "Have you noticed the scars on my face? A wolf cub left them."

My heart careens into my rib cage. The warm solidity of his fingers around mine demands all my attention, and I can only vaguely recall the scratches across his forehead and chin. "You didn't grow up in the wilds. How were you so close to a wolf cub?"

"My aunt had one brought in as a birthday present for me."

I feel the calluses on his palm. Mine must feel the same—all those years of practice, a sword in hand. "Why?"

"I was a timid child—not at all what she expected, since my mother was fearless. She thought that I'd grow more courageous with a wolf cub for a companion. In the middle of the night, she set the cub in a basket at the foot of my bed, so I'd find it in the morning. But the cub woke up and climbed onto my bed. And I woke up to see a pair of glowing eyes right in front of me." He snorts. "I don't think I need to describe the scene that ensued."

I can imagine the chaos. I place my other hand over our clasped hands. "You are obviously still alive. What happened to the wolf cub?"

"My father gave it to a cousin. It died of old age not too long ago."

Now I understand his fear of wolves—and of being alone in a dark room. "Why are you afraid of going down into the encampment?"

"I'm afraid of anything that can kill me."

"You must be frightened of me, then," I say in jest.

"Terrified. My whole life I've been terrified of you."

I almost laugh again, but I don't. He is serious. Stunned, I let go of his hand.

He finds my hand yet again. "When I was a child, I almost wrote you to beg you to consider a more literal version of the contest, because I was so afraid to fight you."

He means the "discourse on swordsmanship," where we would demonstrate our skills rather than fight. I can only imagine how scandalized his aunt would have been if he'd breathed this idea to her.

He squeezes my hand. "But since I find you terrifying, I can't help but think you must petrify everyone else too. And believe it or not, *that* makes me less afraid to venture down into the Rouran encampment."

◆ ◆ ◆

Our descent is painstakingly slow. I don't know how the princeling keeps his fear in check. I feel both that I can't breathe and that I'm drawing in too much air—not into my lungs, but into my stomach, making me bloated and nauseated.

The moon has yet to rise and it's almost pitch-dark in the encampment. We wait until four lantern-swinging patrols pass, then cross an empty expanse to the outermost circle of yurts. We listen at one, then another. They are both silent except for the snoring of their occupants. I recoil when someone speaks inside a third. The princeling listens, then signals me to keep moving.

We pass rings and rings of yurts. My feet march in the right direction, deeper and deeper into the encampment. But my mind quakes. Stealth. Only stealth. We passed the point of being able to fight our way out many rings ago.

We duck a set of patrols. I almost jump out of my skin when I hear a commotion farther inward—surely we've been discovered and Rouran warriors are coming for us. But no. The disturbance doesn't seem to be the kind that comes of spotting intruders at a secret muster.

By the time we reach the five big yurts, which are set in a circle, each with a pair of guards in front, men are still filing into the largest tent. We slip around to the back of it.

I can hear a good twenty, thirty people inside. They move, their clothes sliding on cushions. Some drink, the unmistakable sound of liquid flowing down gullets. One coughs; one clears his throat; one cracks an uncommonly loud set of knuckles.

Despite my two Rouran lessons, I remain utterly useless in that language. I can only hope the princeling will understand enough to make our trip worthwhile.

A man begins to speak, greeting the dignitaries inside.

To my astonishment, the language I hear is Chinese. To my utter stupefaction, I recognize the voice too.

Captain Helou.

15

I glance at the princeling. He is quiet, so quiet—barely even breathing.

"My reverent obeisance to the great and venerable Yucheng Khan," says Captain Helou.

At that name, the princeling seems to wind even tighter. When we discussed his plan to find the meeting ground, he mentioned that the Rouran do have an acknowledged leader, a khan. Is this that khan? If so . . .

My heart thunders.

"My most humble greetings to the gathered heroes," continues Captain Helou. "Your illustrious names have all reached my ears in years past—it is an honor and privilege to at last witness your splendor in person."

It takes a certain gift to make such banal words ring with sincerity. Captain Helou abounds with that force of personality. I don't think any of us ever doubted that he was meant for greater things—but why is he *here*?

I hear the shifting of fabrics and the sound of something striking the carpet. Is Captain Helou kowtowing to the khan?

Someone speaks in a language I can't understand, but does not seem to be questioning him. An interpreter? Then a man with a deep rumbling voice says something.

"His Majesty grants you permission to address the assembled heroes," the interpreter translates, his Chinese accented but fluent.

"My unending gratitude to Your Majesty and all the heroes for your gracious hospitality and your forbearance in agreeing to hear my master's explanation."

More fabric rustling—Captain Helou is standing up again. "The plan was for me to guide our group of scouts to the west once we'd arrived on the plateau, so they wouldn't come anywhere near this encampment. But the fool who lit the beacon, one Bai, got himself caught. And Tuoba Kai, the princeling, was suspicious enough not to kill him on the spot, but to send him away, hoping that he'd escape and lead the princeling's man to my master.

"I couldn't risk that plan succeeding. The princeling sent me to the capital to deliver a message. But first I had to kill Bai, to make sure no word got out, even though I was almost certain he was only a paid lackey and didn't know anything important."

"This man Bai didn't know about you?" asks the interpreter.

"I'm sure he didn't know about me," answers Captain Helou. "I didn't even know about him. I knew someone would be sent to light the beacon, but I didn't know Bai was the man. Nor did I know that the beacon lighter would be traveling with me."

"Was that not reckless on the part of your master?"

"A little risky, yes, but what venture on this scale isn't risky? The plan was an elegant one. Bai hadn't traveled so far north before, and without the team, he would have been a lone man riding toward the Wall. Much better that he was sent as part of the princeling's own group. It should have been more convenient and caused less scrutiny."

"But that was not the result."

"All plans must be adjusted from time to time. I made sure to lay misleading trails before I killed Bai and left his body somewhere difficult to find. The princeling's man must even now be searching for him. There is no trace to lead to me or my master.

"So now the plan can and must proceed forward. My master asks that you will please mount an attack far from here the day after the next lighting of the beacon."

The interpreter confers for a longer time with his master before saying, "The beacon should have already been lit again. We do not have the grain stores necessary to muster men and let them sit."

"Do you wish to throw these men full-on at the defenses, then?" asks Captain Helou. "South of the Wall there has been a realm-wide muster of men. Their granaries are vast and their generals battle-tested and ready. Remember, it is precisely because you aren't sure of victory in a long, drawn-out war that we are proceeding by guile and subterfuge."

He sounds so forcefully reasonable that after the interpreter finishes translating, there is a silence. This time, no one fidgets or makes any sounds.

"What request do you make of us, then?"

"The same," says Captain Helou. "Do your best to make the Northern court think that the most overwhelming attacks will come near the far ends of the Wall. Then wait for the forces now stationed outside the capital to be deployed east and west."

"How long until that happens? We have brought seven days of rations to this muster. They could be stretched out to ten days and supplemented with hunting. But after that . . ."

"In the next valley, you have a fair number of livestock animals. Eat them if you need to. Eat some of your horses if you must. My master will not be able to push too boldly for the central commandery troops to depart. So you must make the situation appear urgent and force the Northern court's hand."

"And how do we do that?"

"The beacons will be lit one after another. And each time one is lit, you mount an attack toward the extremities of the Wall."

"How will you light them so easily again? Surely they will have doubled, if not quadrupled, the guards on the towers."

"There is no need for us to take over any beacon tower—I wish we'd realized this sooner. The towers are ten li apart. The guards at the next tower cannot tell whether a fire is lit on the beacon itself or somewhere nearby. And by the time the matter has been investigated, it will be too late."

"But the signal won't travel all the way to the ends of the Wall. How do we know when to attack?"

"It almost doesn't matter. News will take time to get back to the capital. They will not know whether the timing of the beacons coincides exactly with the attacks. They will only know that we distract them with fire and smoke while real clashes happen elsewhere. At some point they will stop paying attention to the beacons—and the section of the Wall near the capital—and rush to beleaguered forts farther away, especially if you make some real progress there."

The hairs on the back of my neck rise. This is exactly what we feared the Rouran would do.

"When the forces of the central commandery leave the capital, we will send our signal for you to ride south. And Heaven willing, the Rouran heroes will take the capital and replace the current emperor with minimum fuss."

Several Rouran men speak at once. The rumbly voice, which must belong to Yucheng Khan, hushes them and says something.

"It's late," declares the interpreter. "We will show the captain to his quarters and give him good wine, good meat, and other such rewards as we are capable of providing in this camp."

Captain Helou offers his profound gratitude and undying loyalty.

When Captain Helou is escorted out, the princeling gives me a slight push. I understand: He needs to stay and listen to what the Rouran generals might discuss; at the same time, it will be helpful to know Captain Helou's whereabouts, just in case.

My heart thudding in my ears, my legs feeling like over-cooked noodles, I trail behind Captain Helou and a quartet of accompanying guards to a tent almost a li from the one he just left. The guards take up positions outside. I watch for some time from the shadows, then retrace my steps back to the princeling's location.

He is nowhere to be seen.

My mind turns blank, and a thousand blood-curdling fears unleash at once. He has been captured. They are waiting for me. I will be captured any moment now. I will not leave this encampment alive. Worse, when they discover that I am a woman—

I rein my thoughts to a hard stop.

I have not been caught yet. And I've heard no commotion to indicate that the princeling is in any trouble. I've been gone for a while. It's quite possible the Rouran leaders have dispersed—in fact, I can tell they have: The yurt they were gathered in is now silent and dark. It would have been prudent for the princeling to move away a bit, to avoid being seen by those leaving.

Think, Hua Mulan.

Before he hid himself, he would have thought how best for us to find each other again, in the dark, in enemy territory. If he can see me, he would come to me. What if he can't see me and instead wants me to go to him? How would he accomplish that?

Of course, he knows my hearing is more sensitive than that of the typical man or woman. I check to make sure no patrols are nearby, then put my ear down to the ground. It does not take me long to discern a soft double tap that repeats on a regular basis.

The sound leads me three rings of yurts to the south. And there he is, safe and sound.

We grip each other's hands tightly, and then we tiptoe away. I guide him near where Captain Helou is staying. We listen for a while, but there isn't much to hear: Captain Helou, under guard, is soundly asleep.

This part of the valley is less utilized. Captain Helou's yurt is in the next-to-last ring. Beyond, empty space. We head toward it. I'm flabbergasted at what we've learned and giddily relieved that tonight's mission is finished. No one has seen us and we are on the verge of slipping away.

Then I hear footsteps. Light, and closing in fast.

Only a martial artist can move with such quiet speed.

Patrols too are converging in our direction, their footsteps loud as drumbeats. Four men to a group, with two groups about equidistant from us. There is no chance that I can hit all eight guards at once with my hidden weapons. If I try to pick them off one by one, the remaining guards will raise the alarm. And if we try to hide from the patrols, the person who walks with dangerous lightness will catch us.

Is it Captain Helou? Are we going to meet our end here after all?

The softer steps stop. The princeling and I exchange a look, even though I can scarcely make out his features. And we too stop and conceal ourselves behind a mound of earth that has been dug up.

In my right hand I hold three small projectiles. In my left hand is . . . the princeling's hand. Our hands do not shake, but my heart beats so furiously it almost drowns out the patrols' approach.

The two groups salute as they pass each other. And then they recede into the night, continuing their circuit around the encampment, moving farther and farther away.

We run. The light footsteps follow. The valley tapers toward its southern end. We are not far from the slopes. If we can scramble up—

No, our pursuer will reach us before then. Where did the Rouran get such a remarkable martial artist? Even my footfall has become heavier in my rush, but this person's steps remain featherlight and barely audible.

We don't want a fight. We are not so far from the outer-most ring of yurts—or the patrols—that combat wouldn't get noticed. But what can we possibly do to be left alone?

The princeling yanks me to a stop. The loss of momentum is so abrupt I almost fall against him. I stop myself just in time, but he bands his arms about me in an embrace.

My mouth drops open.

"Pretend!" he whispers in my ear.

The touch of his lips on my skin—lightning zigzags through me.

Vaguely I understand that he wants us to pass for a pair of randy Rouran fighters in search of a little privacy. But I only stand like a stone statue. He holds me tighter, one hand on the small of my back, the other behind my head. Is he concerned

I won't respond and he'll need to maintain the pretense all by himself?

I throw my arms around his neck and whisper, "Like this?"

A tremor propels through him. When his hand comes up to my face, his touch scorches. My fingers close over his. But I don't know whether I mean to push his hand away or press it more firmly against my cheek.

His breaths turn ragged. Mine as well. The night pulses with the air we exhale, the darkness heavy yet strangely soft.

"Your Highness, Hua xiong-di," comes the whisper of another. "You don't need to pretend anything. It's just me."

The princeling and I still. He seems as stunned as I am. We break apart and turn to face the man.

"Master Yu, why are you here?"

The princeling's low voice is reserved, almost cold. A gust blows, and all the heat from a moment ago disappears without a trace. I shiver: He suspects Yu of having also committed treason.

Yu drops to one knee, his response just as soft. "I followed Captain Helou here after he killed Bai."

"How were you able to do so without being discovered?"

"For most of the way, I trailed him at a distance. I might not have made it into the valley if he hadn't stopped to wait for nightfall. He didn't want to be seen entering."

The princeling does not speak. I glance from one man to the other and back again, my neck so tense I can barely move my head.

"Your Highness assigned me to find out the identity of Bai's true master, the traitor at court," Yu continues. "That task I have not yet accomplished and have every intention of completing. If Your Highness is satisfied with this interim report, I will offer wishes for your good health and the rations I took from the Rouran stores, and return to watching Captain Helou."

The princeling remains silent for some more time. "Master Yu, please come with us."

◆ ◆ ◆

We make our way warily, aware that a single misstep could alert the encampment to our presence. Still, as I place my feet with care, all my senses alert, the events of the night dart through my head like a pack of unruly children. Captain Helou. Yu. The Rouran khan. The imminent attack against the capital.

But I also reflect on something that has significance only to me: I finally know the princeling's name. Captain Helou called him Tuoba Kai. Yuan Kai, if the ban should come to pass. Kai means victorious—not a bad name for these circumstances.

The moon has risen. I can see him ahead, a dark, agile shape. *Kai*, I say silently. Warmth rises to my cheeks. Other than Murong, Dabao, and a few young cousins on my mother's side, I've never called any men by their given names. But how else am I to think of the man who has held my hand and embraced me? Whose hand I have held and whom I have embraced in turn?

After such close, sustained contact, it would be impossible for him not to realize I am a woman. Since he betrayed no sign of shock, or even of surprise, he must have known for a while. I think back to our first and only night alone together, of him standing by the foot of my cot, gazing down at me. My heart races as if I've been running at a full sprint.

We reach the spot where Kai and I waited earlier and squeeze through the narrow passage to the ravine, which, at its very top, has a bit of a smooth, flat ledge.

"Master Yu, you've had a long journey. Please take some rest," says Kai. "Hua xiong-di, I'd like to speak with you. Come with me."

Heat careens through me. Surely . . .

No, he won't embrace me again. Not with Yu around. And not even if we were alone.

The moonlight does not make it much less treacherous to tread near the top of the ravine, and we trudge on for what seems an unnecessarily long time. I want to ask him outright when and how he learned that I am a woman, but this isn't the right moment. Not when the Rouran are on the verge of sacking the capital.

At last he says, his voice tight, "Now we should be out of Master Yu's hearing."

I put my hands on my elbows, bracing myself. "Are you about to tell me that you don't trust him?"

"I don't."

"But your father trusts him enough to give you into his care.

He's the one who was supposed to look after you outside the Wall, isn't he?"

"At this point, I don't trust my father."

I shudder. *"What?"*

"After you left to see where Captain Helou would be staying the night, the Rouran khan and his generals spoke for some time. Several times they mentioned Captain Helou's master. Not by name, unfortunately, but I was able to confirm that he is a Xianbei nobleman."

"There must be a whole pack of Xianbei noblemen in the capital."

"But my father is the one in charge of the central commandery. He is also the one who sent both Bai and Captain Helou along with us."

"But he's your *father*."

"Most Xianbei noblemen in the capital are fathers. Being a father doesn't mean a man won't betray his country."

What I meant was *How could you suspect your* own *father?* But I should know, shouldn't I, that sometimes one shouldn't trust one's father too much?

I pull my cape tighter around me. "What did the Rouran generals say about this nobleman?"

"I'm not as well versed as Tuxi xiong in languages beyond the Wall. They were speaking fast, and often several voices at once. I don't know exactly what they said. I can only guess that when the nobleman was mentioned, they were debating how much they should trust him."

"What did they decide?"

"Yucheng Khan wished to move forward with the plan, and the others fell in line."

Until this moment I didn't realize how much I want everything to go away. If Yucheng Khan were to doubt the ripeness of the moment, if he came to see that he doesn't want the lands south of the Wall as much as he'd thought he did, if the opposition of his generals somehow outweighed his ambition and impatience . . .

But no. And now we hurtle like Dayuan horses toward a dark and ominous future.

The sounds of agitated breaths echo in the air. They are mine. I force myself to calm down. "So Captain Helou will leave in the morning to arrange for the beacons?"

"Most likely. And that means we have limited time before the central commandery forces are sent away from the capital."

"*If* they are sent."

"They will be sent. If the beacons repeatedly turn out to be ruses, and if pressure is continually applied, the court will become anxious, as anyone would under the circumstances. Those advocating for action will prevail over those counseling patience."

And Captain Helou, of course, never delivered Kai's message to his father. The royal duke, on the movement of whose armies the fate of the realm rests, is now as much in the dark as anyone else with regard to the intentions of the Rouran.

I feel dizzy. "What do we do, then?"

He rubs a hand across his forehead. "That's what paralyzes me. I can't trust anyone else, yet the two of us alone cannot hold back the tide."

He said something similar before. *In matters having to do with the survival of the state, I trust you completely.*

Not that he isn't correct, but . . . "Why do you trust me?"

"Because your father kept your attention focused squarely on the duel and your training. You are involved in this war only because of the conscription, not because you have any connection to either the Rouran or the imperial court. You are no one to the players of this game. Even better, they are nothing and no one to you.

"And that's something I cannot say about anyone else here. Yu is loyal to my father—if my father is not loyal to the country, then there is no telling where Yu's loyalty lies. Kedan worships Captain Helou, and not just as a friend, if you understand what I mean."

I do understand and I think he is correct about Kedan. "But Captain Helou—I don't believe he feels the same way." He doesn't mind Kedan's friendship and adoration, but he doesn't return it in equal or even half measure.

"It doesn't matter what he feels toward Kedan. We already know where his loyalty lies. It's Kedan's we don't know about. Does he love Captain Helou enough to betray his country?"

"Does Kedan even know about all this?"

"I don't know. Then again, I didn't suspect either Bai or Captain Helou. I can't make the same mistake again."

He half turns so that he stands with his profile to me. Moonlight frosts the sharp contours of his face. But I don't need to see his features to feel the tension radiating from him, the palpable fear that one misstep can doom everything.

Whereas I feel as if I'm sleepwalking. I'm afraid, yes, but there is a part of me that can't yet accept that I, a recent exile from the South, am suddenly and inextricably caught up in the fate of the North—one of the central players in this enormous, pivotal game.

"All right, so we watch Kedan because of his devotion to Captain Helou," I say. "But why can't we trust Tuxi? Surely, he must be as much of a nobody to the Rouran as I am."

Kai pinches the space between his brows. "You know how I told you that I was terrified of you? Apparently I didn't know what terrified means. Now I'm truly terrified of this situation. And about you, I feel merely apprehensive."

I almost smile. "What does that have to do with anything?"

"I'm going to tell you something. And you will swear to Heaven above that you will not reveal a word of it to anyone, or we will have our duel right here and I will fight to my last breath."

I swallow—there is a vehemence to his tone that I have never heard before. "All right. I won't tell anyone."

"Tuxi's surname isn't Tuxi. It's Tuoba. His name is Tuoba Xi, and he is my second cousin and the emperor's son."

My lips flap but no sounds emerge. I blink and try again. "Is—is he the crown prince?"

An emperor's successor is almost always appointed from among his sons rather than decided by mere seniority.

"No, he is styled Prince Anzhong of Luoyang and he is not the crown prince," Kai says quickly. And then, after a long silence, "Here's something else you are to tell no one. The crown prince is ill—very ill and deteriorating. Or at least he was when we left the capital. To my thinking, *that* is the reason why those bent on treason are acting now. Without a strong heir, the emperor is weakened. And should the crown prince die—which is almost inevitable at this point—the jostling among the other princes would distract everyone at court and undermine the unity necessary to handle the Rouran."

I thought I was beyond any further shocks, but I still flinch in dismay: He is saying that Tuxi may be conspiring with the Rouran to forcibly improve his own position.

I don't need to ask why a son might wish to overturn his father's rule. Such examples abound in history. Crown princes grow impatient for the reins of power. Princes lower in the pecking order depose their fathers and brothers because that's their best and sometimes only chance at the throne.

"Does anyone else know that he is with us?"

"No one. Not my father, not even the emperor, who thinks he's away from the capital on a different errand."

"No, I mean, does Master Yu know who he is?"

"Tuxi has yet to visit me at home—he has less freedom of movement than I do. I used to go to the palace to study and train with him, and later we met in noodle shops and other such places, when he could get away." Kai sighs. "He wanted to come with me on this mission, and I—well, I was glad to have him because his presence made me less afraid."

And now his presence complicates our already complicated situation.

I rub my temples. The night air bites into my fingers. "Do you really believe that Prince Anzhong of Luoyang would betray his father?"

"Don't use that name—don't even think it. And yes, he is capable of coming up with such a plan. As for why, the emperor can be a harsh father, and he has long underestimated Tuxi, believing him to be unsuited for greater tasks. This would certainly be one way of changing the emperor's opinion."

My brain feels like a piece of paper over which someone has spilled a whole bucket of ink. It's too much. It's all too much. I am not meant to be dealing with matters of such gravity and magnitude. I'm a mere fighter, and not even a reliable one at that.

For Heaven's sake, I'm just a girl.

Patience, echoes Father's voice in my head. *Concentration.*

I can't concentrate and there isn't a moment to lose! I retort.

And then, for the first time, I understand what he wants me to do. He never meant that I should be patient while I wait for my opponent to make the next move, but that I should not become so jumpy and anxious that I lose focus.

That instead of letting my thoughts run wild and take over everything, I can leave some room to allow for the return of concentration.

I breathe deeply, in and out. I am not *just* a girl—no woman is. And if Heaven has deposited me at this time and place, then I *am* meant to deal with these problems, no matter their scale or consequence.

I inhale again. "Yes, Tuxi possesses the intelligence and meticulousness it takes to formulate an ambitious, comprehensive scheme. And so do you."

"What?" says Kai, his response barely audible. Then, "*What?*"

His voice has risen. His breaths turn irregular. I can almost feel the effort he expends to restrain himself so that his next sentence is only a heated whisper. "If I'm behind it, then why would I be telling you about this conspiracy?"

"Because if I suspected you, I could prove a formidable opponent."

"So you *do* suspect me?" His voice does not shake, but it sounds right on the edge of doing so.

"No. I'm sure your aunt made certain you never had time for any such thing."

He lets out a long breath of air.

"You can't suspect everyone because they *could* do it," I go on. "I could be in on the conspiracy too—it's possible! I could hate you and your family and want to bring down this dynasty so when the new Rouran overlords take over, the whole lot of you will perish."

He stares at me, then lets out a soft snort. "In theory my family and I could pledge our allegiance to the Rouran, and

232

thereby save our necks. But I see what you are saying: My fear is overwhelming me again."

I slump against the rock face in my relief. When I pulled myself back from my own incipient panic, I realized that he too was on the verge of tipping over—and that before we could do anything else, we must both be able to think clearly.

He scuffs the bottom of his boot against the stony ground. "If you were in my place, what would you do, Hua Mulan?"

He has called me by my name twice before, shouting at me to get away from the bandits. But this time, he makes it sound as lovely as a magnolia in full bloom. It takes me a moment to remember what we are talking about. "You said yourself that the two of us alone cannot hold back the tide. So we have no choice but to trust more people. Let's start with your father. You've known him all your life. Do you think he would betray his country? Not whether it is possible, but whether he would."

Kai takes a moment to think, then shakes his head. "No. He's a soldier because he must be, but he hates war above all else. And my aunt would put a sword through his throat if he not only got himself into such a scheme, but also endangered me in the process."

"Then we trust him—and if we can trust him, then I think we can trust Yu. Now onto Tuxi. How long have you known him?"

"All my life."

"Would he ally himself with the Rouran to overthrow his father?"

Silence, then, "Highly, highly unlikely. He is a scholar at

heart. He wants to be the court historian far more than he wants to be the emperor. And I believe him when he says that he values peace. He is a great admirer of the philosophical flowering during the Spring and Autumn period—and laments often that the political instability of the past few centuries has slowed the development of new ideas."

That accords with what I know of Tuxi. "So now it's just Kedan we have to worry about."

Kai sighs. "I met him the day you did. I don't know anything about him that doesn't come from what he himself has said."

"Well, he said he's a hunter and a tracker. And he's proved himself to be both. And he has done his best to help us find the Rouran encampment."

"He could have done it because he wants to see Captain Helou again."

"Remember how upset he was when you sent Captain Helou away? If he knew they'd reunite in a few days, he wouldn't have been that dejected."

"He might have been only pretending."

I throw my hands up. "By Heaven, you really are suspicious."

"A fearful mind finds a way to feed the fear," he says, sounding apologetic.

I shake my head. "How do you get anything done if you're so afraid of everything all the time?"

"Well, you know how sometimes something is so delicious you eat and eat and eat—and then one more bite and suddenly you are completely sick?"

"Too much food is something only princelings have to worry about," I mutter. But I can see, theoretically, that twenty lotus seed paste buns in a row might make me sick.

"It's like that with me and fear. My fear will spiral and spiral and spiral, and then all of a sudden I'll be so sick and tired of being frightened that I have to restrain myself from doing something stupid."

I can't help myself. "Well, *I* happen to think you are brave. Exceptionally brave."

What is courage but strength in the face of fear? His fear might be great, but his strength is greater still.

He looks at me, the weight of his gaze a warmth on my cheeks.

Hastily I switch the subject. "Anyway, we were talking about Kedan. I know you still harbor doubts about him, but consider his theft from the Rouran scout. That was done out of mischief and pique. It's not something he would have tried if he were on the same side as the Rouran."

"I don't know if that's enough to prove his innocence."

I sigh. "What would you have done if you had evidence that your father was actually working with the Rouran?"

His hand briefly tightens into a fist. "The right thing, I hope."

"If you are willing to put the safety and security of your country above your love for your father, what makes you think Kedan won't do the same with Captain Helou?"

He does not answer, but at least he signals that we should head back.

We grope along for some time before he says, "If this is a chess match, then the conspirators are the only ones who know where all the pieces are."

"They don't know where *we* are," I point out. "So if this is a chess match, we have just become the chariot—the spoiler of games."

16

When we get back to Yu, he is, as I expected, wide awake, and rises to his feet to greet us. Kai takes a deep breath and thanks him for his tireless work. A moment passes before Yu responds. His words are all the expected ones about devotion to service, but his voice is hoarse with suppressed relief.

Through the rest of the night, we take turns holding watch. Shortly after first light, Captain Helou is escorted into Yucheng Khan's tent. After the time of half a meal, he exits, accompanied by a number of Rouran, presumably the same generals and dignitaries from last night.

Someone brings over a Dayuan horse for Captain Helou. There is talk, followed by a small ceremony—perhaps of oath-taking—that ends with everyone drinking from the same wineskin. Then Captain Helou rides out with a company of twelve, all on Dayuan horses. After he leaves, a number of messengers set out on their own Dayuan steeds, probably to inform

Rouran cohorts farther east and west along the Wall to step up their attacks.

I expected Yucheng Khan's decision the night before to hold. Still, I feel as if I've been punched in the kidney: There is no averting this war now.

When all the messengers have gone, the camp reverts to its normal activities. Men practice fighting with one another, horses are exercised, and more yurts are erected in anticipation of reinforcements arriving. When it becomes clear that further observation will not yield us additional information, we gather our things and depart, Yu to where he stowed his horse, Kai and I in the direction of the valley where Kedan and Tuxi spent the night—and where Yu will later meet us.

When we reach the bottom of the ravine, we take some time to study the steep incline opposite, searching for the easiest route up. My throat is parched, but my waterskin is almost empty. I tilt it back and drain the last drop.

"Here," says Kai, handing over his waterskin.

I hesitate.

"There is a stream on the other side," he says.

I take one swallow and give it back. "Many thanks."

"There's still more."

Only because he's been saving it. I shake my head firmly. He takes a smallish sip and glances balefully at the steep rock face we must negotiate. "When this is all over, I'm never climbing another hill. I'll demand to be carried up every incline in a palanquin."

"I'm giving up horses," I say, only half joking. "And out-doors. Definitely outdoors."

"Cold, for me. I shall sever all ties with cold. Maybe settle permanently in Hainan."

Hainan Island was once the farthest southern reach of the Han Dynasty. It's said to be a beautiful place surrounded by warm turquoise seas, with exotic fruits falling off trees into one's hands. I nearly burst with longing, but I say, "Pah, what's Hainan? Java, that's where I'm moving to, as soon as I can find sailors who know how to get there."

He grins, only to glance at the rock face again and sigh. "All right, up we go."

"Once we get over and tell Tuxi and Kedan what we've learned," I say, testing a toehold, "we'll all be able to discuss what to do. It won't be just our responsibility anymore."

And what a relief that will be.

Kai seems to barely need toeholds, scaling the rock face with the ease of a cat climbing trees. "But we still don't know enough. I suppose I could send Tuxi down to the encampment tonight, but given that they came to a decision last night and set their plan in motion this morning, the Rouran may not hold another discussion so soon. And of course, given who Tuxi is, I'm loath to put him at risk."

I understand what he is saying: We know just enough to be paralyzed. "How far are we from the capital?"

"I've never ridden this way directly from the capital. My guess is three days or thereabouts, depending on the terrain."

"What if we all return to the capital? Even if Tuxi isn't his father's favorite son, his words must carry *some* weight at court. Let him warn the emperor that the forces of the central commandery cannot leave the capital. And since the Rouran don't have enough manpower to overcome us head-on, as long as your father's men remain in place, the Rouran are stuck here, depleting their rations, waiting for a signal that will never come. In ten days they'll run out of food and won't be able to fight anymore."

Kai shakes his head. "First, the Rouran commander understated the quantity of supplies they carry, to give Captain Helou a greater sense of urgency. Before you woke up this morning, I spoke with Master Yu, since he pilfered from their stores last night. He agrees with me that they can hold out for twenty days and still be in shape to ride and fight.

"Second, I have thought about doing what you suggest. While it isn't a bad strategy, it only keeps us where we are. We won't even be able to apprehend Captain Helou for questioning—he will realize the scheme has failed and choose to remain beyond the Wall."

Keeping us where we are seems good enough to me: No war and everyone gets to go home. I maneuver around an outcrop. "What do you hope to accomplish, then?"

"Remove the weed by the root. Captain Helou's master at court needs to be exposed and eliminated. We will accomplish that only if we allow their plan to proceed."

I groan. "For somebody who is afraid of the wind rustling the grass, when did you become so intrepid?"

"I'm just more afraid of the alternative—to go on knowing that such a traitor is among us, lying low and waiting for another opportunity. I don't know that I can take that sort of tension. I might die from it. And you know I'm afraid to die."

He smiles as he says that, and my heart lurches. "I need to say 'I'm afraid' more often. Apparently that is the way to otherworldly courage."

He slithers up another body length. "I'd trade otherworldly courage for some otherworldly astuteness right now. If only I could figure out who Captain Helou's master is . . ."

On this I can't help him at all. I've known Captain Helou all of . . . eleven days? Twelve? "What do you know about him?"

"My father met him at the Mayi garrison several years ago and thought he was a man of great potential. He was hardworking, well-spoken, and intelligent. An accomplished martial artist. Not to mention he looks like a hero from the old tales. My father brought him into the fold, believing he could be a future commander. Possibly a future general."

He tests his weight on the exposed root of a small gnarly shrub that I just used to pivot myself higher. "I haven't known him for as long," he says. "When I was growing up, my father made sure that I got out of the capital periodically, whether to see for myself what life is like in remote villages or to go with my uncle to the South. But because my aunt insisted that the duel was my first priority, he didn't put me to many soldierly purposes.

"That changed this past winter, when our agents north of the Wall noticed greater movement among the Rouran. My father wanted to make sure all the garrisons under his command were at maximum preparedness—and he wanted me to be his eyes and ears where he could not be. My aunt was reluctant to let me go, with the duel breathing down our necks, but she agreed in the end that national peril outweighed personal enmities.

"For three months, Captain Helou and I traveled far and wide, inspecting garrisons, supply chains, and royal granaries. But I'm afraid I don't know much more about him than I did when we first met. My aunt always told me that a man shouldn't say anything unless he has something of value to say. Well, I didn't feel I had anything of value to say before someone like Captain Helou. So I never asked him how long he was at the garrison where my father met him, whom he served under before, or any such questions—and now I could slap myself for that oversight."

And here I thought his silence on those long rides was simply tremendous self-containment.

"It still puzzles me how he managed to keep abreast of the development of his master's scheme. We were constantly on the move, and since we made surprise inspections, he couldn't have had letters sent to our upcoming destinations—that would have alerted me that he wasn't keeping our itinerary a secret. We were always together, from morning to night. If he were to meet with his master's other agents, when could he even have—"

He stops climbing, thunderstruck. "Heavens, the pleasure houses! I have no proof of what he actually did on the evenings he went out for that purpose."

I am equally flabbergasted, and have to refocus my attention to haul myself up to a slight ledge. "I've heard of men using many ruses to go to pleasure houses. This might be the first time a man has used going to pleasure houses *as* a ruse!"

He swears. "Next time anyone I know pulls that out as an excuse, I'll interrogate the madams the next morning to make sure he actually went."

I laugh. Ah, my naïve superior. What if Captain Helou did use pleasure houses as meeting places? I'm about to suggest that to him when my attention is caught by something rolling around in the back of my mind. An idea? No, a memory of some kind. A memory that has faded to almost nothing because what I saw and heard held no significance for me at the time.

It was dark. And I was drowning in unhappy thoughts. I was in an unfamiliar place, walking fast, pulling my cloak tightly around me because the night was bitingly cold.

The royal duke's residence. I slipped out of the banquet, unable to take the gaiety any longer, my head spinning with everything I'd learned about my father. Near one of the alleys that branched out from the path, I heard Captain Helou's voice: . . . *my life or my death I can serve my people, then I will not have lived or fought in vain.*

And another man—one of the royal duke's honored guests—replied, *We who remain in the capital are grateful, Captain. The days ahead will be difficult.*

Kai has by now reached the same narrow ledge. I grip him by the shoulder. "I think I saw Captain Helou with his master the night before we left the capital, outside the banquet!"

"What?"

I let go of him and recount my surfaced memory. He grips me by *both* shoulders. "There were four guests that sat at the head table that night: Minister Buliugu, Lord Sang, General Huniu, and General Li. Describe the man you saw—his features, his clothes, *anything*—and I will forever be in your debt. The whole country will forever be in your debt."

I want to pull my hair out. "But I paid no attention to the guests of honor when your father presented them to the company. And it was dark when I saw him with Captain Helou and I just wanted to be by myself and—I'm sorry, but I can't describe this man at all!"

Kai's disappointment is palpable, but he says, "Still, that's really good. In fact, it's stunning progress that we have narrowed it down to four men."

"I'll think back some more," I say lamely, more to comfort him than anything else.

He lets go of me. "If you're meant to remember it, you will. If not, don't worry too much."

When we reach the top, we lean against a large boulder to catch our breaths. And then it comes to me, not a description of the man's looks or garments, but a sound.

"There was a jingle to that man's walk, as if he were pouring jade beads into a bowl of gold!"

Kai's eyes light up like the sky at dawn. "I know exactly who that is."

We are barely halfway down the slope of the next valley when Tuxi comes running and enfolds the princeling in a bear hug. "Thank Heaven and Earth! We've been sitting on pins and needles—thought you'd be back by sunrise at the latest."

At the sight of this embrace, Kedan looks as shocked as I would have been if I didn't know Tuxi's true identity. For a commoner to touch a man of Kai's elevated station in such a familiar manner—that's a lashing offense if I ever saw one. But Kai puts his arms around Tuxi and embraces him in return.

Kedan relaxes and lets out a breath. He salutes me formally. "Hua xiong-di, it's been a while."

I smile a little and return the gesture. "Have you fared well since we last spoke, Kedan xiong?"

"Exceedingly well, my brother." He sweeps an arm at the panorama. "Heaven was my blanket and Earth my bed—it doesn't get more poetic than that."

"A cold, uncomfortable night, eh?" I reply. "Mine too."

Kedan laughs and slaps me on the arm. "It's good to have you back. We were beginning to imagine the worst."

Tuxi has at last released Kai. "Did you two go down into the Rouran encampment? You did, didn't you? What did you learn?"

"First things first." I toss everyone a strip of dried mutton. "The only thing worse than Heaven-blanket and Earth-bed is poetic surroundings on an empty stomach."

"You raided their store. Well done, Hua xiong-di," says Kedan.

"We didn't," I tell him. "Master Yu raided the store and gave these to us."

"Master Yu is here?" Kedan and Tuxi cry in unison.

I take a bite of the dried mutton. Mulan of the South never would have touched it; Mulan of the North, who hasn't slept in a bed or eaten at a table in an eternity, chomps down with manly fervor. "And Captain Helou too."

"He is?" Kedan's face lights up.

Tuxi's surprise turns into bewilderment. "Were they not sent on separate tasks? How did they both end up here?"

"Well, here's how," I begin.

Kai and I discussed this earlier: I would narrate the events so he could observe Tuxi and Kedan, but especially Kedan.

As my account unfolds, Tuxi's dismay turns into horror. Kedan . . . fades. At first bit by bit, then, as if someone has stuck a knife in him, his animation bleeds out in torrents.

When I finish, he doesn't say anything, but only turns and marches away. Tuxi looks at each of us in turn. When we show no sign of going after Kedan, he takes off. Farther down the slope a thin stream trickles along. By the time Kedan sits down beside it, Tuxi has caught up with him.

They are too far away for us to overhear, but almost in unison, Kai and I start walking in the opposite direction.

"His reaction reminds me of yours," says Kai.

It takes me a moment to understand that he is referring to my disillusionment after learning the truth about my father. My skin prickles.

"So now you believe Kedan isn't conspiring with Captain Helou?" I manage to ask.

He does not answer that, but says, "Perhaps your father had his reasons for keeping the truth from you."

I make no reply.

"Hua Mulan—"

"You are the first person to call me by my name since my mother passed away," I hear myself say. "My brother Muyang died when he was still an infant. But afterward, my name was struck off the rolls. When we arrived in the North, his name was put on the rolls in place of mine. And your aunt still thinks I am him.

"My father has never given me an explanation as to why he erased my name, and I have never asked. I don't know that I can bring myself to ask him about your mother and your aunt—or that he will answer even if I do. So those reasons of his that you speak of, I'm sure they exist. And I'm almost as sure I will never know them."

Instantly I regret my outburst. But it's too late. Now I have not only anger burning in my throat, but mortification stinging my cheeks. I stare at the ground, walking faster and faster.

Silence throbs, broken only by the occasional calls of wild geese flying overhead.

"That day at home, when I learned that my aunt had gone to my courtyard, I feared a bloodbath," says Kai all of a sudden, startling me. "Not the tongue-lashing you received, but a fatal combat."

"Why?"

"Because that is how angry she has been in the past, incandescent with rage at your father. I was especially worried because you had Heart Sea with you."

I remember her ladyship's harsh final words to me, ordering me to hand over Heart Sea if I had any sense of honor.

"I can't tell you how many times she's told me, sometimes with tears, but always with that same seething rage, that I must, at all costs, win back Heart Sea. Even after she left my courtyard that night, I worried that she would come storming back to compel us to fight our duel that very instant.

"Once upon a time, she would have. But now I know that even though to you she might still come across as wrathful, she has changed in some subtle yet substantial way. So don't be so certain that your father will always maintain an obdurate silence. He is not the same person he was last year or last month. None of us are."

I don't say anything. In the distance, horses neigh in the Rouran encampment. Underfoot, pebbles disturbed by our boots slip and slide down the slope. The corners of my cape and his lift in the wind, sometimes overlapping each other.

Kai sighs and says, "To answer your earlier question, Hua Mulan, no, I no longer believe that Kedan is involved in the conspiracy."

◆ ◆ ◆

Not long afterward, Yu's figure becomes visible over a slope, leading his horse. By the time he reaches us, we are all gathered to greet him, even Kedan, who still looks as if he's been ill for three months and nearly died several times. Yu's eyes soften with sympathy as they land on Kedan. He greets Kai first, and then the rest of us in order of age.

Kai thanks him gravely for his dedication, then he addresses the entire company. "It is good fortune that has brought us together again. It is perhaps better fortune than we can appreciate at this moment to have discovered Captain Helou's betrayal. But our greatest fortune may be that Hua xiong-di decided to come with us north of the Wall. Hua xiong-di, will you tell everyone about the night of the banquet?"

I redden, unaccustomed to such praise, and give my account.

"That's Lord Sang, no doubt about it!" exclaims Yu. "I remember that jeweled chain. But isn't he only half-Xianbei?"

"I've always suspected that the mastermind behind all this doesn't have any great desire to preserve Xianbei ways, but instead means to exploit the high emotions roused by the possibility of the ban for his own gains," says Kai. "The important thing to remember is that Lord Sang is in charge of the security of the capital."

Tuxi clutches himself by the temples. "And should the royal duke's men deploy, Lord Sang would have the largest force in the region!"

"Captain Helou served under him at Mayi," says Kedan, in a low monotone. "At the wedding where we first met, his mother, who was still alive then, told me that. She was very proud of his having been singled out by Lord Sang for attention and praise. I thought he would rise high in Lord Sang's service and was surprised when I learned that he had instead become one of the royal duke's trusted lieutenants." He shakes his head. "But it makes sense, doesn't it? If they always planned to attack at the center, then Lord Sang needed someone with a deep understanding of the central commandery."

Kai grimaces. I wonder if he's thinking about just how deep an understanding Captain Helou has of the central commandery, from all those months of unannounced inspections they undertook together. "The court must be informed," he says.

Tuxi swallows.

"But we shouldn't stop there," continues Kai. "We should kill the snake with a strike to the head."

"How?" asks Tuxi, his voice anxious. "If it's just my—our word against Lord Sang's, I'm not sure we can prevail. He is supremely favored at court. That jeweled chain? The emperor took it off his own person to pin it on Lord Sang, to express his pleasure and gratitude."

He looks at Kai. "And would you not say, Your Highness, that the emperor trusts Lord Sang just as much as he trusts your father? Had the traitor been the royal duke, would the emperor have believed you, if you yourself went before him and made the claim? Or would he suspect *you* of being in league with the Rouran before he would lose faith in your father?"

Kai expels a lungful of air. "I agree with you on the difficulty of the task, and I don't know how to go about it either. Earlier I thought, since Captain Helou has to get word to Lord Sang at some point, we could lie in wait for him, follow him to the capital, and catch him and Lord Sang in the act. But even this stretch of the Wall is hundreds, if not thousands, of li in length, and I haven't the slightest notion where he will choose to come through."

"I might know something," says Kedan, his tone still completely flat. "Captain Helou guarded the Wall for a while."

"That's right!" I can't help interjecting. "I remember you two talking about it while we were on top of the beacon tower."

"That might have been the first time I spoke to him about it directly—before that, I heard it from a cousin of his." Kedan's lips pull to one side, as if he's vexed that he spent so much time talking about Captain Helou with the man's relatives. "I don't know the name of the fort, but he said it wasn't far from where we were, and the commander he served under is still there."

"When did he guard the Wall?" asks Kai, his voice tight.

"Eight, nine years ago, I gather."

Kai closes his eyes for a moment. "Then I know where it is."

17

"That's right!" cries Tuxi. "Along this stretch of the Wall, only one garrison commander has served continuously at the same post for that long. Captain Helou plans to come through Futian Pass."

"Never heard of it." Kedan's voice is still quiet, but not as listless.

"It's not a major pass," says Kai. "In fact, it doesn't even merit the term *garrison*. It's mainly there because a beacon tower was needed at the location."

"Where is it, exactly?" I ask.

"Southeast of here. Not too far, but I don't know the precise distance."

"But can Captain Helou actually get through it? Does he have the necessary pass?"

Before I left the garrison, I was given a new pass that enabled me to travel beyond the border under Kai's supervision. But I can't use it alone. If I rode up to a border garrison now, from the north, by myself, I'd be escorted to a holding cell until it could be determined whether I'd deserted my mission.

Kai nods. "He, Master Yu, and I were given comprehensive passes. That's one reason I sent the two of them off in the wake of Bai's trickery, because they wouldn't be stopped on the imperial road for lack of authorization. So, yes, Captain Helou will be able to come through Futian Pass—or any pass along the Wall.

"But the pass applies to only him; his Rouran escorts will present a problem. Which is why I think he will come through not at a random pass, but at a place where he served—served well, no doubt—and is still fondly remembered by the commander. A stranger asking to come in with twelve passless riders would be refused outright. But a well-liked old subordinate, who now has the favor of a royal duke? He might be able to fool the commander with some grand excuse and manage to get those Rouran riders through."

"Your Highness, are thirteen men sufficient to take control of Futian Pass?" asks Yu. "I assume that is Captain Helou's goal, and not simply to get past the Wall."

"There are eighty men at the pass. In open combat, Captain Helou and company would be at an overwhelming disadvantage. But suppose they win the commander's favor, then poison the food or wine . . ." The princeling nods grimly. "Yes, they can take charge of the pass that way."

Tuxi sucks in a breath. "I haven't been to Futian Pass myself, but I remember riding by the crossroad that leads to it. The way is little used, as it leads to no village or settlements, but it joins the imperial road only thirty li northeast of the capital."

We are all silent, digesting his words.

"So . . ." says Yu, sounding a little less imperturbable than usual, "if Captain Helou takes control of the pass, that is where the main Rouran force will come through. And if they do, they will easily get within thirty li of the capital."

"And if they reach the imperial road at night," says Kai, "and mow down the sentries—or if Lord Sang orders the sentries to stand down—then they could be at the very gates of the palace before the emperor is any wiser."

Alarm pulses through me. "Who is responsible for the security of the palace? Not Lord Sang?"

"No, not him," answers Kai. "The palace guards are selected for their loyalty and skill at close-range combat, and they serve under Captain Chekun, one of my father's cousins. But Captain Chekun and Lord Sang are on very good terms—which is not to say that he's personally involved in Lord Sang's schemes. Only that if Lord Sang wants to deceive him, it should not be difficult to accomplish, given the trust Captain Chekun has in him."

"Is there no end to Lord Sang's reach?" moans Tuxi.

"Of course there is an end to his reach," says Kai. "Our problem is that he has orchestrated this scheme so that it takes place at the very center of his web of power."

"So . . . we go into that web of power?" I hear myself ask, my voice hesitant.

Kai looks around. "Any objections, my brothers?"

No one speaks.

"Then it will be as Hua xiong-di suggests."

◆ ◆ ◆

The time of a cup of tea later—not that we have such luxuries now—I'm still rolling my eyes at the princeling's pronouncement.

It will be as I *suggest?*

I would never suggest such a thing. I very distinctly remember recommending that we make sure the forces stationed in and around the capital do not leave, so that the Rouran never come south of the Wall.

Fortunately, my companions are all highly intelligent and understand very well that this is *the princeling's* intention.

Still. Grumbling is good. Grumbling keeps me from thinking about the madly nonsensical feats we are about to undertake. If my mind strays even remotely in that direction, the soles of my feet tingle, as if I were standing above a bottomless precipice, about to lose my balance.

As it will take Captain Helou several days to reach Futian Pass, we decide to rest ourselves and prepare for our next course of action. Kai also wishes to spy further on the Rouran encampment and get a better sense of their numbers. I do some chores—grooming my horse, sorting through my few belongings. Yu takes some rest—his has been an even more arduous road than ours. Kai and Tuxi are engaged in an intense discussion, presumably on how Tuoba Xi, Prince Anzhong of

Luoyang, can convince his father that one of his favorite nobles is conspiring against him.

Kedan has gone back to the stream again. I waver over whether he'll want any company, least of all mine, but after some time, I join him anyway. "Dried apricots, my brother?" Mutton jerky wasn't the only thing Yu took from the Rouran stores.

Kedan sighs. "How can I say no to such a delicacy?"

We each eat a dried apricot, him wolfing it down, me taking the smallest bites possible to make the preserved fruit last. The tiny brook meanders by, a scant trickle. Still, plants grow lustily on its banks, and to my surprise, I discover a few wildflowers among the green leaves, the blossoms so tiny they are scarcely bigger than pinpricks.

I scour my brain. Nothing. Confronted with Kedan's pain, I draw a complete blank on appropriate things to say.

And then I see my mistake: *Inappropriateness* is the only way forward.

"Remember what you said about the special affection His Highness feels for me?"

Kedan shifts in place. Good, I'm getting a reaction.

"You were right. Last night he held me tight and whispered into my ear."

Kedan stares at me, then glances surreptitiously at Kai, still deep in conversation with Tuxi. He proceeds to study my face with an almost humorous concentration. "Nooo," comes his conclusion. "He would never do that."

But underneath the denial there is definitely a twitch of hope.

I lower my voice. "Oh, he did. Embraced me so hard I could scarcely breathe. Touched my face too."

Kedan's jaw drops. He casts another look at our austere leader. *"Him?"*

"I know, right? Such a cold fish by the looks of him."

Kedan shakes his head. "You are jesting, Hua xiong-di."

I point my right index finger at the sky. "I swear on the Heaven above."

"Don't swear idly. There'll be consequences."

"If you don't believe me, ask Master Yu. He saw us."

Kedan's jaw drops farther than it did last time. "Master Yu would have given you such a lecture that you wouldn't even have dared to look at him today."

Finally I burst out laughing.

"I knew you were joking," said Kedan, both relieved and clearly disappointed.

"I'm not. It really happened. I just didn't tell you the circumstances."

I describe for him, in as vivid detail as I can, our fear that we were about to be caught and our last-ditch effort at portraying ourselves as nothing more than a pair of amorous Rouran fighters. Neglecting to mention, of course, my own turbulent reactions.

Kedan listens with scandalized delight. When I finish, he blinks a few times, and then bumps his shoulder into mine. "I was right, Hua xiong-di. Trust me, if it had been me down there with him, he would never have done that. Not even if we were about to be chopped to pieces by a horde of Rouran fighters."

There is a hint of a smile in his voice.

"I don't know. Should we go ask him?"

Kedan sucks in a breath. "For that, Master Yu *will* beat you."

"Not if His Highness stands in front of me and shouts, 'If you are going to beat Hua xiong-di, you have to use the rod on me first!'"

This time Kedan does smile. "I didn't guess it in the beginning, but Hua xiong-di is a brat."

"Better watch what you say about His Highness's beloved. Or Master Yu will beat *you*."

Kedan laughs softly. At the sound, both Kai and Tuxi look toward us, astonished. Which only makes Kedan's mirth spill over even more. When he finally gets himself under control, we sit for some time in companionable silence.

I have accomplished my aim: All I wanted was for him to feel like himself again, however briefly. But after a little more hesitation, I say, "Speaking of special affection, Kedan xiong, I think Tuxi xiong has been really worried about you."

"Hush. Don't go around spreading rumors," he says, but without any real heat to his words.

I say no more, giving him time to chew on the idea.

Sure enough, a while later, he says, "Tuxi xiong is far too superior a man for me. I mean, have you seen his handwriting? It's as handsome as any great calligrapher's. He's so learned and I'm not even literate."

"Illiteracy isn't a permanent condition. We are all born illiterate. I can teach you to read right now."

But Kedan shakes his head. "I don't know what he can possibly see in me."

I roll my eyes. "We men are shallow. You know this—you are as shallow as the rest of us. Of course Tuxi xiong is besotted by your outstanding beauty."

His beauty isn't quite as outstanding as Kai's, but he has an adorable face, especially when he laughs. Kedan shakes his head again, but he is blushing, the color spreading all the way to his ears.

I give him a slap on the back. "His Highness is watching us. I'd better go do something else before he decides to beat you for taking me away."

This earns me another smile. "Let's by all means avoid that sort of trouble. And by the way, Hua xiong-di, you're a good man."

I smile back at him. "That I am, my brother. I'm nothing if not a good man."

◆ ◆ ◆

Not long after, Yu gets up from his nap. Kedan approaches him. The two speak briefly, then Kedan walks away toward the southern end of the valley.

The princeling, Tuxi, and Yu confer for some time. After that, as I expected, Tuxi seeks me out.

"Where did Kedan xiong go?" I ask.

"Master Yu says he asked for permission to go for a walk. Said he'd be grateful if he could range farther afield for a bit."

I sigh. "Did you ask him about Captain Helou?"

"I did. He said he stopped hoping long ago that Captain Helou would return his affections, but he thought that it was all right to engage in one-sided hero worship, since Captain Helou seemed destined for greatness."

That potential for greatness might yet blossom if Captain Helou's side prevails. Greatness tends to be measured only by the height, breadth, and duration of power achieved, with little attention paid to the suffering incurred in that achievement.

I look in the direction in which Kedan disappeared. Most of the ridges and spurs we have encountered in this mountain range have a roughly north-south orientation. But the southern end of this particular valley runs into a sharp slope that cuts crosswise, a rocky surface with its share of stubborn shrubs and small, twisty trees. Kedan was ambling across the slope earlier, easy and graceful in his progress, but now he is no longer in sight.

I wonder if I'll ever see anything but lean, sparsely clad mountains again. But I'd be content with this less-than-ravishing panorama if it meant I wouldn't need to go anywhere near Captain Helou and his master. I inhale the clean, cold air, thankful to be still safe.

For now.

"So what did Hua xiong-di do to cheer Kedan xiong-di up like that?" asks Tuxi.

Aha, the question I've been expecting.

I grin. "Gossip."

Kai commanded me never to call Tuxi by anything but the name he gave us—never even to think of him as anything but Tuxi. At first I thought it would be difficult. But the opposite is true: I keep forgetting his extraordinary background because he is still the same kind, sincere, and slightly diffident man I first met, still the same good, comfortable friend.

"Gossip?" he says uncertainly.

"Yes. Kedan xiong enjoys scandalous news, so I was telling him . . . stories."

"Oh." Tuxi looks crestfallen. "I don't know that much gossip. No wonder I couldn't make him feel better. Kedan xiong-di clearly responds to someone more fun, like you."

I tsk. "You are too hard on yourself, Tuxi xiong. If anything, Kedan xiong is in awe of you. He feels inferior next to your erudition and penmanship."

And he will drop dead if he ever learns that Tuxi's father is the emperor of the North.

"Really? You don't think he finds me boring? Or . . . awkward?"

"No. And if you ever get the chance, teach him to read and write."

Tuxi brightens. "You think he'd like that?"

"Yes, I do."

Tuxi's expression turns dreamy, as if he can already see the two of them seated at a desk, the four treasures of the study spread before them. Then he says shyly, "I do know *some* gossip. Court gossip, mostly."

I smile. "Regale Kedan xiong, then, when you teach him."

"I think I will." He takes a deep breath. "If we ever get the chance."

◆ ◆ ◆

I take a nap too. At dusk I wake up, groggy and disoriented. My body is stiff, but unlike the first few times I slept on the ground, I barely noticed how uncomfortable my bed was: I've never been so deprived of sleep in my life and fell supremely unconscious as soon as I lay down.

Tuxi is keeping watch; Kai, like me, is slowly sitting up from a nap. In the distance, Kedan approaches. He's too far away for me to make out his features in the deepening dark, but his gait evinces a bit of bounce and jauntiness. I glance at Tuxi, who sits a few paces from me; he looks both nervous and hopeful.

But they do not get an opportunity to speak alone. As soon as Kedan reaches us, Yu distributes food, and the topic turns to our next course of action.

"Your Highness," says Tuxi, "I know you are against my going down to the Rouran encampment. But I feel I should attempt it in case I learn something important."

"No," says Kai instantly. "Besides, it's too late. You can't cross the ravine when it's this dark. You could break your neck going either down or up."

"But Master Yu knows a more straightforward way into the encampment."

"*No.*" Kai stands up. "And I'll hear no more of it."

Tuxi leaps to his feet. "But there is still so much we don't know. The signal you mentioned, for example, that Lord Sang means to send when the royal duke and his men have left the capital. If we don't know what kind of signal he'll use, then how will our side know what to watch for?"

"If Tuxi xiong goes, then I'll go too, to help keep him safe," says Kedan quietly.

We are all on our feet now. I glance at Kai, unsure what I should say or do.

Yu bows. "With your permission, Your Highness, I will also accompany Master Tuxi, since I was the one who inadvertently gave him the idea."

Kai sighs in exasperation. "At this rate, all five of us will be going down to the Rouran encampment. Is the specific nature of the signal worth the risk?"

I cringe at the thought of repeating the trip from last night. Real danger or no, the fright alone probably took several years off my life.

And then I see something in the southern sky and an even worse fear sears my spine.

"Brothers." I manage to push the word past my suddenly closing throat. "We will not need to find out what the signal is. Look behind you. That's it!"

18

We do not have a clear line of sight to the Central Plain because the slope that cuts across the southern end of our valley is just high enough to block the view. But there is a gap at the top of the slope, and through that gap, a golden nimbus shines in the night sky. When I squint, the nimbus resolves into hundreds if not thousands of pinpoints of light.

"Sky lanterns!" cries Kedan softly.

Tuxi rubs his eyes. "Surely they weren't launched from the capital itself!"

"No, but if the forces of the central commandery marched out earlier in the day, there would have been plenty of time for Lord Sang to send a rider to a town close to the border." Kai's voice is grim. "If those sky lanterns had been stowed earlier, the rider could pretend to be an imperial messenger and order the town's residents to light the lanterns—an entreaty to Heaven above to protect us from the Rouran."

"Or maybe Lord Sang found an actual imperial messenger willing to do his bidding," I mutter.

"So what do we do?" asks Tuxi, his voice shaking just a little. "This is too soon. Even the Rouran weren't expecting to head out so quickly, were they? Your Highness, Hua xiong-di, you said they thought they'd have to hold out for some time."

And Captain Helou went so far as to counsel them to slaughter their horses, if they ran out of stores.

Before Kai or I can say anything, cries erupt from the Rouran encampment. They have seen it too—the signal they were waiting for.

"Don't we need to go right now, so we can get ahead of the Rouran?" I ask. My voice doesn't shake, but my fingers do. I grip the edge of my cape.

Kai swears. "There is no way we can get ahead of the Rouran. Their vanguard will be riding out now. By the time we exit this valley—and remember, we'll have to take a more circuitous route—we'll be caught between their vanguard and their main column. Not a good place to be."

"Let's not go in that direction, then," says Kedan. "I didn't just take a walk to clear my head. I also wanted to see whether we could leave to the south. From the bottom that ridge looks impossible for horses, but halfway up, I found a fissure that cuts across to the other side. And that side has a path leading south—I could see the Wall in the distance."

"But even if we get to the Wall, there won't be a road that leads directly to Futian Pass," points out Tuxi. "We will have to go in the opposite direction, probably, until we can join an imperial road."

I blink. "But there *is* a road that leads directly to Futian Pass. The Wall itself goes there. And last I saw, two can ride side by side on the top."

Silence.

Then Tuxi grabs me and lifts me bodily. "Hua xiong-di, just for that, the court owes you a reward of five thousand *mu* of land." He sets me down and looks around. "Well, what are we waiting for? Shall we go?"

Our gazes are fixed on Kai.

He exhales. "Yes, let's go."

◆ ◆ ◆

We do not leave immediately: The princeling wants to make sure that the Rouran vanguard takes the route we assume they will—north out of the encampment, then along the edge of the plateau to the nearest pass—and not a southerly course that would lead them far too close to us.

Yu busies himself seeing to the horses. Tuxi pulls Kedan aside, probably to inquire if the latter feels any better. Or who knows? Perhaps there is no time like now to share some court gossip.

I sidle up to Kai, who is pulling daggers out of what seems like a dozen hidden places and checking them.

"Give me one," I say.

He does. The dagger is small, from hilt to tip barely longer than my forearm. I test its weight and balance, then stow it in my boot. "Scared?"

"When I saw the sky lanterns, I thought I had become a ghost then and there."

His honesty only makes him braver in my eyes.

"You, Hua xiong-di?"

"I'm so scared the backs of my knees are perspiring—in *this* weather."

It's getting too dark to see his features, but I hear his smile. "You know what they say: *That which is near vermilion becomes red; that which is near ink becomes black*. You may blame your cowardliness on me."

"I do so unreservedly."

We both laugh a little.

And then I admit my real fear. "I hope I won't freeze again, when it's time to fight."

"You won't," he says simply. "I don't look forward to fighting, but I do look forward to fighting alongside you, Hua Mulan."

✦ ✦ ✦

We proceed on foot, leading our horses. Kedan has the vision of a cat. In the dark he advances without fear or hesitation, calling back from time to time for us to watch out for a sudden dip or a boulder in our way. The Rouran vanguard has already departed—to the north, easily verified by an ear to the ground—and their main column will soon follow.

The entrance to the fissure Kedan mentioned is hidden behind an outcrop. I catch a glimpse of small, cold stars just before we enter the passage. It is so narrow that at one point I worry my horse won't fit through. It does, thankfully, but I stop anyway: Behind me I do not hear Yu's footsteps, only his agitated breathing.

I lead my horse forward to where the passage widens a little, then squeeze past the horse to reach Yu, who is leaning with his back against one side of the fissure. To my ears, his breaths sound as loud as bellows.

"Are you all right, Master Yu?"

"I'm—I didn't anticipate that this space would be so constricted—and so long."

His answer doesn't make sense. But there is a well-trained princeling who has spent his life in terror of *me*, so anyone can be afraid of anything.

"How about we get you on your horse and I'll attach a rope to your horse's bridle so I can lead both our horses along?"

"All right," he agrees, still breathing heavily.

We catch up to our companions, who have stopped to wait for us, and soon find ourselves on the other side of the ridge. The sky lanterns are long gone. The starlight is only bright enough to make the terrain ahead seem treacherous and impenetrable.

But Kedan, sure-footed and confident, starts down the hill.

And we follow.

◆ ◆ ◆

The moon rises, providing enough illumination for us to mount and ride. We are in a long valley not very different from the one we rode in after leaving the border garrison. The floor of the valley is even, almost smooth, and the grass is already noticeably thicker than on the plateau. Trampled underfoot, it releases a fragrance that makes me think of spring outings in the South, to take in the sight of peach and apricot trees in full blossom.

The ease of our progress makes me nervous. I catch up to Kai. "If this route is as good as it appears to be, why isn't it used more? In thousands of years, surely someone must have come upon it, even if the entrance is a little hard to spot."

"Eh, I hear that, Hua xiong-di," answers Kedan from ahead. "Yes, our road will probably drop off a cliff—that's why we are proceeding very carefully. But for a while yet we should be fine. A good long while, I hope."

"Well, Hua xiong-di, you heard him," says Kai.

I turn around in my saddle. "Tuxi xiong, did you hear that? How about another thousand *mu* of land for me if I have to go over cliffs?"

"Let me petition the court the next time I'm in the capital," says Tuxi, with exaggerated seriousness.

We all laugh.

But nobody laughs a little past midnight, when we stand at the edge of a seemingly bottomless chasm. Five hundred paces along its edge in either direction do not bring us any closer to a better route. Even Kedan, with his ability to see at night, cannot tell us where the canyon ends or at least tapers off.

He swears volubly and with great wrath.

After he falls silent, Kai asks, "Kedan xiong, you said you saw the Wall in the distance during your walk. How far do you think we are from the Wall now?"

Kedan rubs his temples. "Twenty li or thereabouts."

Kai turns to me. "Hua xiong-di, what would you do now?"

I swallow. "I would wait until morning—if we had time. But since we don't, I would cross this chasm as soon as possible."

He nods. "So would I. And if anyone wishes to wait until morning, you may."

Kedan and Yu immediately declare that they will come with us. Sounding squeaky, Tuxi joins the chorus a second later.

"All right, then, ropes out," says the princeling. "This is where we leave our horses and everything that isn't essential."

Kedan descends first, coming back up three times before he finds a viable way down.

"It's not as deep as I feared," he shouts from below. "Only about the height of ten men."

Plenty enough for a fall to break a leg—or a neck.

Yu and I climb down next, the princeling and Tuxi last. The bottom of the chasm is pitted but dry. We scale the opposite rock face without too much trouble—if one doesn't count Tuxi nearly falling off twice—and come up the other side.

Kedan sets a strenuous pace, but nobody complains. We go

down and up a series of gullies, big and small. Twenty li isn't a negligible distance. On a flat stretch I can probably cover it in twice the time of a meal, but this is not a flat stretch. After I lose count of the number of gullies we cross through, I begin to wonder how much distance we have covered as the arrow flies. What if all we've done is five li? Or worse, three?

The sky is turning pale when we trudge up the last hill to the Wall. Here at least the Wall is working as it ought to: A line of soldiers awaits us on top, bows drawn.

"Who goes there?" shouts their lieutenant.

Kai sighs and holds his hand out toward Tuxi. Kai's own pass is enough to get the lieutenant and his men to stand aside, but we need a great deal more than that, and we need everything right away and without questions asked.

Tuxi hesitates before handing over a pass. Kai brandishes it. "This is His Royal Highness, Prince Anzhong of Luoyang. His Royal Highness is here on official business. You are to immediately welcome us and provide our company with everything we will requisition."

The lieutenant's mouth opens and closes a few times. "May I—may this humble lackey request to see the imperial pass a little more closely?" he asks in a trembling voice.

Kai walks several paces forward.

The lieutenant kneels. Despite my fatigue, I almost laugh aloud, because he disappears behind the crenellations of the Wall.

Realizing his mistake, the lieutenant rises hurriedly. "My most abject apologies to His Royal Highness. We weren't expecting his august presence."

"Forgiven," says Kai. "Now catch these ropes and help us up."

Atop the Wall, we learn that only the lieutenant arrived at this spot by riding. The princeling sends him off to fetch more horses without delay. We five sit down with our backs against the parapet. Kedan seems stunned by the revelation of Tuxi's true identity, but too exhausted to say anything. Yu appears no less flabbergasted.

Tuxi just looks spectacularly embarrassed to be the center of so much attention. The soldiers gape at him and his lackeys, sitting on the paving stones like a gaggle of peasants. After a while, the lieutenant brings horses, food, and water. He also brings his garrison commander, who apologizes profusely for not having been there to welcome us in person, as if commanders typically patrol the Wall first thing in the morning.

Kai, speaking for Tuxi, thanks the commander and apologizes that we cannot stay to enjoy his hospitality. He does, however, take the time to ask about possible breaks in the Wall. "I hear that sometimes walls do not extend over ravines and such. Are there any such ruptures between here and Futian Pass?"

The commander assures him that the Wall runs as smoothly as an imperial road all the way to the pass. Kai then asks about the distance remaining, the number of garrisons in between, and the best place to leave the Wall to reach the capital in haste.

The commander answers all the questions. Kai relays a series of instructions and thanks him again. The commander pays his obeisance once more to His Royal Highness.

We mount and rush off.

◆ ◆ ◆

We ride as fast as we can but not as fast as we'd like.

The top of the Wall is in good repair. But as the Wall takes the contour of the landscape, winding along sharp crests and precipitous drops, we keep coming across stairs in the steepest stretches. The garrison's horses are trained to handle stairs, but for the sake of our own necks, Kai requires us to dismount each time and walk our steeds.

At one point, guiding my horse down yet another set of steps, I happen to look up toward the south. For days we've been stuck with a limited sight line, deep inside valleys and ravines, but now I feel as if I'm standing on top of the world. Under a bright sun the mountains stretch endlessly into the distance, green spurs and ridges gradually fading into lilac-blue shadows against the edge of the sky.

I sigh softly at this vast, beautiful panorama before returning my attention to the road under my feet.

At the next garrison we requisition fresh horses. At the garrison after that, the same thing, except this is where Tuxi leaves us for the imperial road—and the capital—to present our case against Lord Sang to his father.

He forestalls Yu, Kedan, and me when we are about to sink to our knees. "No, no, please, my brothers. Please let us not have that."

Instead, he salutes us and one by one takes us by the arms, his hands remaining on Kedan perhaps a fraction of a moment longer. Then he enfolds the princeling in an embrace. "Look after yourself, Kai di. Be safe."

The princeling hugs him hard. "Same for you, Xi xiong. Be careful going into the center of the web."

And then it's just the four of us.

"Let's go," says the princeling. "We have no time to lose."

◆ ◆ ◆

Late in the morning we arrive at Futian Pass. Our request for a private audience with the commander is promptly granted. Commander Wu and Kai have met once, when the commander was in the capital the year before. He obviously thinks well of Kai. Still, as our conversation progresses, he becomes increasingly incredulous.

"Captain Helou has betrayed us? Captain *Helou*?"

"He and a number of Rouran riders will come through *here*? And take control of this pass so tens of thousands of Rouran fighters can advance toward the capital?"

"And you want us to—Your Highness, please forgive this mediocre old soldier. Did I hear Your Highness correctly?"

To which His Highness smiles slightly and answers, "Yes, Commander Wu, you heard me perfectly well. I intend to kill all of you."

19

Kai and I stand on the ramparts, watching the rising dust cloud in the distance. The Rouran's Dayuan horses must have traveled a great distance, possibly without much rest since the morning before. Still they run briskly and tirelessly. At this pace they will be here in the time of a cup of tea.

My hand grips the hilt of my sword, now worn on my hip. My heart beats so hard it hurts. And I very nearly see double when I stare too long at those who are fast arriving.

"I told you that I saw your father when I was in the South," says Kai.

I blink repeatedly before his words penetrate the thick dread in my head. Yes, he told me. His hired pleasure craft went past our house on Lake Tai. And that was the first time he learned that Father had been paralyzed in the duel.

I turn toward him. "Yes?"

"When I decided not to call on your father in person, I had

the pleasure craft steer toward open water. In the distance a small boat shot shoreward. As chaotic and preoccupied as my mind was at that moment, I couldn't help noticing its swiftness.

"The boat was punted by a young woman in a peach-colored overrobe. At first I paid attention solely to her technique, wondering how she achieved such spectacular speed. It was only as the boat drew near that I saw she was as lovely as Lake Tai itself."

I hold my breath. Is he speaking of . . . of . . . ?

"Just then the boat slowed to a drift. It was the type with a covered middle. The young woman ducked under the covered portion and drew the curtains. A short while later, a young man emerged."

"So you knew from the very beginning!"

He turns toward me at last. His gaze, stark yet fierce, reminds me of how he looked the day we first met at the encampment. I know him better now. This is him keeping his fear in check. This is his strength and fortitude fighting through.

"Later I learned from the referees that your father lost a child not long after the duel, one of a pair of twins. They thought it was the daughter who perished. But I knew that it was the daughter I would meet someday, in the guise of her brother.

"I feared you no less, but I—" He takes a deep breath. "But I kept thinking of the young woman on the boat. I wanted to see her again. And I wished with a futile intensity that we weren't headed for a fateful clash. That we could have met under other circumstances."

Pain and sweetness both pierce my heart. "So you arranged our three meetings."

And how I hoarded those memories.

"But when news of the Rouran attacks came, I thought I'd seen the last of you. Imagine my shock and . . ." He smiles slightly. "Imagine my shock—and elation—when you marched onto that training ground to challenge Captain Helou."

My lips quiver when I smile back. We've had so little time together—and very possibly none left. "Only because I thought I'd be safe if I stuck to you."

"That's the reason I didn't ask you to come with us beyond the Wall. But I can't tell you how grateful I am that you did."

I have wondered why, quiet and reticent as he can be, he has told me so much about himself. Now I know: He does not believe we will survive our mission. And what he confessed just now is further confirmation that while we are exceptionally fortunate to have made it this far, we are still hurtling headlong toward our final fight in this world.

I let go of the hilt of my sword and take his hand. "At this moment, I don't wish to be anywhere else."

Our eyes meet.

His gaze turns ever starker, ever fiercer. "And here comes Captain Helou."

❖ ❖ ❖

Perhaps it is because my head is full of *us*, of secret yearnings that are no longer so secret. Perhaps it's because, despite my brave words, I *do* wish we were anywhere else but here—gliding across Lake Tai on a painted boat, playing go while a spring breeze ruffles our hair, or walking down a busy street in the capital, stopping to buy a freshly made sesame bing.

Whatever the reason, when I look upon Captain Helou, instead of paralyzing fear, I feel only consternation. He does not need to do this. He does not need to bring war to the Central Plain. There have been two centuries of it. And as a result of what he intends, the North could splinter again into dozens of warring factions and suffer two more centuries of upheaval.

Earlier I meant to smile at Captain Helou—part of the reason I felt sick to my stomach. But now I won't. What he is doing—and what *we* are doing—is no smiling matter.

"Your Highness. Hua xiong-di." He squints up at us, his voice even but suspicious. We must be the last people he expected to find here, where he plans to let in the Rouran.

"You made good time, Captain," I say. "We've already secured the place for you. Let me come down and open the gate."

The gate isn't visible from the north. An invading force would see only a negligible fort bestriding the Wall. But there is a gap between the part of the fort that protrudes north of the Wall and the Wall itself. One must come into the gap—the length of a short corridor—and reach the very end of it before entering, because not only does the gate face the south, it opens toward the dead end, rather than the other side.

When I unbar the door, Captain Helou is already waiting, his hand on the hilt of his broadsword. My hand, hidden from view, grips my own sword. I say, "I don't need to let you in, if all I want is to kill you."

With an upward tilt of my chin, I guide his attention to Kai, who is standing almost directly above him and could have easily shot him with an arrow.

"You could torture me for information," Captain Helou says.

I roll my eyes. "You think you know something that His Highness doesn't? Lord Sang isn't at the top of the pecking order. There is someone he answers to—and that august personage speaks to His Highness directly. We have no need to fish for information from a lackey like you."

Captain Helou hesitates another moment, then his hand leaves his broadsword. "In that case, my gratitude to His Highness and to Hua xiong-di."

His horse just manages to squeeze in and then has to turn itself around in a tiny space before walking down a stone passage to a courtyard at the back of the fort. I stay in place as the other riders, all hard-looking Rouran fighters, bring their horses in the same way. I keep my face impassive, but my knees quake. When the fighters have all come through, I secure the door and walk behind them into the courtyard, where Kai is now standing.

Captain Helou must have already made his obeisance, for he is asking tentatively, "And Your Highness, if you don't mind me inquiring, is His Grace directing this whole operation?"

Kai is as aloof as I have ever seen him. "That isn't something you need to know, Captain."

"Forgive this humble soldier, Your Highness. But Your Highness, where are the men of this garrison?"

My turn to speak. "Captain, why do you bother His Highness with so many questions? I already told you we took care of this place."

"But—but this place had eighty soldiers."

"And in the South, my forefathers are famous for their powerful, fast-acting, yet practically undetectable poisons. Eighty men are easy enough to dispatch, Captain, when seventy-five die on their own."

I step closer, so he can see me better. There are splatters of blood on my clothes. Specks on the princeling's too, if one looks closely.

"I thought—I thought—I must have been mistaken in thinking that Hua xiong-di isn't so used to actual combat."

So he remembers my cowardice before the bandits. "That was for the benefit of Master Yu, so that he wouldn't become suspicious. You will recall that the night the beacon tower was lit, Master Yu singled out His Highness, Bai, and me for questioning. Impeccable instincts he had. Too impeccable."

"So . . . Hua xiong-di was never a stranger to His Highness?"

"I first came across Hua xiong-di years ago," says Kai, "at the edge of Lake Tai."

"But what has been done with the bodies of the men?"

I sigh. "Come with me, Captain."

We climb up. The fort overhangs a gully to the south. The drop from the bloodstained ramparts to the bottom of the gully is the height of eight men. The gully is full of bodies that have been dumped in a heap. Most lie facedown, but the man on top stares at the sky, his helmet askew, his mouth wide open.

Captain Helou glances at me. "Hua xiong-di and His Highness moved this many bodies?"

"Hardly. I saved a pair of strong, stupid soldiers for the job. Pushed them over while they inspected their handiwork at the end."

Lightning fast, he whips his bow off his back, nocks an arrow, and fires. The arrow buries itself deep in the chest of the man at the top of the heap. The corpse, of course, reacts not at all.

"Why not fire a few more?" I say. "I hear that in war, whenever there's a sizable pile of bodies, there's usually someone still alive lumped in with the dead."

Captain Helou clears his throat in embarrassment. "That will not be necessary. Hua xiong-di, please forgive my action. And there is no need to mention it to His Highness."

"You are lucky, Captain, that His Highness appreciates underlings who can think for themselves. A different master could have you lashed. Now, if you are satisfied, shall we set out for the capital? I'd offer you some hospitality, but at the moment nothing in this fort is safe to eat or drink."

This clearly disappoints Captain Helou. But he must be relieved that the task of securing the fort is already behind him, because he only murmurs, "We will make do with our rations and find water on our way."

"I assume you have already chosen the men you will leave behind to hold the fort for Yucheng Khan?"

"Yes. Four of them will remain behind."

"Good. His Highness and I will take two of those Dayuan horses."

"Yes, Hua xiong-di," says Captain Helou, more deferential now. Slightly fearful, even, before the remorseless poisoner of the South.

Maintaining my bored expression, I gesture him toward the steps that will take us down. "When do you expect we will reach the capital, Captain?"

"Before midnight, certainly."

"And Yucheng Khan?"

"By first light, at the latest. I will have the men I leave behind here send up sky lanterns to signal our success as soon as it's dark enough."

I nod. "Good. Speak to your men, make sure they know what to do, and let's go."

✦ ✦ ✦

Having the men of the fort lie at the bottom of the gully was my idea. But Yu quickly pointed out that Captain Helou would not be so easily convinced, and we had better make some dummies from straw and blankets in case he decided to throw a stone at the bodies or worse.

Here, fate came to our aid, as tragedy had struck the fort

only the night before. One of the guards, trying to impress his fellows, had climbed on the rampart to do some tricks and slipped off. So we had an actual corpse on hand.

Several chickens at the fort met their end so we would have blood to smear on the rampart, on our clothes, and on some of the soldiers who would be playing dead. There were only twenty soldiers in the pile, lying on sacks of provisions brought down to make the pile look bigger, with stuffed pairs of trousers and boots artfully arranged to achieve the proper number of legs and feet. On top of the soldiers we arranged the dummies, and on top of the dummies we placed the actual dead man.

Commander Wu sent out scouts. We of the princeling's company took a brief, much-needed nap while his men rehearsed getting into the heap formation. Soldiers from forts we had passed earlier began arriving. The princeling had requested reinforcements, but specified that they must not come marching in columns—only in pairs, spaced well apart, as if they were simply patrolling the Wall.

When the first scout returned, reporting that Captain Helou had been sighted, the body heap was constructed. Yu hid himself in the fort and everyone else, including Kedan, disappeared into the mountains.

And that is how things stand as the princeling and I depart with Captain Helou and his Rouran escort, all of us now dressed in imperial uniforms.

I barely manage not to groan as I swing myself into the saddle. Every part of my body aches, and my head teems with all the ways everything could go wrong. The remaining Rouran fighters might discover Yu and slaughter him before he can let in our reinforcements. The men in the heap might make some sound or movement that gets them noticed and spoil the entire plan. Or everything might go off without a hitch, but—and this worries me most of all—because our numbers are so few compared to the incoming Rouran, Yucheng Khan and his followers might overpower the fort's defenses and come through anyway.

I would have preferred never to light the sky lanterns. But Captain Helou will check. And if the sky lanterns do not rise, he will know that something has gone wrong at Futian Pass. In which case, all his suspicions would roar to the fore, and the princeling and I would find ourselves in a fight for our lives.

We are taking an enormous gamble, and I'm not at all sure that luck will tilt our way. But Kai successfully argued that Lord Sang has worked with such meticulous cunning, unless he in fact shows his hand, we could not convince the emperor that his favorite—indeed, beloved—advisor has turned against him.

So now, we ride. The path leading from Futian Pass to the imperial road isn't awful, but we proceed at such a pace that I'm always just short of crying out in alarm, as my mount descends with the speed of a darting deer.

We slow down a little when it becomes completely dark. And sure enough, Captain Helou begins to look back frequently. Whenever he does so, the princeling and I do likewise. The third time we turn around, a handful of sky lanterns rise from Futian Pass into the night—stars that sway and twirl on the wind.

How close are the Rouran forces? Are they already at the gate, breaking it down? Will they have archers? Will they have ladders and grappling hooks to ascend the Wall? And how long can our defenders hold out?

My heart seizes at the peril Yu and Kedan will be in. Will they outlive this night? Will any of us outlive this night?

But all I can do is hold on to my seat and let my Dayuan horse carry me swiftly down the hills toward the imperial road.

Toward the capital.

20

As we ride, my anxieties shift to Tuxi, who was so apprehensive about his task. Has he arrived in the capital yet? Has he spoken to the emperor? Does the emperor believe him? Or does the emperor instead punish him for going beyond the Wall without leave?

To my surprise, just before we reach the imperial road, Captain Helou calls for a stop. "Let the horses rest for a bit."

The horses, these amazing, amazing horses, seem fresher than any of the riders. I wonder if Captain Helou, faced with the enormity of what he is about to do, needs a moment to collect himself. Or at least to put it off ever so slightly further into the future.

I pull him aside. "We didn't secure Futian Pass just to help you, Captain," I say without preamble. We are well past the hour for preambles.

Suspicion, mixed with exhaustion, emanates from him.

"What do you mean, Hua xiong-di?"

I carry on with the scenario Kai and I have constructed, in which Lord Sang isn't the architect behind the Rouran invasion but only a lieutenant to the actual mastermind—Kai being another trusted lieutenant, perhaps more trusted than Lord Sang. "I mean Lord Sang may not be proceeding as he has been instructed. Were you ever aware that he had someone else to answer to?"

"No."

"Well, neither was Yucheng Khan. And that might present a problem, don't you think? After our glorious deeds tonight, when the time comes to distribute honors and rewards, the one who deserves the most accolades is at risk of being left out."

"I—I see."

Probably the last thing Captain Helou expects, as he fights his own trepidation, is to be thrown into the middle of a territorial dispute on which important man has contributed more to treason. But that's what's so good about this lie. He has made a career as a soldier; if nothing else, he understands the scramble for glory.

"His Highness and I will be on hand to make sure that Lord Sang does not claim more than his share of credit. Lord Sang, of course, does not need to know that we are there."

Captain Helou is silent, pondering my request, which verges on an order.

"*Your* work here will not be disputed," I assure him. "Your reward is certain. In fact, your reward will be all the ampler,

287

when we get *our* fair share." I pause and let my words sink in. "Do you understand me—and His Highness—Captain Helou?"

After a long moment, he says, "Yes, Hua xiong-di, I do."

◆ ◆ ◆

When I return to Kai, he tilts his head in Captain Helou's direction.

I nod. We—he, especially—need Captain Helou not to direct Lord Sang's attention our way.

"You are very good at this," he says softly.

At deception, he means. Perhaps I am better than some, but every woman has a great deal of experience presenting herself as someone other than who she is, since no girl is ever everything the world wants her to be.

But if Captain Helou said yes only so that I would stop pestering him, if he means to inform Lord Sang about us once he sees his master . . .

I turn my mind aside. This might be the last opportunity I have to speak to Kai, and I don't want to waste any more time on Captain Helou or Lord Sang or how we are all going to meet our end.

But I don't know what to say.

Kai sighs. "According to the monks, it takes five hundred years of karmic cultivation for two people to share a journey, a thousand to share a pillow. If that's correct, we must already have at least fifteen hundred years of karmic ties between us."

I haven't heard of the saying, but I'm pretty sure the monks weren't referring to the way we shared a pillow, with five other men snoring on the same platform. I smile a little. "Fifteen hundred years—that's thirty lifetimes?"

"I think so," he murmurs. "Do you believe in reincarnation?"

"I . . . I don't know."

"I do. Next lifetime, let's not waste years upon years. Let's be friends from the very beginning."

Tears sting my eyes. "Where should we meet in the next lifetime? In the South or the North?"

"It doesn't matter. Anywhere under the sky."

"Let's go!" calls Captain Helou.

Our hour has come.

"All right," I say. "Next lifetime, I'll expect to have met you when I turn five."

"I'll be there when we're three."

We laugh. Then he is walking toward his horse. I wipe the corners of my eyes and swing back into the saddle.

Now to our fate—and the fate of this country.

◆ ◆ ◆

A pass from Lord Sang, brandished by Captain Helou, gets us through the checkpoints without any fuss.

Thirty li on the imperial road go by in a blur. As the city walls materialize in the distance, lit by torches and lanterns, my heart thuds uncontrollably. I lower my gaze so that I see only what lies directly in front of me.

At the city gate, someone is waiting for Captain Helou. I tense, fearing it will be Lord Sang himself. But it's only a senior gate guard, with a sealed message. Captain Helou thanks the man, reads the message, and rides on. Kai pulls his helmet low and enters the capital unrecognized.

It's late, but not so deep into the night that the entire city is dark. Though the streets are empty except for night watchmen walking in pairs, here and there we pass a window lit from within.

We ride past places that seem vaguely familiar, and now the streets are even wider and smoother. We skirt a large square. On the other side of the square, high, crenellated walls loom, with large, lamp-lit gates, and behind them, roofs rising like mountain ridges against the night sky.

Are we approaching the palace?

We are, but not from the front. Even at the back of the palace, the arched entrance at the center is reserved only for the emperor himself. Kai may be of sufficient stature to use the smaller gates immediately to either side, but officially the highest-ranking man in our party is Captain Helou, and we go to a gate that is second from the center.

The two palace guards stationed there greet Captain Helou quietly, but with familiarity and respect. I have no idea how often Captain Helou comes to the palace, but I suddenly wonder whether these are real palace guards or Lord Sang's men in palace guard uniforms, disguised as we ourselves are.

We are about to ride through the gate—is it really so easy

to gain admittance into the imperial palace?—when another guard, an older man in a fancier uniform, appears.

"Who are these people? Why are we letting anyone in so late?"

One of the guards salutes, bending from the waist. "Lieutenant Tufulu, this is Captain Helou. He just came back from the Wall with urgent news. But the central commandery forces have left, so he needs to see Lord Sang, who is visiting with Captain Chekun tonight."

"He can come inside by himself and wait here for someone to inform Lord Sang. And why is Lord Sang still here so late? Captain Chekun should know better than that." Lieutenant Tufulu sends a disdainful glance our way. "The rest of you wait outside."

He turns to leave, but pivots back to the guards. "And who are you two? Why have I never seen either of you before?"

The guard laughs incredulously. "Lieutenant, how can that be? Why, we—"

A dagger flashes and buries itself to the hilt in Lieutenant Tufulu's chest. Another in his back. Lieutenant Tufulu's eyes widen, then he stumbles and falls.

Blood roars in my head. But I do not make any sound. I do not even look at the dead man as we ride past.

Beyond the wall of the palace lies a long, narrow space paved in granite and lit with a few lanterns, their light dim but sufficient. We dismount. Captain Helou once again consults the message he received at the city gate and marches us east.

A short time later, near an alley that looks very much like the ones I saw in the royal duke's residence, except wider and with higher walls, we are met by a man who herds us forward.

As we approach the gate of a courtyard, another man walks out. Even before I see his face, I know he must be Lord Sang. I have not forgotten the distinctive jangling of his jeweled chain.

Captain Helou goes down on one knee. "My lord."

I doubt Lord Sang would recognize me even if he saw me in broad daylight, but I keep my gaze averted. Beside me, Kai does likewise.

"You have worked hard, Captain," says Lord Sang softly. "Is the pass secured?"

"Yes, my lord."

"And is the khan's representative with you?"

A Rouran fighter steps forward and says, in stiff but passable Chinese, "I am Anake. Our khan sends his greetings. He will be at the city gate in the morning."

"It will be the pleasure of three lifetimes to see Rouran banners flow through the streets of this city," replies Lord Sang smoothly. "Now, to our task."

We have taken no more than ten steps when a man comes running. "My lord, the emperor has left his own dwelling for the crown prince's. The men aren't sure what to do."

Lord Sang does not sound pleased. "So late? Why is he visiting the crown prince?"

"I'm not sure, my lord. The crown prince's condition grew worse yesterday and today. Maybe . . . maybe . . ."

Maybe he won't last the night? The man is obviously forbidden to speculate on the likely mortality of as exalted a personage as the crown prince, but is that what he means to convey?

"Tell the men to follow the emperor to the crown prince's. They are to be anywhere that he is."

Does this mean that the guards outside the emperor's personal residence, within the palace, have all been replaced by Lord Sang's men? How many of them are there? Counting Lord Sang, Kai and I are already outnumbered five to one.

"Yes, my lord." The man takes off running.

We, on the other hand, set off at a leisurely pace, which makes me feel as if ants are crawling all over me. Screams keep rising to my throat. My hand is so tight on my sword that my wrist is in agony. And I can barely keep myself from turning around and sprinting in the opposite direction.

The only thing that keeps me going is the knowledge that Kai is in the throes of the same terror, and he is putting one foot in front of the other.

We go down a long, narrow alley, cross a stone bridge that arches over a small stream, and pass through a garden in which all the trees and ornamental rock hills appear intent and sinister.

Once, we are stopped by guards who are not Lord Sang's men. Without any hurry, Lord Sang tells the guards that Captain Helou has just returned from the Wall with news that must reach the emperor without delay. We are allowed to continue: Not only is Lord Sang a familiar figure in these parts, but he is also holding a pass from Captain Chekun, the head of palace security, which the guards dare not challenge.

I expect to be assaulted by the bitter smell of simmering medicinal herbs as we step into the crown prince's courtyard. Instead, I smell incense. There is one guard at the gate and another stationed by the house, which is situated against the north wall of the enclosure.

Lord Sang shows Captain Chekun's pass. "I have urgent news from the front. Where is His Imperial Majesty?"

Judging by the gate guard's puzzled expression and his uncertain glance at all the men in soldiers' uniforms, he must think the proceedings at least somewhat irregular. Nevertheless, he bows and answers, "He is with the crown prince, your lordship."

Footsteps, distant but fast approaching—Lord Sang's men, running over from the emperor's private residence.

Lord Sang sounds more pleased as he says, "Announce me."

The guard, after a long moment of hesitation, goes to the house and kneels outside the door. "Begging Your Imperial Majesty's instruction—Lord Sang implores to be received."

"It is late," comes the voice of a man. "What is the matter?"

"Urgent news from the front, Your Imperial Majesty," answers the guard.

His Imperial Majesty sighs. "Let him in, then."

I swallow a whimper. There are too many of them and too few of us. We should have incapacitated Captain Helou and all his men while we were at Futian Pass. That way Yucheng

Khan wouldn't have received the signal to proceed, and Lord Sang, for all his scheming, would have no Rouran army to back him up.

But here we are, and the *emperor*'s life is in our hands.

Lord Sang signals for his men to advance. At the door he declares, "Your Imperial Majesty, your servant Sang offers his greetings."

"Enter," says the emperor wearily.

Anake, the Rouran khan's representative, follows Lord Sang, but both the guard from the courtyard gate and the guard who was already at the door move to block him.

"Only Lord Sang," they say in unison.

Anake reaches out two enormous hands and pinches the guards on either side of their necks. The guards drop in place, and Anake enters. My legs feel as if they have been stuffed with cotton. At any point, they could fold under and I'd collapse in a heap.

Lord Sang's men, the counterfeit guards who were stationed outside the emperor's private residence, have now arrived and are busy taking up positions in the courtyard. I count at least fifteen men.

I squint. Is that a large *gong* standing in a corner of the courtyard? The strong lingering scent of incense suddenly makes sense: A temple rite has been performed here recently for the crown prince, in the hope of banishing his illness by supernatural means.

Still more men pour in. Kai and I are now outnumbered

twenty to one. We exchange a glance. His is stark with both fear and resolve; I can only pray that I will not disgrace either myself or my family.

I don't know how, with my wobbly limbs, I manage to step over not one but two high thresholds, but now I'm inside a reception room. A man sits behind a low table at the head of the room, nursing what appears to be a small, shallow bowl of wine. He is in his late forties, dressed simply in black, slightly portly, slightly round-shouldered.

The emperor looks up from his wine. "Lord Sang. What news from the front brings you here so late?"

I've never been near an imperial court before, but I'm certain that under normal circumstances, Lord Sang would have already knelt in greeting. Tonight he remains standing, his back as straight as a sword's edge. "Enemies beyond count have converged on Futian Pass, which is barely a guard tower. The pass will soon be overrun, and the Rouran will be in the capital by morning."

The emperor takes a sip of wine and sighs. "The central commandery forces have gone off to fight enemies at the ends of the Wall. But now I learn that my real enemies have always been closer to home."

He looks grim. Somewhere in his eyes, there is a trace of heartbreak, that a favorite advisor and friend has betrayed his trust. But he is not puzzled by Lord Sang's lack of deference or confused by the appearance of so many armed soldiers where they do not belong.

I let out the breath I've been holding. Tuxi has spoken to his father.

"My son gave me an account of events at the Wall and in the Rouran encampment."

Lord Sang draws back a little, as if in surprise. Like most everyone else, he had no knowledge that a imperial prince ventured outside the Wall.

"To think that however briefly, my doubt fell on my trusty cousin," continues the emperor. "It is deep treachery indeed, Lord Sang, to place your minions under the royal duke's command."

"And so easily too." The traitor chuckles. "A forged letter from his brother, and he was happy to welcome a snake into his household. As for Captain Helou here, I needed only to set him in the royal duke's path."

Lord Sang has a golden, honeyed voice. Even speaking treason, he sounds mellifluous. I can imagine how agreeable it must be to listen to him when he aims to please.

"Have you always been the sort of man who mocks others for their virtues and boasts of his own malice?" The emperor stares at him. "Never mind that. What do you get out of this, Lord Sang?"

"Don't be so bitter, Your Imperial Majesty," says Lord Sang. "Dynasties rise and fall. Many have risen and fallen in the past two hundred years—yours has already lasted longer than most. As for me, my daughter will marry Yucheng Khan's heir, and my grandson will sit on the throne of the North. And perhaps, if he is capable enough, the throne of a China once again united."

The emperor gives a dry, short laugh. "For fifteen years I have honored and promoted you—while you harbored the heart of a ravening wolf."

Lord Sang oozes smugness. "Your Imperial Majesty cannot know everything under the sun, no matter how your lackeys flatter you otherwise."

"Have you come to kill me, then?" asks the emperor, before taking another sip of his wine.

My innards twist. We are moments away from drawing swords. My eyes flick around the room, taking in where everyone and everything is.

"No, sire," answers Lord Sang. "We have come to help you relocate. Have you not said, more times than I can count, that the responsibilities of the Son of Heaven are myriad and heavy, and you long for the pastoral life of your ancestors? Well, the Rouran are eager to welcome you in the open simplicity of their grasslands, where you can look after sheep and horses to your heart's content."

The emperor's knuckles are white around the wine bowl. "And my family?"

"They will go with you, of course, provided they first swear allegiance to Yucheng Khan and renounce any claim to the throne of the North."

"You have been thorough in your machinations."

"I have been in your service many years, sire. That has given me time to think. But now it's time to act." He turns to Anake. "Bind the emperor. The crown prince too. And anyone else in these rooms."

A large figure leaps out from behind a painted wood screen, sword drawn. "No one will dishonor my father or my brother, not while I still live."

Tuxi!

Lord Sang's brow furrows, as if he is having trouble placing Tuxi. "Ah, Prince Anzhong of Luoyang. I heard you returned today from your travels. I didn't know you had chosen to become involved in matters of state."

"When the survival of the state is at stake, every man must do his duty. That isn't something you would understand, Lord Sang."

Lord Sang laughs, not at all chastened. "Your Royal Highness, you are a budding historian. How do you not grasp that the founder of every dynasty is a usurper? Power confers all the legitimacy and respectability anyone needs."

"Not on you. You will never have any power," says another man, stepping out from an inner room.

I have no idea who he is, but Lord Sang turns to the emperor and says, "I've been meaning to tell you, Emperor, that your personal bodyguard is utterly useless as a martial artist. Devotion is a fine attribute, but devotion in the absence of skills is worth nothing."

On the tail end of those words, he rips off his jeweled chain and throws it at the bodyguard. The chain hits the bodyguard on the forehead. The next moment a dagger from Anake buries itself in the bodyguard's chest. He collapses.

Three small metal spheres leave my hand, one each for Anake, Lord Sang, and Captain Helou. Several things happen at once. Tuxi rushes forward with his sword. Anake leaps to meet him, and my hidden weapon misses him by a hairsbreadth. The fighter standing immediately behind Lord Sang draws his broadsword, and the sphere intended for Lord Sang glances off the blade with a sharp clang. But the third one hits Captain Helou squarely on the side of the temple, and he goes down with a thump.

"Hua xiong-di!" shouts Tuxi. "I knew you'd come!"

The two Rouran fighters in front of me turn around, their faces twisting from shock to anger to a furious bloodlust. Suddenly I don't feel my arms or legs. I don't feel the floor beneath me or the sheathed sword in my left hand. All I feel is a fear so enormous that I will suffocate if I don't scream.

So I scream, and draw my sword.

Heart Sea skewers one Rouran before he can lift his own weapon in defense. His companion raises a huge battle-axe, but Kai blocks it for me. The man impaled on Heart Sea is still standing, gurgling and staring. Behind him, two Rouran fighters launch themselves toward me. I put my foot against the man's abdomen and kick hard. He falls and I yank Heart Sea free just in time to parry two broadswords.

Even as I do so, I spin to one side of the men—my back was to the wall and I didn't want to be pinned in place. Another

Rouran comes at me. I hook the toe of my boot under a nearby low table and send it flying in his direction. It splinters against his battle-axe.

Not counting the emperor's unfortunate bodyguard, Lord Sang's side had ten men to our four. Now, with one Rouran run through by Heart Sea and Captain Helou out of commission, they are down to eight. And the more men Kai and I can draw to us, the easier it will be for Tuxi to defend his father.

Kai is now across the room, close to the door, fighting two Rouran. The emperor and Lord Sang are locked in combat near the head of the room. And Tuxi has taken on Anake and another Rouran.

Tuxi is a decent fighter, but Anake is both bigger and better. In one glance I can tell that Tuxi is behind in his countermoves. After kicking the other fighter aside, he barely catches Anake's broadsword before it meets his shoulder.

A battle-axe comes my way. I leap backward. It comes again. I sidestep and it embeds itself in the pillar behind me. I round the pillar and run Heart Sea through the Rouran with the stuck axe.

Kai fells one of his attackers. Six against four.

I slash at the two Rouran fighters still besieging me—they are a little more careful now, knowing that their light armor is no defense against my blade. When they retreat a few steps, I somersault backward and land next to a low table on which has been set two bowls, one full of oranges, the other walnuts.

Tuxi cries out in alarm as he barely ducks under Anake's broadsword. I grab a walnut and hurl it as hard as I can. It hits Anake on the jaw, just outside the protection of his helmet. The big Rouran roars in pain.

I can make getting hit with a lotus seed paste bun hurt. Give me a walnut and I will break a man's jaw.

In Anake's moment of inattention, Tuxi's sword slices through his leg. I almost lift off the floor with a rush of energy. Anake is their strongest fighter. With him hobbled, our chances suddenly look a lot better.

I launch myself at my two Rouran. Thrust. Parry. A slash from the side. They fear me now—I hear it in their panicked breaths and see it in their disorderly footwork. I bloody the arm of one Rouran and very nearly shave off the nose of the other.

We can do this. Subdue all the Rouran fighters, then take Lord Sang. Without him, this whole scheme falls apart. And once—

"Drop your weapons or I'll kill your emperor!"

Captain Helou.

I leap away from my enemies before I glance in his direction. He has his arm around the emperor, a dagger at the latter's throat.

"Drop. Your. Weapons."

Tuxi takes a step toward his father. A line of red appears at the edge of Captain Helou's dagger.

Hastily, Tuxi drops his sword. It clangs loudly against the floor.

Kai puts his down carefully, barely making any sound. He

looks at me. I lower my sword likewise, then I stumble backward until I collapse onto the floor, panting.

The next moment, the dagger from my boot—the one Kai gave me in the mountains—sails through the air and buries itself in Captain Helou's neck. I sat down so that my hand would be closer to it, and I stumbled back to achieve a better angle for the throw.

Captain Helou drops in a heap.

Before I can calculate how many of our enemies are left, Lord Sang whistles, three short, abrupt trills. Men rush in from the front door—the counterfeit guards who have been standing outside, waiting to be summoned.

I scream in frustration as I dive for my sword. I thought we had neutralized Lord Sang's advantage. I thought we might even have taken the upper hand. But I forgot how long he had prepared for this. He had men at the ready.

So many of them. Too many. It's fortunate that the room isn't large and only so many can fit inside, with weapons swinging everywhere. I'm fighting four men, which is one more than I can comfortably handle. I stop one blade a handspan from my forehead and another barely an inch from my shoulder.

"Xi xiong, where are the off-duty guards right now?" shouts Kai, his voice carrying above the din of battle.

The off-duty guards? Of course. The palace is guarded day and night, so there must be several shifts.

"In their dormitory!"

"How far is that?" Kai and I ask together.

"I'm not sure. Half a li?"

Half a li is too far for them to overhear us fighting inside. And even if we leave the crown prince's rooms, the noise of our battle wouldn't be enough to carry that far, penetrate walls, and awaken sleeping men.

But I know what *will* wake them up.

"Outside!" I cry. "We need to go outside!"

"Keep them inside!" commands Lord Sang.

I knock aside a spear. "Kai xiong, help me!"

"Let's fight together, all of us!" he shouts back.

I dispatch two men, he probably more, before we meet. We give up a few paces to join with Tuxi and the emperor. But Kai was right: We are more tactically sound as a unit. He and I serve as the wedge of the spear, kicking, pushing, and thrusting men aside.

Lord Sang's men cluster near the door to prevent us from leaving, but we were never headed for the door. Kai leaps onto a table, kicks open a window, and jumps out. I somersault out after him, not even bothering with the table.

The men left behind in the courtyard and those clustered at the door scramble toward us. But we have the advantage of speed and a clear idea of where we are headed.

"The gong!" cries Lord Sang. "Don't let them get to the gong!"

This has the effect of slowing down his men, many of whom have no idea what he is talking about. The courtyard is dark, and I noticed the gong earlier only because it was where one fake guard stationed himself.

Kai and I run and slash, slash and run. The fake guards are catching up to us.

Kai stops. "You go. I'll hold them off."

But I take no more than three strides before a mountain of a man steps into my way. My mind goes blank—is it Anake, somehow recovered from the injury to his leg? No, it's a different man altogether, even taller, even broader. He assumes a wide stance and shakes his battle-axe at me.

Without thinking, I take a running start and dive between his wide-spread legs. As soon as I get to my feet, before he realizes where I've gone, I leap, spin, and kick him on the side of the head.

Something whooshes in the air. I catch the spear and throw it back.

Send me another, you pigs. I can do this blindfolded.

I cover the remaining distance, yank the wooden hammer from its slot, and strike the gong.

The deep yet piercing metallic reverberations nearly deafen me. The sound should carry across the city and halfway to the mountains.

I steel myself and strike again. And again. And again.

The emperor and Tuxi are in the courtyard too. Lord Sang limps out of the reception room. He leans against the doorjamb and reaches down toward his boot. Before he can pull out a hidden weapon, Kai throws a dagger, pinning Lord Sang's hand to his boot. Lord Sang screams.

"Kill them. Kill them all!"

A spear flies toward Kai's back. I hurl the gong's hammer. The wooden hammer knocks the spear off its trajectory and falls near Kai's feet. He pushes off three attackers, hooks his boot under the hammer's handle, and sends it flying back to me. I catch it and strike the gong three more times.

Now all the able-bodied enemies are in the courtyard, pressing in on us. How many are there? Still too many. And why has no one come to our aid yet?

I groan with effort. Sweat rolls down my temples. My sword becomes heavier with every sweep of my arm.

Still we fight.

My ears ring with the clashing of metal. My eyes are blind to everything except the flash of deadly weapons. My legs grow tired and unwieldy, as if I stand not on flat ground but on the deck of a ship caught in a storm.

Still we fight.

Tuxi grunts in pain—he's taken a slash to the shoulder. The emperor's footwork is lagging—he is no longer a young man, and it has probably been years since he last had to exert himself so. Kai is still fighting well, but I know his reaction time has slowed. I myself barely duck the fall of a broadsword, which I should have heard from half a li away.

How long can our enemies last?

How long can *we* last?

"If I don't make it," shouts Kai, "tell my aunt—tell her that I wish I had the good sense to call her 'Mother.'"

My eyes sting with tears. "And if I don't make it, tell my father that I'm grateful for everything!"

There is no time left for anything except gratitude.

And then, footsteps. Scores upon scores of men running in our direction.

21

The real guards, at least eighty strong, have come to the Son of Heaven's defense.

My exhaustion evaporates in an instant. I kick one counterfeit guard in the throat and knock the broadsword of another clean out of his hand.

"Protect the emperor!" shouts Tuxi. "Arrest the traitor Lord Sang!"

"And let none escape!" cries the emperor.

But Lord Sang is already near the gate of the courtyard, the inrush of guards almost obscuring him from sight.

I half turn to Kai. "Give me another dagger!"

The men attacking us earlier are now busy defending themselves from the real guards, giving Kai room to pull a dagger from his left vambrace. I grab it and throw it halfway across the courtyard toward Lord Sang's sidling form.

He screams.

But only in fright.

The dagger has pierced through his topknot and the handsome toque around it, and embedded itself in the wooden courtyard gate, pinning him in place.

The real guards apprehend him. His men, now leaderless, quickly give up. Suddenly I'm exhausted again. I drag myself to the gong, slump down onto the ground, and lean my back against its framework.

Vaguely I hear several voices asking the emperor whether he is unhurt. He calls for a physician to see to Tuxi's shoulder and speaks to Kai. I pant, wipe the sweat from my face, and pant some more.

"Hua xiong-di," calls Kai.

Weakly I flick a hand in the air, trying to tell him that I don't want or need anything.

"Hua Mulan," Kai calls again. "Present yourself before His Imperial Majesty."

My head snaps up—this isn't a request I can ignore. Kai is peering out from the crown prince's house, beckoning me. I leap to my tired feet and hurriedly cross the courtyard.

At the door he stops me, his hand on my arm. "Are you all right?"

"Just spent. You?"

He smiles a little, as dirty and bedraggled as I've ever seen him. "Same. Now come."

The emperor sits at the same table where I first saw him, but now the table is notched from the fight and the wine bowl he used earlier in fragments. Two steps into the room, I kneel. "This humble conscript presents his greetings to His Imperial Majesty."

"Your Imperial Majesty, this is Hua xiong-di, Hua Mulan, who has proved himself a hero for the ages," says Kai. Then, to me, "Hua Mulan, express your gratitude to His Imperial Majesty, who has bestowed upon you the great honor and charge of seeing to his personal safety."

In my astonishment, I almost forget to kowtow.

For our night is only beginning. The Rouran could be here by sunrise, the capital is without an army, the city guards have been compromised, and Captain Chekun, from whom Lord Sang stole that all-important palace pass, is badly wounded from fighting Lord Sang's men, once he realized what was going on.

Tuxi, despite his injuries, takes charge of the palace guards, as he is familiar with the inner workings of the palace. Kai is tasked with commanding those city guards who have not conspired with Lord Sang. And I follow a few paces behind the emperor as he oversees the organization of a civil defense.

The residents of the capital are roused from sleep. The armory empties. Barricades go up. By the middle of the night, I can map the capital from memory, with all its streets and landmarks.

From time to time during the frantic preparations, my mind strays to the men I pierced through, wondering whether they are dead or still drawing breaths. My skin crawls, recalling the stomach-churning, indescribable sensation of Heart Sea meeting flesh and bone. Once, I run to a corner to empty the contents of my stomach.

Not long before dawn, we return to the palace. While the emperor meets with group after group of officials in his personal study, I fall ravenously upon my breakfast. I haven't had anything to eat since Futian Pass, and any nausea pales before the hunger of a woman who has ridden, fought, and worked all night.

A nobody like me eating in front of—or, in my case, behind—the emperor must be a breach of etiquette severe enough to make entire rows of courtiers faint. But the sovereign himself told the servants to give me a portion of everything. And I did not need more permission than that to begin.

The officials leave. I expect another group to come in. But when no one enters, I realize that the emperor has now met with everyone. We have done all we can. It only remains to be seen whether what we have done will be of any use.

The emperor turns around. I am caught with one sweet fried honey bing in each hand.

He smiles. "Ah, the appetite of the young. Eat as you wish, Hua xiong-di."

Not with him looking at me. I set the goodies down, even as I bow and say, "Yes, Your Imperial Majesty."

He shakes his head a little. "Are you married, young brother? Will your wife thrill to the prospect of welcoming home a hero?"

"I'm not married, sire."

"But a match has been arranged for you?"

"No, not yet, sire."

The emperor raises a brow. "How old are you, my boy?"

"Nineteen, sire."

"Nineteen and not betrothed? I was three years married by that age. Should everything go well today, I will see to it that you will have a beautiful and loving wife."

And wouldn't *she* have a surprise coming. I sink to one knee. "Thank you, sire. Your Imperial Majesty's kindness is that of springtime sun."

He smiles again. "Eat more."

And very considerately turns his back to me. I gobble down the honey buns and swill another cup of tea—ah, what nectar!— just in time for him to turn around again.

"Where did Kai-er find a martial artist of your caliber?"

Er is often attached to a character of one's name by one's elders, to make a "little name" to use at home and among intimates. Mother always called me Lan-er. As for Father—I can't remember him ever calling me by my name.

"His Highness knows me because of a family connection. We are to fight a duel against each other." It's been a long night and I can't manage any prettier answers.

The emperor's eyes widen. "He spoke to me about the duel after he returned from the South. He said that the young man he thought he would be fighting did not live past infancy. And that his opponent would be a girl."

It becomes my turn to be taken aback. "Oh, he did?"

The emperor scrutinizes me more closely. Then he smiles widely. "I *was* wondering how he managed to locate a martial artist who is both fiercer and prettier than he is. I have my answer. Shall I seek a beautiful and loving husband for you, then?"

I can't help smiling a little myself. "Thank you, sire. But I shall need to consult my father first."

"Of course." The emperor nods with approval. "Were you a man, I would have offered you an excellent position. But I don't suppose that is what you seek."

Do I want an excellent position? I've never thought about it. Such choices are not given to women. "I . . . I seek nothing, sire. There are no able-bodied men in my household, but I am more than able-bodied, so I answered the conscription."

"Kai-er chose a dangerous course. You needed not have traveled this path with him. From his account, you are barely a Northerner."

"But the North has sheltered my family and me, and for that I am grateful. And one does not abandon friends in their hour of need. So one might say, sire, that I traveled this path for duty and friendship."

"That is the answer a man would have given," says the emperor.

"I beg a thousand pardons, sire, but that is the answer any right-thinking person should give."

The emperor gazes at me a moment. "Well said."

He turns his back to me again. My heart thumps and my

fingertips shake. I've just held a conversation with the emperor. Well, the emperor of only the North, but still.

"And since you are a right-thinking person, my child," says the emperor, still with his back to me, "what do you think of what Lord Sang said, that every founder of a dynasty is a usurper? That would make me but the descendant of a usurper. Do I really have more right to sit on this throne than Yucheng Khan, who will at least have won it for himself?"

My mind stutters. The emperor, asking *me*, whether the throne he occupies is rightfully his? Obviously I believe so—I've just risked my life to keep him from being usurped, and will risk my life again when the Rouran cavalry arrives before the gates of the city, any moment now.

Except I didn't do it for *him*. For duty and friendship, for the peace and security of the North, but not for this man, who was only an idea to me.

Yet now I have fought alongside him and been given a glimpse into his private doubts. I remember talking with Tuxi and Kai about the proposed Xianbei ban and saying to Tuxi, *I would be happy if the emperor gave half so much thought to these questions as you do.*

I know now that he does. That like his son, he thinks on and struggles with the weighty issues before him.

I sink to one knee. "Sire, that you ask yourself these questions, that you believe you should prove yourself worthy of the throne—I would rather have you as emperor than anyone who believes the throne should be his simply because he wants it."

The emperor is silent for what seems an eternity. Then he turns around and smiles at me once again. "Dawn comes, my child. It is time we face our next test—for duty and friendship."

◆ ◆ ◆

We stand atop the city gate, the guard towers rearing up behind us, the emperor at the center, Kai to his side, and me on Kai's other side.

But when an army materializes, it isn't the Rouran cavalry, but the central commandery forces led by Kai's father, the royal duke.

I have never heard such a roar of joy, nor cheered so much myself. Kai and I throw our arms around each other, tears streaming down our faces.

We have done everything we have set out to do, for the peace and security of the North, for duty and friendship.

And we have lived to see another sunrise.

22

Kai rushes down to greet his father—and his aunt, who rides into the capital beside her husband, a sword at her side. She is not dressed as a man, but in a scarlet brocade cape lined with fur, beautiful and proud.

I do not leave the emperor's side—that is my post until he dismisses me. But also, I wasn't entirely jesting when I told Kai that I was deathly afraid of his aunt. On any other day, I would hide behind others when she and her husband come before the emperor to pay their obeisance. But today I'm so eager to find out what happened that I actually press forward a little to hear the royal duke's account.

The letter Kai sent via Captain Helou, of course, never reached its intended recipient. But Kai dispatched another letter via the border garrison's messenger. In case that letter fell into the wrong hands, he was much more circumspect in both his description of events and his warning about a ruse to empty the military presence around the capital. And for that reason he never mentioned this second message to us, because he himself was convinced that it was too cryptic to be of any use.

But his father, reading between the lines, did understand his hints and decided to play a ruse of his own. Ostensibly, he allowed himself to be persuaded by the more anxious voices at court to lead his men to the eastern end of the Wall, where the commanders were in need of soldiers. Except he decided to hedge his bets and keep half of his units within two days' march of the capital.

At his first bivouac, he saw the sky lanterns—the batch numbering in the thousands that alerted us to the fact that the central commandery forces had left the capital. He felt it was too much of a coincidence to ignore. The next day he kept his troops in place, pending further news. And when the beacons on the Wall were lit again—this time in truth, to signal Yucheng Khan's attack at Futian Pass—he immediately headed back.

And so when the imperial messengers met him, he was only hours outside the capital, and had already sent two of his most capable lieutenants and half his soldiers to Futian Pass to aid the units guarding the Wall.

The emperor walks forward and places his hands on the royal duke's arms. "My dear cousin, on any other occasion, yours would have been the greatest contribution to the defeat of our enemies. But today that credit must go to your remarkable son and his equally remarkable companions—including, I am happy to say, Prince Anzhong of Luoyang, who is currently in charge of the defense of the palace. Hua Mulan?"

Startled, I say tentatively, "Yes, Your Imperial Majesty?"

"Come here, young man," says the emperor with a twinkle in his eye.

I am set next to Kai. The emperor gives a quick account of the previous night before all the important courtiers and ministers gathered atop the city wall. The royal duke beams. His wife looks upon her nephew with so much pride and fierce joy that she doesn't even bother to glare in my direction.

"Great rewards will follow in the wake of great deeds," says the emperor. "But our peril has not passed yet. Let all go to their stations and be vigilant."

Around noon, however, more good news comes in the form of a messenger from Futian Pass. By the time Yucheng Khan reached the Wall, enough soldiers from nearby garrisons had converged on the Pass that they managed to hold it. And when the royal duke's men arrived with news that Lord Sang's scheme had failed, Yucheng Khan decided to cut his losses and retreat. Commander Wu especially asked the messenger to convey that Yu and Kedan are safe and sound, and will be headed for the capital once they've recovered from the rigors of battle.

With joy and relief comes the exhaustion that need alone has been holding at bay. The emperor orders double sets of guards and patrols, and everyone else is given leave to rest.

I almost fall asleep on my horse, riding beside Kai. Not until I see the front door of the royal duke's residence do I remember that his aunt probably won't want to see more of me. I'm too drained to care. Kai still has to speak with his father, but I'm conducted directly to the same suite of rooms I occupied earlier.

I scratch out a quick note to Father, telling him that the war is over and that I have not dishonored the family name. After entrusting the letter to Xiao Yi, Kai's attendant, I fall into bed and do not wake up until sunset. After dinner and a wash— with steaming hot water!—I sleep again until dawn.

When I open my eyes, the room feels a little too warm—a completely foreign sensation—because of all the braziers Xiao Yi set blazing. I put on the men's clothes that have been provided, made of blue embroidered silk. They are a bit long for me—Kai's garments, most likely. When I'm dressed, I open a window. Are those actual flower buds on the trees in the courtyard? Has spring finally arrived in the North?

Kai emerges from his rooms, with faint dark circles still under his eyes, but looking alert, clean, and very handsome. I half expected that it would feel awkward between us, after, well, having made promises for our next lifetime. But all I feel as I look upon him is a great swell of affection and happiness.

"Good morning, Your Highness. What are you afraid of today?" I call out as my greeting.

"That you wouldn't be here when I got up. But, as usual, I see I was afraid over nothing," he says brightly. "Ah, here comes Xiao Yi with our breakfast. It's nothing but coarse food and weak tea, unfit for a refined palate such as yours. All the same, will you forgive the inadequacy of this rough repast and deign to partake of it in my rooms?"

I laugh, remembering his similar words the first time we dined together. Confucius would clutch his chest in shock and disapproval, but I feel no compunction about sitting down with Kai in his reception room. "This lowly conscript overflows with gratitude at Your Highness's beneficence. This morning's bountiful meal will be a kindness never to be forgotten."

As we feast on freshly steamed pork buns, pickled radish, and bowls of hot porridge, he tells me that his father and his aunt have gone to Futian Pass for an inspection—and teases me about my evident relief. "You're more afraid of her than you were of the bandits."

"I'm more afraid of her than I was of Anake, the Rouran warrior last night," I joke right back. "And he almost made me drop in a dead faint!"

On my third bowl of porridge, I remember something from my conversation with the emperor. "Why did you tell the emperor that you'd be dueling with a girl?"

"Ah, that." He sprinkles some finely diced pickled radish on his porridge.

He is . . . blushing.

"Yes?"

He clears his throat. "The emperor knew that my aunt would not allow a marriage to be arranged for me until after the duel, since the outcome could be uncertain. But he had some matches in mind for me."

I stop eating and stare at him. It didn't occur to me that his marriage might be something the court would take a hand in—a matter of state interest.

"I declined all his suggestions!" he protests, a hint of apprehension in his voice. "He asked if I had any preferences. By that time I'd returned from the South, after having seen you and met you twice for sparring. I told him that I would not marry anyone else unless you first rejected me absolutely."

I breathe again, even as my cheeks grow warm. "And what did he say?"

"He teased me for my presumption and told me that I had better render a great service to the country first, before I dare think of such things as choosing my own wife."

But he has now rendered a great service to his country, which the emperor publicly acknowledged.

It becomes my turn to clear my throat. "Will your aunt ever allow such a thing?"

"I don't know, but I have told her the same thing as I told the emperor."

"What? When?" When her ladyship met me, she believed me to be Hua Muyang, my father's son.

"The morning we left the capital, when I said my goodbyes to her."

"And what did she say?"

"Nothing. But her opinion will matter only if you are amenable to the match."

His gaze is direct, this young man who is afraid of everything and yet fears nothing.

"I—I will not reject you absolutely," I say, my face burning. And then, because I'm braver than that, "Yes, I am amenable."

He smiles. I smile back.

Then he asks, "Can I still come and find you in the next lifetime, when we are three?"

We dissolve in laughter.

◆ ◆ ◆

After breakfast, I am free to spend my day as I wish. While we were riding all over the plateau, I would have said that I wanted to spend the rest of my life doing exactly nothing. But now that the rest of my life is here, doing nothing seems rather . . . boring. Especially when I'm filled with such a sense of energy and well-being.

"What can I do?" I ask Kai, still smiling.

He too is still smiling. "If you don't have anything else you'd rather do, you can always come with me. I have to deal with the capital guards some more."

I haven't the slightest idea what to do with capital guards. "Well, why not?"

As it turns out, there is a great deal of work to be done, from poring over documents, to tracking how Lord Sang might have misused state funds to finance his treasonous activities, to checking for shortfalls in equipment and maintenance because money has been siphoned off elsewhere. I listen to Kai question some capital guards and speak to two dozen guards on my own.

The next morning we draft a report for the imperial court. That afternoon I go out and shop, because I have been one of the royal duke's men, and his men are paid regularly. With silver and coins I've earned on my own, I buy books for Father, calligraphy brushes for Murong, a supply of sweets for Dabao, and several lengths of silk for Auntie Xia.

That evening Yu and Kedan reach the royal duke's residence. Kai sends a message to the palace for Tuxi. He isn't sure whether Tuxi will be able to come—the movements of royal princes being typically rather restricted. But soon Tuxi arrives to round out our group.

Yu stays only a short time—there are too many household tasks for him to see to. But the rest of us linger over a plentiful dinner and talk and laugh. At first Kedan is uncharacteristically bashful, but once he realizes—as I did earlier—that Tuxi is the same person he has always been, he relaxes and entertains us with an account of the defense of Futian Pass. It must have been a most harrowing night, yet he makes us laugh uproariously with stories of soldiers in the overcrowded fort tripping over its few remaining chickens.

We are obliged to give an account of what we went through that same night. To my surprise, Kai proves himself an exceptional storyteller, and I find myself listening with my mouth open to events I have lived through.

Kedan has already been informed of Captain Helou's fate, so Kai glosses over that part. But when he nears the end of his narrative, as he describes me fighting my way toward the gong, he says, "Hua xiong-di catches a spear thrown at him without even turning around. Then, as he hurls the spear right back, he yells, 'Send me another, you pigs. I can do this blindfolded!'"

Kedan hoots and claps.

I'm astonished. "I said that aloud? I thought it was only in my head."

"Oh, everyone in that courtyard heard you, Hua xiong-di," confirms Tuxi. "I think at least half the men shivered, including me."

"Me too," says Kai. "You know I did."

Which makes me choke on my wine laughing.

After he finishes the tale, I turn to Tuxi. "You were worried, weren't you, Tuxi xiong, that your father wouldn't believe you?"

Tuxi reddens. "Horribly worried—not to mention I thought he would be angry that I went beyond the Wall without his leave. But"—he beams—"today he told me that sometimes boys become men when their fathers aren't looking."

We bellow with approval and drink to his elevation in the eyes of the Son of Heaven.

"Wait a second," says Kedan after a while. "Nobody ever mentioned why the emperor was in the crown prince's rooms that night."

"My horse went lame on the way, so I didn't reach the palace until perhaps two hours before Kai xiong-di and Hua xiong-di," explains Tuxi. "And by the time I half convinced my father that Lord Sang was expecting the Rouran, we weren't sure we dared trust anyone. We wanted to distance my father from the guards who had been placed around him, and going for a visit to my brother's residence seemed a plausible reason, since my father had been doing that frequently of late."

"And where was the crown prince all that time?" asks Kedan.

"On his bed, in the next room from where we were fighting."

"What?" Kedan and I cry in unison.

"Those of his household hid in a storage room, but he himself refused to move. He said he'd die with his father and brother if it came to that." Tuxi exhales. "Fortunately that didn't happen. We were all lucky."

He raises his bowl of grape wine. "To good men, men of great might and stalwart hearts."

Kai and I glance at each other and raise our bowls obligingly, but Kedan clears his throat. "Tuxi xiong, I regret to inform you, but one of us isn't that good a man."

"What do you mean?"

"Just that. There is someone at this table who is no kind of man at all."

Tuxi looks concerned, as if wondering whether Kedan already had too much to drink.

Kai and I exchange another glance. I turn to Kedan. "How did you know, Kedan xiong? And when?"

He grins. "Remember that day we first saw the Dayuan horses, and you asked me to show you how to read tracks and prints?"

I see where this is going. "My prints gave me away?"

"Exactly. You were too light for a man of your height and build."

"What?" Tuxi stares at me, then looks around the table, his eyes settling on Kai. "Is Kedan xiong-di saying what I think he's saying?"

"Yes," answers Kai. "More wine for you, my brother?"

Tuxi thinks about it for a bit. Then he grins. "Yes. More wine for everyone."

✦ ✦ ✦

We talk and laugh late into the night. Fortunately, I do not imbibe too much: The next morning, Kai and I head to the palace for a private audience with the emperor, to discuss what should be done about the city guards.

When we arrive back at the royal duke's residence, Yu greets us. "Your Highness, Hua xiong-di, Master Hua awaits you in the Court of Indigo Pine."

Master Hua? "My *father* is here?"

"Yes, Hua xiong-di," answers Yu, and withdraws discreetly.

Kai waits until he is out of earshot. "Along with your letter, I sent a message to your father and asked him whether he would like to come to the capital, since you might be here for a while. I told him that we have fought together, that I would like to meet him formally, and that perhaps it is high time he and my aunt met again."

"And you didn't tell me?"

"Your father, in his return message, asked me not to. He isn't sure how you will receive him."

Neither am I. I don't know that I'm ready to see him.

"Let me take you to the Court of Indigo Pine," says Kai.

We walk silently for some time. Then, as we pass through the main garden, he says, "For the longest time, I couldn't understand my aunt. She goes on retreats to mountain monasteries, where the nuns expound on wisdom, compassion, and the impermanence of everything. And yet her hatred of your father has remained a permanent fixture in our lives."

I stop. So does he. With a faraway expression, he gazes at a small tree, its slender branches dotted with creamy white buds, ready to bloom. "And then one day, I overheard her saying that if only she hadn't fallen ill, then whatever happened during the duel, it would not have been her sister who came out the worse. That's when I understood that she blamed herself more than she blamed your father.

"She drove me as hard as she did because she did not know what else to do with all her anguish. And when she meets with the nuns, she asks for their help in forgiving your father, but she never thinks that she needs to forgive herself too."

I bite the inside of my lower lip. "You are suggesting that perhaps my father feels as your aunt does about what happened?"

Grief-ridden and full of self-blame?

He turns to me. "I'm only saying that I can never fully experience how difficult my aunt's life has been. And that I regret all the resentments I used to carry."

❖ ❖ ❖

I enter the Court of Indigo Pine by myself. It is a small courtyard, but more ornately decorated than the princeling's, with a grove of shapely pine trees, their needles brilliantly green even after a long winter.

A house occupies the northern half of the courtyard. I'm not sure when Yu arrived, but he opens the door for me and ushers me in.

Father has been set behind a low table, on a raised side platform. He is dressed in his most formal overrobe, but it hangs loose on him. He has become thinner in the time since I left home, his eyes sunken. My heart aches.

Yu pours tea, urges us to taste all the different pastries and delicacies that have been laid out, and excuses himself.

Father and I regard each other. I sink to one knee—so much deference isn't expected in daily life, but it is before and after a major trip away from home. "I offer my humble greetings, Father. My apologies—I should have rushed home to look after you. It is unforgivable that you needed to come all the way to the capital."

"Take a seat," he tells me. "It is good for me to get out once in a while. I visited the North in my youth, but I had never seen the Northern capital."

There is another raised platform opposite the one on which Father sits. I settle myself behind one of the low tables there—not the one directly across from him, but one further from the head of the room, as a gesture of respect.

"Has Father been well in my absence?" I ask.

He assures me that he has been well, given that the war was blessedly short. I ask after Murong, Auntie Xia, and Dabao, and he replies that they are also doing well, extremely relieved that I am safe and exceptionally proud of my deeds.

He does not say that *he* is exceptionally proud of me, but I am not as disappointed as I could have been. Everything I have done, I did for duty and friendship. Every decision I have made, I made so that my conscience would be at ease.

I am, I realize, proud of myself.

We speak of some household matters. I begin to sense his distraction. He picks up a candied lotus seed and sets it down again. He picks up his teacup and sets it down again. At last he says, abruptly, "You have met the princeling's aunt."

My chest tightens. "Yes, I have."

"Then you know what happened."

Is he not going to dispute anything? "I have heard what her ladyship and His Highness had to say."

Father's hands clench in his lap. "I was—I was not a young man who deserved his good fortune. My father always taught me that character is more important than swordsmanship. But I believed swordsmanship to be character enough. Because no matter what I did, I would always be a great swordsman.

"I did not like the matrimonial agreement my father made with Master Peng. I thought I wouldn't get along with his elder daughter at all—nor with Master Peng, for that matter. And I was rankled by the fact that the Peng ladies seemed more adept at swordsmanship than I was.

"But I wouldn't have broken the agreement if I hadn't loved your mother. The thought of marrying Miss Peng so that the swords would be reunited—that meant nothing to me. The thought of giving up your mother, of watching her someday marry another, that was unbearable.

"What I did was egregious, but it was the only thing I could have done at the time. Even now, all these years later, knowing all the tragedies that have followed in the wake of that decision, I don't know that I could have acted differently."

I look down at my hands. "You know I can never truly blame you for marrying Mother. But why did you not tell me the truth about what happened at the duel?"

He turns his face to the front of the room. A water-and-ink landscape painting hangs there, that of a sword-sharp peak. "I went into the duel thinking that it might be fatal for me. I thought I'd reconciled myself to it. But when the moment came, when I was lying on the ground, helpless, and the princeling's mother came at me, her sword dripping with my blood, I . . .

"The thought of never seeing you, your brother, or your mother again burned through me like a wildfire. I cannot recall ever making up my mind that I would use the poisoned bronze lilies. I simply acted. The moment they left my hand I knew that I had not only condemned my opponent, but myself.

"I was in a state of delirium from my injuries when I was carried back home. I woke up days later to the sight of your mother weeping by my bedside. We had lost a child, she informed me. And I was stricken with horror. For the first time it occurred to me that perhaps in my fear and agony, I had mistaken my opponent's intention. Perhaps she had meant only to take my sword, and not to murder me in cold blood, in front of many witnesses.

"Without cause, I had killed the beloved sister of the woman I spurned. I had robbed a man of his wife and a son of his mother. What I now faced was divine retribution.

"I shook as I asked your mother which one of the twins we had lost. She told me it was our son. My heart shattered, yet— yet such a fierce relief washed over me. I had feared that *you* were the one who was taken before your time, and *that* would have been too heavy a blow for an already broken man."

I stare at his profile. I can't have heard him correctly. He has always wanted me to pretend to be his son.

"The moment I saw you as a newborn, I knew that I would not trade you for ten sons. You were going to be the bright pearl in my hand, and I wanted nothing but a life of ease and plenty for you. So when I learned that you were still alive, despite my sorrow, my joy was sharper than Heart Sea or Sky Blade.

"And immediately I was terrified. A man who has committed as many wrongs as I had does not deserve to feel such joy. I was convinced that moment of feverish relief shone a light on you and exposed you to all the infelicitous elements in the universe. I used to tremble when you so much as sneezed. And whenever you were the slightest bit unwell, I would be beside myself.

"Finally I traveled a hundred li to consult with a famous priestess. She said that if I wanted to keep you safe, then I should fool the lords of the Underworld into thinking that you did not exist. 'Have her pretend to be Hua Muyang, your son,' she said. 'The lords of the Underworld already have Hua Muyang and won't send their minions for him again.'

"Your mother thought it was the stupidest thing she'd ever heard, and I don't blame her for thinking so. But after she died, I did as the priestess advised. I'd already lost her and Muyang; I couldn't lose you too.

"And I never mentioned what happened with the princeling's mother because—because to this day, I cannot bear to look back on the man I was then, or face all the suffering that I have caused."

He still has his eyes on the painting, and I'm still staring at his profile, trying to understand everything he has said.

He has always loved me. He has never wished I were my brother.

I could have gone to my death not knowing that. I could have drawn my last breath wishing that I mattered to him. I could have—

I'm only saying that I can never fully experience how difficult my aunt's life has been. And that I regret all the resentments I used to carry.

Let me not be angry at him now for things that did not happen, or for things that should be left in the past. And let me not give myself resentments to carry—that cannot possibly be the reason I survived impossible odds to live to this day.

I go to him and take his hands.

Tears spill from his eyes. "I'm sorry, Mulan. I'm so sorry."

"You are my father," I tell him. "I can never adequately repay you for raising me, and you do not need to apologize to me. But there is a family here . . ."

He grips my hands. "That you do not despise me—you don't know what that means to me. And as for the family, I knew before the start of my trip that I must face them this time. And perhaps I'm at last ready to—"

"Hua Manlou, you come out here!"

The voice can only belong to her ladyship, back from Futian Pass to find the man she hates the most in her own home, invited by her own nephew.

"We'll go out there together," I tell him.

A tremor passes beneath his skin, but he looks at me with tired yet clear eyes. "Yes, Mulan. Let's go out there together."

◆　◆　◆

A pair of strong manservants under Yu's supervision carry Father out and place him on a cushion on the ground.

Kai, his father, and his aunt stand in the courtyard, the latter two still in their traveling capes, her ladyship's flying about her like a flame.

"Kai, give your opponent's sword to her."

I notice only then that Kai, who looks openly apprehensive, has both Sky Blade and Heart Sea. I left Heart Sea in my rooms earlier, as one does not, under normal circumstances, enter the royal palace fully armed.

I accept Heart Sea from Kai while glancing between him and her ladyship. The royal duke looks as if he wishes to say something to his wife, but he doesn't.

She announces coldly, "Today is the day of the duel. Both opponents are present. The rules stipulate that three martial arts experts should serve as referees. Master Yu, Master Hua, and I will fulfill those roles. You may begin."

I have lost count of the days. Today *is* the day the duel would have taken place had the Rouran not attacked.

Kai and I look at each other. I can tell that all kinds of disastrous possibilities are racing through his mind, but when I behold him, I feel only affection and happiness.

Discourse on swordsmanship, I think to myself, remembering what he said about wishing for a more literal version of the contest.

I smile at him and mouth the words, putting the emphasis on "discourse." Startled, he stares at me a moment before returning a tentative smile.

And then a full, radiant one.

I lift my still-sheathed sword. "I begin with a maneuver called 'the crane glances back.'"

Which is an elegant name for an attack that switches direction midthrust. I perform the move, but at a fraction of its normal speed—and seven paces away from Kai.

"I would counter with 'the meteor crosses the sky,' which neutralizes the risk posed to my right flank by your move, and exploits the fact that your move exposes your left shoulder."

Standing where he is, he sweeps a still-sheathed Sky Blade

before him, his motion slow and majestic.

"But my move was a feint," I say. "Just when I've convinced you that I am using 'the crane glances back,' it mutates into 'the dragon's tail tangles the clouds,' which takes advantage of your unguarded torso during 'the meteor crosses the sky.'"

"And I have anticipated that, because 'the meteor crosses the sky' changes easily to a centered stance that seems defensive but is in fact an ambush waiting to happen."

He smiles again at me.

"What are you two doing?" shouts her ladyship.

"Discoursing on swordsmanship," answers her nephew. "But in a manner befitting our surroundings. In the beginning, the point of this contest was that both sides improved their skills."

"We have fought four times now, and we have come to know each other's style and tendencies very well," I add.

Father looks almost as stunned as her ladyship. The royal duke smiles in relief. Yu is too dignified to smile, but his eyes soften with approval.

Kai and I continue to discuss our craft. He points out something that I have failed to notice myself, which is that I tend to overadjust when I attack to the left. And I tell him that his stance is slightly insecure in certain maneuvers, leading to a slower reaction time.

He salutes. "I am fortunate in your instruction, my esteemed opponent."

I return the salute. "As am I. I have learned much from you,

Your Highness."

"I might have learned something too," says the royal duke mildly.

His wife doesn't take it in the same spirit. She glares at me. "Are you mocking me?"

I bow to her. "No, your ladyship. Your nephew and I have fought real enemies together and come through as friends and comrades. We will not raise our swords to each other again, save as sparring partners, training for mutual improvement."

"So I am to consider this travesty a tie?"

"Your ladyship, if I may," says Father. He gestures for me to come to him. With my help, he gets up on his knees. "I am at fault in all this. My selfishness has brought dishonor to me and pain to many. I have no words that can make up for what I have done, except sorrow and regret."

He kowtows three times each to the royal duke, her ladyship, and the princeling—the three people most affected by the death of the princeling's mother. While supporting him, I follow his lead.

"And if your ladyship will accept this token of my humble contrition . . ."

Father takes Heart Sea from me and holds it above his head.

I feel a twinge of regret, losing the great sword that I can finally call my own. But this is the right thing to do, and the feeling of solidity and substance in making such a choice outweighs any vanity or possessiveness.

With a deep bow, Kai takes Heart Sea from Father and

hands it to her ladyship, who regards this object she has so long desired with a strangely detached look. As if she is realizing for the first time that what she has desperately yearned for all along was peace in her own heart, which no blade, however legendary, can bring her, not even when it is offered by her nemesis on his knees.

The royal duke comes forward, lifts me with his own hands, and helps me to settle Father back on the cushion. Tears rise to my eyes at the kindness in his. This is a man who has suffered a grievous loss, but still chooses to see my father's pain and self-reproach.

Kai comes forward too. With another deep bow, he places Sky Blade, his own sword, in Father's hands.

Both Father and I stare at him in incomprehension. Her ladyship gasps. "Kai, what are you doing?"

"Master Hua, please accept this as a token of my appreciation and gratitude to your daughter. I am convinced that if it were not for her, neither the emperor nor I would be alive today, and the streets of this city would be awash in blood."

Kai bows yet again and returns to the side of his aunt, who doesn't appear half as furious as I expected her to be, though she does glower at him. "Oh, and it's yours to give now?"

He leans in and whispers in her ear, but to those of us whose hearing has been sharpened by years of training, he might as well have shouted his words from the rooftops. "If you wish the swords to be reunited, Mother, perhaps you can see your way to arranging a match between me and Miss Hua?"

EPILOGUE

Kai and I sit shoulder to shoulder as our small boat drifts lazily in a field of water lilies.

I never thought I would see Lake Tai again, yet here I am, surrounded by her clear, abundant water, breathing in the fragrance of high summer.

We have been on assignment in the South, a delicate yet dangerous mission which we have just concluded. And Kai has arranged for this small holiday near my old haunts before our return to the North.

"Thank you," I murmur in his ear.

"I'll do anything to make you happy," he murmurs back. "You're less terrifying when you're happy."

I laugh. I *am* happy. And I am happier yet to realize that while the South is as beautiful as I remembered, this time, when I leave, I will not miss it as much. That even as my heart sighs over the absolute loveliness of the lake turning gold and red in the light of sunset, I am looking forward to returning to the North, my new home.

And to all the challenges and rewards of my new life.

AUTHOR'S NOTE

In June of 2017, my agent emailed me out of the blue and asked if I had any interest in doing a YA retelling of the ballad of Mulan. My first reaction was laughter, not in derision, but in sheer astonishment. On paper I seemed a good candidate for such an adaptation: I grew up in China; I'd made a career out of historical fiction; I'd even produced two books, set partly in China, featuring a young woman who is a highly skilled martial artist. But in reality I'd never had the slightest interest in the legend of Mulan.

But now I was intrigued.

The original ballad tells the very simple story of a girl leaving home in her father's stead to go to war and then coming back. I could have taken it in any direction I wanted, and I chose to infuse it with elements of wuxia, a uniquely Chinese literary genre that explores themes of honor, sacrifice, vengeance, and forgiveness through the adventures of almost mythically adept martial artists. The editor who suggested the retelling, Cheryl Klein of Lee & Low Books, liked that approach, and we decided to go forward on the project.

And then I realized I knew next to nothing about China in the fifth century AD, when the story of Mulan is most commonly inferred to have taken place. I didn't know what people ate—it turned out that many staples of my childhood diet, like potatoes, tomatoes, and peanuts, originated in the New World. I didn't know what people read—most of what I considered ancient Chinese poetry dates from the Tang Dynasty and later, hundreds of years after Mulan's day. I didn't even know whether Confucius had been born by then. (He was, in fact, born about a thousand years earlier—which should tell you a lot about the depth of my ignorance.)

So I set out to learn about the time period. And what I learned challenged, even upended, many of my own notions of what it means to be Chinese.

Though I remembered little of the animated Disney version of the story, I did remember that the invaders were called the Huns. (Whether any of the nomadic tribes that clashed repeatedly with the Han Chinese were, in fact, the Huns is a matter of debate—there is no definitive evidence.) So while I was not surprised that in the fifth century, the dynasty that controlled the northern half of China had to contend with incursions from a nomadic confederation known as the Rouran, I was shocked to learn that this northern dynasty was itself nomadic in origin.

After the fall of the Han Dynasty in 220 AD, and until it was unified again under the Sui Dynasty in 581 AD (approximately a hundred years after the setting of this book), China was in a state of almost constant reconfiguration. The Three Kingdoms, the Six Dynasties, Sixteen Kingdoms, Northern and Southern Dynasties—those are just some of the names used to describe various periods within this generally tumultuous era.

Northern Wei, the dynastic time and place where the ballad of Mulan is typically assumed to have occurred, was one of these Northern and Southern Dynasties. It was founded by the Tuoba clan of the Xianbei tribe, one of the nomadic peoples that had settled in northern China centuries earlier.

In discovering this, I realized the north of China—and the south, too, with its indigenous peoples—was far more diverse than I'd supposed.

The debate concerning Sinicization you read in this book was also real. What is Sinicization? Think of it as the Chinese counterpart of Americanization, where peoples from many backgrounds converge into a single national identity. For example, the policy of giving Xianbei families Han Chinese names was later actually implemented. This meant that what I always took to be a rather monolithic Chinese identity was actually forged of the collision and melding of many cultures and many peoples.

Through writing this book, I learned that in its day, China had been quite the melting pot. (The founder of the Tang Dynasty, often considered the pinnacle of Chinese civilization, was himself half-Xianbei.)

That the age-old story of Mulan can actually be a timely exploration of whose voices are heard and whose stories get told.

That a girl who goes to war and finds her courage can at the same time unlearn ingrained biases and unpack her own assumptions.

All of which have made writing *The Magnolia Sword* one of the most rewarding experiences of my career, and for that I could not be happier.

NOTES ON LANGUAGE AND HISTORICAL MISCELLANY

Xiong means elder brother in Chinese, *di*, younger brother. *Xiong-di*, as a term, can refer to brothers in general, or it can be how one addresses a man younger than oneself. Di by itself would have been a more intimate address. Had Kedan not revealed to Tuxi that Mulan is a woman, at some point Tuxi would start addressing her as Mulan di, to indicate the depth and significance of their friendship. That's also why he addresses Kai, once his own position is known, as Kai di.

Jiejie means elder sister. Mulan would call Murong *didi*. *Gu-niang* is a generic respectful address for a young woman.

While words for members of a family are always gender-specific—and often convey relative seniority between parties—Chinese as a whole is less gendered than many other languages. Gendered third-person pronouns did not come into use until the twentieth century, and the language makes no grammatical changes in response to gender. So it would not be terribly difficult to speak of someone without revealing their gender and without lying about it.

The Huns—a nomadic people of Central Asia—have entered the Western cultural imagination as barbarian invaders, thanks in part to their attacks on the Roman Empire a few decades before the start of this book. There have been scholarly arguments but no definitive evidence that the Xiongnu and the Huns are one and the same, or that they even belonged to the same loose confederation of nomadic tribes. I elected to refer to the Xiongnu once as "the Huns" so that readers will have a better understanding of what, culturally, the Xiongnu symbolized to the Han Chinese.

At the time of the setting of this book, the Chinese divided a day into twelve *shi*, each approximately the equivalent of two modern hours. I didn't want to introduce yet another concept here, so occasionally I did use "hours" to express lengths of time.

During my research, I kept coming across references to wine in the time period, which puzzled me. Grape wine was available, yes, but I was pretty sure I was reading about alcoholic beverages made from grain. Weren't all such beverages hard liquor? And then I learned that distillation, as a common practice, didn't start in China—or elsewhere in the world—until centuries later. So the grain wines the Chinese drank then were probably around 10 percent alcohol by volume, stronger than beer but less potent than your average modern-day wine.

There are no definitive dates on when chairs began to be used in China. There were stools earlier, introduced by the nomadic tribes, but the general consensus is that proper chairs probably did not come into use until the Tang Dynasty, several hundred years after the setting of this book, and probably did not entirely replace sitting on mats at or around low tables until the Song Dynasty. Until then, in formal settings, Chinese people sat on their knees and shins, with the buttocks on the feet.

At the border garrison, Tuxi, Mulan, Kedan, and Captain Helou play Chinese chess, or *xiangqi*, which dates back to the Warring States period (453-221 BC). Like Western chess, the game represents a war between two opposing armies. During the Tang dynasty, the playing pieces were renamed, so it's possible that the piece nowadays referred to as the chariot was known as something else in Mulan's day. But chariot sounds cooler, so chariot it is in this book.

The legendary swords Sky Blade and Heart Sea are based on an archaeological artifact known as the Sword of Goujian, unearthed in 1965 in Hubei Province, China. The Sword of Goujian is estimated to have been made during the Spring and Autumn period (771 to 403 BC). And when it was discovered, nearly two and a half millennia later, it had not rusted and still held a sharp edge.

ACKNOWLEDGMENTS

Kristin Nelson, for herding this opportunity directly into my lap.

Cheryl Klein, for the sheer amount of work she put into this book. I didn't even know editors edited like this anymore. Her dedication, energy, and vision guided me to produce a work that I am enormously proud of. Although I am still embarrassed that she read my first drafts, even partials—I haven't inflicted those on anyone in quite some time.

Christina Chung and Neil Swaab, for the beautiful cover.

Linda Yu, for pointing me in the right direction on research.

Chris Stewart, for generously sharing his knowledge and expertise.

Janine Ballard, for always making my books better.

Cheryl Etchison, for telling me how excited her daughter is for this book. I tend to exist in a cave, so it's really helpful to be reminded from time to time that I'm not doing this solely to honor a contract.

My family, for always being there.

And you, dear reader, for everything.